The
Language
of
Everything

KATHLEEN EVANS

LifeRich Publishing is a registered trademark of The Reader's Digest Association, Inc.

LifeRich Publishing books may be ordered through booksellers or by contacting:

LifeRich Publishing
1663 Liberty Drive
Bloomington, IN 47403
www.liferichpublishing.com
844-686-9607

ISBN: 978-1-4897-3099-2 (sc)
ISBN: 978-1-4897-3100-5 (e)

Library of Congress Control Number: 2020917997

Print information available on the last page.

LifeRich Publishing rev. date: 09/23/2020

For everyone I love and have loved at 2 Baker Street

PROLOGUE

9 years earlier

He'd brought only a map, three horses, and two soldiers to scout with him in Devoran; it was too early in the process to trust more than a loyal few. Unfortunately, neither Price nor Bernhardt seemed up to the challenge. Years of cautionary tales had painted Devoran as a dangerous, magical country, and both cowards shuffled along as though every rustling leaf could turn them to stone.

Marten snarled and spurred his horse. His objective was far too important to indulge such childish superstitions. The precious parchment stowed away at his side had fallen into his possession only a few weeks before, and ever since its secrets had consumed him. It had been confiscated material, taken during a routine arrest back in Cantor. He shuddered to remember how those foolish guards had almost thrown it away. He, alone, had realized its potential.

His mind wandered to the painted green flames that flickered from the hills of Devoran on the intricate map. He felt as though they were dancing for him, calling out to him— and he would answer. Long had there been rumors of potent materials and energies stored away in the wild forests of Devoran. With the growing hostilities exhibited by the Rie—falsely reported and spread by Marten himself—the time had come to wield the full might of the Cantic nation. Those green flames, so delicately drawn, had the potential to deliver all that he needed to succeed, and his desire for them burned through him as he rode.

If Marten Landsing had been the kind of man to care, he'd have taken the time to look about as they rode, and appreciate the wonder of this uncharted land. Devoran seemed to alternate between every biome imaginable. As they went, deep forests gave way to rainbow deserts which bled into breezy fields.

Of course, he was *not* that type of man. For as long as he could remember, Marten had been two things: practical and calculated. Nothing of value was to be gained from sightseeing, and so he made his way through Devoran as though it were nothing more than a brisk ride through a bustling Cantic street.

Eventually, Marten thrust out his hand, bringing his companions to a sudden stop. They had arrived at a wide plateau layered with years of multicolored sediment, but Marten hadn't come all this way to marvel at geology. He was interested in the opening that lay at the base of a cliff a mere hundred yards from where they were standing.

"Bernhardt!" Marten snapped, gesturing for the man to come forward.

"Yes, sir?"

"Do you see the cave over there? I need to you take a stone from inside and bring it back to me."

"Yes, sir." Bernhardt brought his trembling hand up for a short salute before sliding off his pony and jogging off.

In his absence, Marten and Price waited in silence. He had found that this tactic not only limited unnecessary chatter, but was also an effective intimidation technique. Marten accomplished more with silence than a foolish man's bellowing ever could.

When Bernhardt came back with the sample, Marten grabbed it wordlessly and held it up toward the sun. He squinted intently, and from the stone's crannies he could make out a green glint that shone incongruously with the dull mix of rock around it.

Inside, Marten's thoughts soared. *This was it!* But his was a private celebration. He turned towards the two soldiers and nodded once as he wheeled his horse about.

"Okay. Let's head home."

Both mounted their horses without question, eager to leave Devoran unscathed.

"Price," Marten snapped again, burying his joy long enough

to deliver the next, crucial order. "I nearly forgot. Before we left, I received a report of dangerous activity along our border with Rien. See to it that we circulate news of the insurgents. People must be informed of the threat.

"Of course, sir," Price saluted.

And so it begins. Marten thought. He kicked his horse and started home. *There is much to be done.*

PART ONE

Long after embers whiten
—each cool and dulled to black,
look twice, that every speck is out
before you settle back.
Look deep within those dying coals
—as lights they dim and wane.
One searing bit may be enough
to blaze the fire again!

Cal

Emilee and Eleanor Hanson ran through the sitting room in a blur of color and giggles. Cal watched with fondness as the girls chased an ancient cat, their hands full of skirts and gowns they'd ripped from their dolls, hoping to play dress-up with the poor creature.

Unlike other siblings with such a large age difference, Cal adored his sisters and even now felt only slightly inclined to put an end to Fendrel's humiliation.

Sighing, he took a few big steps, scooped up the animal, and, much to the girls' protest, carried him away to safety.

Cal bore him through the hallway that connected the livingroom and kitchen. Large panes of glass lined the walls around him, and Cal watched as raindrops splattered against them. The sound was comforting, the irregular *tap tap tap* accompanied by the faint smell of fresh earth. The clouds outside had necessitated an early lighting of lanterns and candles, and flames flickered about as Cal passed.

Eventually Cal dropped the cat at its food dish. The beast gave him a contemptuous glare before bending to munch on whatever scraps remained. Cal thought this ungrateful, considering the charity he'd shown Fendrel only moments before. He raised a dubious eyebrow and turned away, wandering over to his mother, Caroline, who was sitting at the kitchen table reading the afternoon paper and ignoring a cup of tea. Cal inhaled the scents of ginger and lavender coming from the cup, and decided the drink shouldn't go to waste. He edged over to Caroline's side and cradled the warm porcelain, delicately shifting it into his hand.

Without looking up, Caroline said, "I have been waiting ten minutes for that to cool. If you drink it, you will pay."

Cal laughed and put the cup back, settling for a seat next to his mother and a glance at the news.

Peering over her shoulder, he could just make out the first story:
Council meets today to decide the fate of 28-year-old Antony Blaise.

"The man needs consequences," Caroline Hanson muttered, seeing Cal's eyes on the story. "He's been caught out past curfew one too many times. A slap on the wrist clearly isn't going to work."

If Caroline was anything, she was fair. She was a Cratian lawyer and loved order almost as much as she loved her family.

Cal didn't disagree with her. Rules were important; they kept things in working order and allotted them the freedoms they enjoyed in Cratos. He did wonder, however, if there weren't the occasional grey area.

Cratos certainly didn't offer a lot of grey area. It was a heavily governed country in the Northeast corner of Colliptia that provided much social freedom. Cal knew that when he grew up he could choose whatever future he wanted, but that meant adhering to strict regulations, taxes, and government mandates—the price of a comfortable life.

Not everywhere was this way, however.

Could he ask her now? Cal had been mulling over some travel plans for the last few weeks, but had been hesitant to bring them up with either of his parents. Between lectures on Colliptian history and droning mathematics drills, it had been hard *not* to let his mind wander to more exciting topics. He just wasn't sure that either of his guardians would be quite as keen about those wistful adventures.

As if summoned by the changing trajectory of his thoughts, Cal's other mom, Cora, came walking in that very moment, rain following her as she hastened to close the door and fasten the latch.

Her entrance made Cal smile. Most people come in from the rain, embodying the storm around them. Not Cora—she stretched luxuriously after stepping across the threshold, taking her time as she hung up her jacket, and smiling when she met Cal's eyes.

"Afternoon, you two," she called into the kitchen. As she made her way over to them, Cora grabbed an apple from the counter, kissed Caroline, and sat down next to Cal before biting into her fruit.

"Hey, sweetheart, how's your break going?" Cora asked between crunches.

To Cal's immense relief, his lessons had closed a few days earlier, and he had spent several days basking in his ample leisure time, all the while plotting to fill it in other, more interesting ways.

"It's amazing, Mom," Cal answered.

This seemed as good a time as ever. He was determined to spend the precious months of his break doing something worthwhile. Cal took a quiet breath before taking the plunge, willing whatever chance he had to be in his favor.

"I'm thinking of taking a trip down to Cantor in a few days. I thought it might be a nice change of pace."

His parents exchanged almost identical eye rolls. They didn't seem entirely surprised, but that did not mean they would go along with the plan. Cal waited a few agonizing moments, calculating possible counter-arguments, before Caroline answered.

"You can go, but you have to remember that things are different down there, Cal." Her voice was firm as she added, "You just have to be careful. I know you're sixteen and I know you're smart, but Cratos is more accepting than other countries in Colliptia. Cantor is not as open-minded as we are."

Cal knew this, of course. It was why he wanted to go. He lived a comfortable, pleasant, but regimented life in his country, and he was *utterly* bored. He wanted to experience risk for once—to stay out until the trees were mere shadows in the darkness of night, and maybe even go to one of the races Cantor was so famous for. Cal thought of the Cantics as brutish and old-fashioned, yes, but he was willing to put that aside for a bit of adventure.

"I'll lay low, Mum," Cal promised, thrilled that his request had been granted so easily. All those weeks of worrying had been for nothing.

Cal smiled at his mothers, but the moment was interrupted by the abrupt sound of something shattering, followed by a mixture of tears and laughter that came trilling from somewhere in the house.

"What do you think? I'd guess they broke Grannie's plate." Caroline shot Cora a challenging look. They had long argued over the wisdom of placing the plate on top of the mantle.

"Not a chance! Emilee wouldn't be laughing." Cora crinkled her eyebrows together in thought. "Eleanor was balancing the clay vase on her head again, and it tipped."

"I'll take that bet!"

They walked off, and Cal could see them transitioning from scheming partners to somber parents as they made their way to the source of the chaos.

He watched them, the familiar realization of their wonderfulness settling in. Caroline and Cora were incredible, and he couldn't help but smile as he thought of the life he had somehow lucked into.

Garreck

Garreck took a deep breath, and then punched a hole in the wall. Well, not so much a hole as a small dent. His knuckles absorbed the brunt of the damage, and he looked quickly around for something to help staunch the bleeding.

He had just finished the most infuriating dinner with his family and had released every ounce of pent-up rage on the hard, limestone surface.

How did the rest of them deal with their own passive-aggressive garbage? Were *their* walls likewise littered with anger-driven imperfections? Somehow Garreck doubted it.

In the wake of his fury, he threw himself on an unyielding mattress and looked around at the sparse decor of his small bedroom. A square, wooden clock hung at a perfect right angle on the opposite wall, and under it stood a desk that exactly matched its deep brown hue. The windows loomed with dark, simple drapings, and there were no decorations. Garreck's slate-grey blanket drooped haphazardly from the bed frame, and a single pillow embroidered with the flag of Cantor lay beneath his head. Garreck's mother had stitched the cushion herself—tiny black threads joined together to form a fearsome horse that reared across the length of the fabric, with three grey stripes rushing up in the opposite direction. Those three lines, though subtle, were the cornerstones of the Cantic creed: *might, valor, and vigor.*

Garreck lay like an ancient, entombed knight, legs straight and hands folded over his chest. His mind sank further into itself with each passing moment, suffocating him as though he actually *was* one of the long-buried.

As Garreck lay there, he thought of his father, Marten, who was a leading politician and military general in Cantor. Because of his position, Marten had high expectations for his children—ones that Garreck never quite seemed to reach.

Men in Cantor were expected to practically pound their chests with pride at the idea of a career in either the government or the military. At some point in their childhood, Garreck's father had decided that his sons were better suited for the latter. Ever since, they had been pushed through multiple sports, trainings, and tactical drills that only fueled the flame of Garreck's loathing for the man.

Truth be told, he'd found true joy when he was introduced to archery. He was a damn good shot, even from early on, and still went shooting when he needed to relieve stress.

Garreck remembered the first time he'd hit a bullseye. He'd run as fast as he could to tell his father, proud of the accomplishment, but Marten had simply replied, "It only matters when there's someone to see you triumph." Ever since, confusion and rejection had been two of Garreck's most constant companions.

The rest of the Landsing boys didn't seem to foster the same resentment toward their father. Ronan and Benji embraced the hard parenting, waiting sickeningly to lap up whatever slight approval Marten decided not to withhold. There had been a time when Garreck was right there with them, but as the years went on he suspected that there was no hidden center of approval buried deep within his father—only tradition and contempt for those who lacked a respect for it.

Garreck had a hard time entertaining his father, which had lead to the trouble at dinner. Marten had suggested Garreck begin training as a recruit on the weekends. Without really thinking, Garreck replied with something to the effect of, "What, with all of those canks?"

Silence.

Marten clutched his fork with a ferocity that should have broken it in half. His brothers jeered at him from across the table, while his mother, Jana, muttered something unintelligible about potatoes before exiting the room. The rest of the meal was spent in uncomfortable, earth-shattering stillness, until finally Garreck heaved himself from the table, stomped upstairs, and took his anger out on a surface almost as hard as his father's head.

He obviously hadn't been serious, and that was the problem. He couldn't even joke about not wanting to submit to every want and whim of his father. Garreck almost wished the man had yelled; it might then have ended in a discussion. But no, the slightest denial was met with silent scorn. God forbid he have his own thoughts, ideas, or ambitions.

Garreck stayed in his room a long while, vitriol coursing through his veins. When his thoughts became too much, he went to the closet, grabbed his coat, and left through the window to go for a drink.

Cal

The streets of Cantor were bustling as Cal stepped off the wagon he had taken from Cratos. Hangings of deep scarlet and cerulean stirred in the breezes over busy marketplaces. People from every station of life scuttled about their errands. Statesmen and official-looking individuals passed each other casually, all the while mingling with fire dancers, hagglers, and other common folk.

In addition to his rucksack, Cal carried a bulging package of cured meats, hard cheeses, and thick loaves of bread that Cora had prepared for him before he left. She'd also snuck in some homemade soaps and oils, and he had not put up a fuss. Yes, he wanted an authentic experience traveling the world, but that didn't mean he had to smell like a vagrant while it happened.

Weighed down by his luggage, Cal walked over uneven cobbled streets so dissimilar from the smooth, mosaic ones he was used to, marveling at the exchanges around him. In Cratos, everything had a specific price that was paid without contestation. Here, however, Cal listened with intense curiosity as people haggled and bartered over various goods.

"You there, little one," Cal's wonderment was interrupted by the voice of a small, hunched man whose eyes barely met Cal's shoulders. The man was pointing at him with a smile, his grin spreading wide enough to reveal several missing teeth.

"Me?" Cal asked him, an eyebrow raised.

"Yes, of course!" The stranger took Cal's shoulder and shuffled him over to a drab booth that was stocked with rucksacks. The entire supply were almost identical to Cal's bag, and some were in rather worse shape than his own. "Why would you settle for that flimsy thing, when you can have a custom Cantic creation?" The man's little arms spread out wide over his head as he emphasized each word in "custom Cantic creation." The movement made him look more like a miniature scarecrow than a human booth worker.

Despite the poor quality of the products, Cal was nonetheless intrigued. Something about the man was compelling. Cal felt himself warming in an agreeable way, and it was only with much effort that he turned down the salesman's offer.

Cal hurried to put some distance between himself and the tiny salesperson, the latter of whom had begun hurling swear words the moment he realized there would be no sale.

The insults troubled him little; Cal was sure he would be called much worse during his visit in Cantor. What bothered him more was the unpredictability of this place and the resulting inequality. There was nothing fair about a more persuasive person getting a lower price. What madness had allowed such a horrid man to sell cheap products for a small fortune?

Then again, it was really quite compelling. It made every day a constant competition—life itself was addicting here.

This initial excitement propelled Cal through several days of eager exploration. He did, in fact, go to the races. Not only that, he won a few rounds to boot. He visited the statehouse and several museums during his days and drank until dawn a few nights. As it was forbidden in Cratos, Cal had never been able to drink—publicly or privately. But in Cantor there were no alcohol restrictions. And while he thrilled at a world without curfew, it also made him pause. How much crime happened in the dark corners of this country?

Cal had been in Cantor for nearly a week before he realized "crime" meant something very different there than it did back home.

On the night in question, Cal was having a jovial night out drinking with a few men he had met in town. All were likeable enough, and their knowledge of the area had been invaluable to Cal as he traipsed about the city. On any given night they could be found bouncing between several rowdy bars, but, without fail, they would find their way to the Pallary Pub.

Such was their routine that when the group walked through the doors on Cal's sixth night in Cantor, a few people greeted him by name, and the bartender had his drink waiting for him at the counter. Cal smiled and waited while the others got their drinks and spread out—a tight squadron advancing on the unassuming bar folk. Some in their army planned to pursue a conquest, others wanted nothing more than to put their boots up by the fire. Cal remained at the bar, surveying the scene with a broad smile, feeling warm and thoroughly content.

Spying the bottom of his glass, Cal was about to order another when a young man, probably two or three years older than Cal, handed him a pint and came to sit by his side.

"Night going well?" the young man asked, and Cal could not help but admire the stranger. He was stocky and handsome, with chestnut hair that curled a bit at the ends. He stood in stark contrast to Cal himself, who was a lanky six feet two inches tall and still growing—his blond hair the only part of him truly within his control.

Both men had the same dark brown eyes, however, and when they met, Cal felt at ease. "Going great," he replied, "I've been here just under a week, and I must say I've been making the most of it."

"Yes, you have! I saw you the other night at Darcy's. Quite a crew you bring around with you." He gestured to Cal's friends around the bar.

"They're good men. They get me around the city, and I help them get a few girls."

The man raised an eyebrow. "I didn't take you for much of a ladies man."

Cal laughed, "Oh, you underestimate me. Women love me! I'd just rather let my friends take over once I've worked my charm."

With a broad grin, the stranger held out his hand. "I'm Sam."

"Cal." He smiled and took another swig of his drink.

Sam, Cal discovered, was a blacksmith of fairly good renown. His primary work was in armour, but he dabbled in other areas when demand was low. His parents had both recently passed away, so he owned the business outright. It was work he enjoyed, but he felt the pressure of owning his own shop. Cal listened with rapt attention to Sam's story, a bit embarrassed by the sheltered life he led back home. He *did* tell Sam about his studies and about some of the main differences that he had observed between Cratos and Cantor.

"Take this bar, for instance." Cal spread his arms out to indicate the pub. "*Everything* here is illegal back home. No alcohol, no late-night happenings, no gambling!" He nodded his head towards a table of men who were playing a complicated card game called "Grunt." Cal had played it a few nights before but had lost a sizeable chunk of coin and still wasn't entirely sure of the rules.

Sam laughed, "What happens when you break a rule?"

"Oh, you're warned right away, and if you don't listen you're punished. But people rarely break the rules. We all believe in them." Cal said with earnestness.

He reached out and picked up his glass, leaving behind a thin curve of condensation on the countertop. "Our symbol is the ripple," Cal told Sam, using his finger to draw two smaller, concentric circles inside the first. "It represents balance, but also that our actions have consequences. We're taught from a young age that by following the rules, we're benefitting others as well as ourselves"

"That sounds very dull," Sam said, barely suppressing a smirk.

"That it is, Sam, that it is," Cal laughed, reaching to clink his glass to Sam's before draining the rest of its contents.

Their conversation continued, and the two sat at the bar for some time, talking as the night passed around them. When a few hours had elapsed, Cal's friends called over to him. They eyed his drinking partner suspiciously, and told Cal they were ready to head to the next haunt.

"Want to come?" Cal asked Sam. He declined, opting instead to give Cal a firm handshake before walking out the pub's front door.

Cal joined his group as they stumbled from the pub, laughing and teetering down the moonlit street. When he was sure none of them were looking, Cal read the bit of paper Sam had slipped into it moments before.

Smithy. 6 Brim Street. Be Careful.

Cal's pulse quickened and his face flushed with an intensity that made him thankful for the dark, night air. It would not be hard to break from his crew; they had many drinks and flirtations ahead of them. It took him only a moment to make a decision before he gathered his things, waved to a few of his fellows and turned to pad quickly away. He thought he saw one of the lads grimace as he made his exit, but he couldn't be sure.

The smith shop was not difficult to spot once Cal reached Brim Street. In a row of dusty brown houses and stores it was a deep, muted red. He smiled when he saw Sam leaning casually against the entrance.

"You came." A broad smile illuminated Sam's face as Cal approached.

"Of course," Cal said, grinning at how pleased Sam seemed. "Now, what is on the agenda for the rest of the night?"

"I wanted to be able to talk candidly. How would you feel about a nighttime stroll? Let me show you my Cantor."

Cal nodded eagerly and Sam laughed. "Alright then, let's go."

They wandered about, their conversations unhindered by the possibility of prying ears. Now and then they enjoyed a silent moment or two, taking advantage of dimly lit side streets whenever they were able. It was only when the grey beams of early morning began to shine orange and purple that Sam hurried them back to his shop.

"How about some breakfast?" he asked Cal, motioning him into the building.

"Wonderful," Cal said, a bit confused by Sam's haste, but intrigued by the idea of a good meal. "I'm starving."

As Sam busied himself in the kitchen, Cal wandered about the small home. It was cozy, and while there was not much natural light, paintings and tapestries had been hung on the walls, making the space quite welcoming. Cal lingered at a portrait of two people who he assumed were Sam's parents. The artist had done a fine job, and Cal could tell from the faint sparkle in their eyes that they had been kind. With a sudden pang, Cal missed the parents he had left back home. How brave of Sam to stay afloat in the face of such tragedy— Cal couldn't imagine a world without Cora and Caroline.

The aromas of good cooking pulled Cal from his sudden sadness, and he followed his nose to a tiny kitchen just off the main entrance. Sam had finished his preparations, and was spooning eggs and sausages onto two plates in heaping portions. When he saw Cal, Sam put down the pan and walked over to him, kissing him once before returning to the meal. Cal flushed, pleased, and followed Sam to the table. It did not take long for them to clean their plates.

Leaning back to stretch his now-satisfied stomach, Cal asked, "Alright, Sam, what shall we do with the rest of the day?" In truth, he needed a nap, but he didn't want to waste any time that could otherwise be spent with Sam.

"It wouldn't be a good idea," Sam looked sad as he said it. "Cantor is no place for us, last night was more than we should have had together, I'm afraid."

"Even if we just walked around as friends? I mean, after all I am a foreign traveler, what if I go astray?" Cal gave him a pleading face that had little to no impact on its target.

Sam just laughed and rolled his eyes. "You were doing fine on your own before I met you. You can last a few more days in the city without a guide."

"But it will be entirely boring to know that all the fun is happening back here." Cal paused and then brightened, "Maybe I'll need something smithed!"

They went back and forth, but despite Cal's best attempts, Sam was steady in his conviction. Last night was to be a happy memory, nothing more. Disappointed, but understanding Sam's position, Cal eventually left 6 Brim Street feeling dazed. How could he possibly top *that*?

"Hey, cank!" A gruff voice yelled from behind him.

Cal turned just in time to see a fist, followed by flashing lights that gave way to total darkness.

Garreck

Ever since the incident at dinner, Garreck had gone out almost every night. He never left before the last bits of sunlight had flickered out, because he was not looking for bustling crowds. Instead, he craved the solitude that a quiet street provided. He roamed about, letting evening candles light his way, never knowing where exactly he would end up. More often than not, he found himself a corner in whatever dive he came across and proceeded to drink himself into an even more ill-tempered state. This night it was at Morissey's, though the place was livelier than he would have liked.

At least he wasn't at home. In these taverns, his mother could not lie to him about his father's intentions, and his brothers could not get on his case. Still, he wore their condescension like an extra skin, and he tempered his ever-present fury by ordering another pint.

Drink after drink, Garreck glared about, cursing the much happier people surrounding him. Everywhere he looked were the drunk faces of individuals who, sip by sip, allowed their problems to slip away. Garreck wished he could join them, but his bitterness ran deep. Who were *they* to enjoy themselves?

One particular couple in a wide armchair was painful to look at. They were nauseatingly in love; Garreck wished them only the harsh pain of reality.

With a grunt, he motioned to the bar keep for another ale. Instead of the bartender, a burly man came up to Garreck, his expansive arms folded across a wide chest.

"Keep says you've got to leave," he told Garreck in a firm voice, challenging him to contest.

"Like hell," Garreck returned with similar finality. Unfortunately for the bouncer, Garreck was in the mood for a challenge. He stood up from his stool, stumbling a bit from a dizziness brought on by too many ales. This did not bode well for the forthcoming brawl, but Garreck didn't care.

A massive arm grabbed Garreck's collar and yanked him forward, attempting to pull him towards the door. In response, Garreck aimed a surprisingly strong right hook at his challenger, hitting hard despite his intoxicated state.

In an instant, three or four other men came to assist the bouncer as Garreck continued to lash out, throwing wild punches at whomever he could reach.

This felt good. The physical act of hurting someone other than himself was a gift. He fought and he fought, scrambling like an animal, savoring the rush of adrenaline that came with each thrusting blow. It wasn't until a pair of cuffs were snapped around his wrists that he realized he had gone too far.

Garreck

The next morning, Garreck woke up hungover and annoyed.

As he sat up to stretch, Garreck assessed the sizeable bruises he had all over his body. At least he'd put up a decent fight. He'd be no match for his dad when Marten heard what happened. The man was going to flay him alive.

A cough interrupted his thoughts, and Garreck realized he wasn't alone in the cell. *The police have been busy*, he thought to himself as he gave his neighbor the once over. The gangling boy was younger than Garreck by at least a year or two. His mop of blond hair lay in disarray, and his shirt was a bit torn. He also sported a shiner that rivalled a few of Garreck's finer bruises.

"You're up." The boy's voice was almost chipper from his corner of the cell.

"Observant," Garreck muttered.

"I'm Cal," the boy offered, straightening up a bit. "Why are *you* here?"

Why the hell do you care? Garreck took a deep, annoyed breath before answering. "Garreck," he muttered. "It's a bit foggy, but it looks like I got in a fight with half of Cantor last night." Garreck was still trying to piece together the brawl through the drunken haze of his memories. "You?"

Cal seemed to ponder that for a moment, then answered, "Got into a bit of mischief with a friend."

Garreck, altogether unimpressed by the vagueness of the answer, was too apathetic to pursue the point further.

Garreck leaned back and pressed his eyes together, hoping that when he opened them again his vision would be a bit more concrete. Instead, he found his cellmate gazing curiously at him. Garreck could tell Cal was trying not to bother him, but in the end, Cal's need for knowledge outweighed any attempts at consideration. "What do Cantics do to get out of here? Will I have a trial? In Cratos, things like this can stretch on for some time."

So, this guy was Cratian. That added up. Only a Cratian would be stupid enough to think the state would waste precious time on a petty arrest. "You really think they care about proper procedure here? It's about who you know, or how much coin you have. Without either, you'll rot here."

Garreck reached into his pocket and pulled out a heavy leather purse. Cal watched him, mirroring the act in an almost childlike manner. Garreck rolled his eyes and bellowed to a guard about fifteen feet away.

"Hey! You! Come here." The guard turned and walked with tentative steps toward their cell. Once he was within reaching distance, Garreck said, "We've got ten dourns a piece if you let us walk out right now."

The guard studied Garreck for a minute before looking over at Cal. "Ten for you, but twenty for him," he replied, disgust dripping from the words as he spoke.

Such abhorrence was generally reserved for Rie or canks, and since he'd already surmised that Cal from Cratos, Garreck could only assume the latter was the root of the guard's distaste.

Well that was one mystery solved. *Mischief* indeed.

Garreck looked over at Cal, who was already taking out the extra money. "Done," he told the guard, who took the coins, paused, then opened the gates. "Been a pleasure," Garreck nodded as he walked out of the cell and through the doors of the small jail.

Behind him, Cal stumbled a bit, but looked rather pleased. "Well, that was easy, wasn't it?" he said as he followed Garreck down the street. "Thanks."

"No problem," Garreck told him, stopping to assess the situation. His father may not have heard the rumblings from the previous night, but he would eventually. He always did. The very thought of facing a lecture from that man was more than Garreck's dehydrated brain could take.

As he began to spiral, Garreck felt a firm tap on his shoulder.

"Garreck?" Cal asked. "Where are you off to, then?

It made Garreck redden to realize that he didn't know. Cal seemed to recognize, if not understand, his confusion. Before he could answer, the kid intervened.

"I'm on break, you see, and I'm not too keen to continue here. I've heard Aelemia is interesting, though. I might head that way."

Interesting was putting it lightly. In Garreck's opinion the Aelish were a crew of oddities, misfits. But in that moment he didn't much care how strange they were or how much of a cank Cal was. He only knew that if he went home, he'd do something he was sure to regret.

"And you'd like me to come along?" he asked.

Cal nodded, "Better to travel with a companion than alone, don't you think?"

"All right then," said Garreck. It was foolish. A stupid idea that only patched the enormous crater he'd have to fix when he got back, but Garreck didn't care. In that moment, this was the only option that didn't involve him going home to Marten.

"Let's go," he said to Cal, who smiled and turned to move. After a few steps the boy paused, then spun back around with an apologetic look on his face. "One moment," Cal said, taking off his bag and rifling through the contents. "I have to find my map."

Good god, Garreck thought. What had he just agreed to?

Mauria

The summers in Marcan West were beautiful. Mauria Hoan sat on the branch of a large yew tree, looking out at the wide pasture her family shared with nine others. The entire community included several thousand people. Children ran through lakes in great splashes that sprayed the sandy shoreline. Men and women bustled about, gathering and sharing their crops and hunts.

Sharing was everything here, as it was in all of Aelemia. Whether it was land, or food, or gifts, everything circulated among families and communities in order to reach those who needed it most.

Gifts. Mauria sighed as she thought of her own. Almost half the population was born with the ability to heal, and it was evident even as a child that she was gifted in this manner.

When she was five, Mauria's brother had fallen from the very tree in which she now perched. Kent howled at his clearly broken leg, writhing from the pain of the injury. Mauria had gone to his side, and in an instant his shrieks transformed to whimpers. The gentle touch of her hands numbed him long enough for her to craft a crude splint, and together they'd made their way back to camp.

Only a few days after the incident, she was training as a healer. Her parents had been thrilled, of course. Warren and Robin loved that their family was now able to contribute in this way, and Mauria enjoyed being able to help her community. It was an Aelemian's call to serve and save others. There was a piece of her, though, that was not satisfied by this trajectory in life—a part of her that craved a different fate. She could not claim to be unhappy, for most of the time there was happiness in her life. She had a warm bed and good food and people who loved her dearly. Somehow, though, these assets did not leave her fulfilled.

Perturbed by the direction of her thoughts, Mauria swung with practiced grace from the tree and began a swift run through the woods. The forests were thick in Marcan West, but she knew them well. She dipped and swerved through the brush until she came to a sizeable clearing.

It was hers, perhaps the only thing that she never had to share. Light fell patchy on the thick grass of the opening, and every now and then sprigs of common ragwort shot up in yellow tufts. She had secreted this place away for occasions when the weight of the community became too heavy or when she simply needed peace and quiet. Here, Mauria was far enough away that the chaotic sounds of community members were gone, replaced instead by the quiet whispers of nature.

She threw herself onto the soft ground, but realized within seconds that she was too restless to nap. Her muscles screamed to be used. She heaved herself back to her feet and began to fight. It was not any combat that others would recognize; in fact, to the watchful eye she could have been dancing. If Kent happened upon her, he probably would have thought she was losing her mind. But she was neither crazy nor a dancer.

She was a fighter. Twice a year, Cantic troops used the woods of Marcan West for practice drills and, every time, Mauria hid and watched them with a fierce intensity. She took in everything and adapted it accordingly. She loved the control it gave her, loved the feeling of ownership over her body and mind that the movement provided.

On some occasions she stole away, just like this, to hone her skills. She would never need to use them—Aelemia was a peaceful land. But it would always be a part of her, and that knowledge made her smile. Sometimes it felt good to be a bit selfish.

Cal

Cal had some regrets about inviting Garreck. The man was frequently hostile and sullen at best. He stomped about and complained more than anyone Cal had ever known and was something of a broken person. Cal didn't begrudge Garreck his baggage but also thought he could carry the burden with a bit more grace.

Still, it seemed worth the bouts of moodiness to have someone to share the road with. Even Cal, a sheltered Cratian, knew that a single wanderer was doomed to be robbed. While it may have grated a bit on Cal's nerves, Garreck's grunting provided a feeling of security as they made their way down the eastward road toward Aelemia.

Aelemia was, at least, a socially forward society. Cal wouldn't end up in prison there, but then again he doubted there would be anyone quite as appealing as Sam. The Aelish were notorious for their lackadaisical interpretation of "hygiene." No, he didn't see himself falling for an Aelish man.

Cal looked ahead to Garreck, who was trekking through a thicket of trees. Garreck looked the part of an upstanding, Cantic man. He possessed broad shoulders and brown skin that had the glow of someone who often trained outside. His dark hair was short and his posture straight, clearly taught to him from an early age.

So why had Garreck agreed to come? Cal was certain Garreck had correctly assessed the situation back at the prison and was also quite sure that Garreck held many Cantic prejudices. There was no reason for him to have said yes to Cal's request, and yet he had.

Was he military? The theory fit well with Garreck's physical appearance. A deserter perhaps? Cal wanted to know.

"Hey, Garreck!" he called. A few yards away, Garreck slowed so that Cal could catch up.

"What's your story?" Cal asked, his tone direct. "You go around getting into midnight brawls, but what else do you do?"

To Cal's amazement, Garreck replied, "I enjoy archery and work in my father's office every once in a while. That is if he needs the help or I want the coin."

Encouraged by a response that was something other than a single word, Cal pushed on. "Are you a recruit? A bowman of Cantor?"

At this Garreck stiffened, and Cal knew he had struck a chord. Garreck simply answered, "'No, I'm not,'" and his tone invited little else.

Switching topics to avoid an abrupt end to their conversation, Cal asked, "Do you have a knack?"

At this Garreck loosened a bit, but looked confused. "What's a knack?" he asked.

"In Cratos, some of us have a "knack." It's usually of the mind. My moms both have one. Caroline is the best at it. She's able to guard herself, strengthen her mind against falsity or persuasion. It makes her an amazing lawyer."

Recognition crossed Garreck's face and he smiled a bit. "We call it a gift. I think the Aelish do as well."

This bit of etymology was interesting, but not entirely surprising. Cal could see why the Cratians didn't use the same word as the other countries. His people were logical, valuing fairness. While a "gift" implied something out of one's control, a "knack" was more tangible.

"I've got one," Garreck told him, and Cal could detect a hint of pride in his voice. "My dad's the only other one in my family who has one. That's how he got his position." After a blank look from Cal, he clarified, "We're gifted with persuasion. Kind of a funny counter to your parents' knacks. Some Cantics can bring crowds together, others might just be able to get some extra dessert at mealtimes. Mine and my dad's sway more toward the first variety."

Cal gawked at him. Such a knack was dangerous; even he could see that. It created an automatic hierarchy if people like Garreck's father could talk their way to the top. And if the knacks turned out to be familial? Then a cycle of power was inevitable.

Thank goodness Colliptia was divided into separate lands. More than any other difference he'd encountered so far, this gift of persuasion disturbed Cal the most.

Garreck seemed to understand Cal's anxiety and dropped the issue. For a while the two did not speak, and in these moments Cal realized that the light around them had changed. Although the sun was still high in the sky, it was obstructed by wide leaves overhead. He looked down at his hands, which were cracked with dancing shadows, and reached out to touch a thick vine that wound down from some distant canopy. The beauty of the woods, enchanting as it was, only briefly blocked out the whirring of Cal's mind; his brain buzzed with questions and possibilities. Garreck's imprisonment, in particular, did not add up with his newfound knowledge of "gifts."

When he was unable to reason it out himself, Cal turned to Garreck and asked, "If you can persuade others, how did you get yourself thrown in jail? Couldn't you just talk your way out of it?"

Garreck took a moment to formulate his answer. His face worked through several different emotions, and it was some time before he spoke. "There are a couple reasons," he began. "One, booze dulls the gift—as does rage. You need your wits about you and I was far from that. Two, I don't use my gift, even when I'm not tanked."

As Cal's mouth opened to ask the obvious question, Garreck just smirked and said, "Father issues," before walking away.

Soaking in this new information, Cal followed. Perhaps Garreck wasn't a typical Cantic as he had assumed. Cal had little time to contemplate this, however, for within moments of continuing on their route, he heard a loud yell just ahead.

Garreck lay with his ankle twisted at an unnatural angle, a gnarled root encircling it like a primitive bear trap.

Shoot. Cal thought. *Now what?*

Mauria

Mauria was halfway through her practicing when she heard a faint cry.

What could that be? Her first thought was that someone had found her clearing. In that instant a wave of sadness swept over her. But no, surely not. She was far from her family's cluster, and the shout had been from even deeper in the trees, away from the community. Her panic subsided, but her curiosity was piqued.

She gathered herself and moved toward the disturbance. If it was someone in trouble, she wanted to help. If it was something else, well, perhaps she could finally test her training.

As she jogged further west, she began to hear voices. There were at least two: one male voice, certainly. The other was so distorted that she couldn't tell. *They must be in pain*, she thought, and her steps quickened as she did.

Mauria soon reached the source of the commotion. She ducked behind a thick trunk to peer at a tall blond boy and a darker man only a few yards from where she hid. For a brief moment, Maura considered the danger these two might pose, but was quick to brush her fears away. She could tell that the blond was not a fighter, and the other man's leg was mangled in a way that neutralized any threat.

Making up her mind, Mauria emerged from her hiding place and approached the strangers. She bypassed the blond and went directly to the man spread out on the forest floor. She crouched down next to him, assessing the situation as he swatted her away.

"My name is Mauria," she said, dodging his hands. "I can help."

"What are you going to do, sing it back to not-broken?" The man asked through his teeth.

Rude, thought Mauria, but she was undeterred. Clearly this man harbored some biases.

"No, actually, and I don't think it's broken. But I can help all the same." She edged a few inches closer to him. He followed her with wary eyes, but after a moment gave her a curt nod.

Mauria smiled with satisfaction. She took the ankle gently in her hands, and smirked at the surprise on its owner's face as she did. Then, with the careful touch of a healer, she untangled him from a particularly vicious root. Mauria finished by ripping three inches from the bottom of one of her sleeves, then wrapping and massaging the injured bit of his leg.

The man winced, but was an otherwise willing patient. Mauria could see the pain recede from his eyes, and his breath became less ragged.

She'd performed this act dozens of times, but there was still something satisfying about watching someone benefit from her touch. It was almost worth the sharp pain that accompanied each healing moment. Aldra, her mentor, described this discomfort in terms of energy when she had first asked about it. "You are drawing energy from the sufferer, and it does not just disappear," she'd said, matter-of-factly. "You are gifted with a body that can imbibe and accommodate their pain, but you will feel it each time."

Mauria smiled at a job well done, but knew that in order to get him back to the community they'd need more than a mild reprieve from the pain. As such, she left the two of them to gawk at her gift, and made her way over to a nearby sapling. Using the knife that she carried at her waist, she hacked away until the branch eventually yielded. The blade was not meant for anything thicker than line rope for a boat, and she made a mental note to sharpen it the second she got home. Mauria measured to her shoulder and then cut there as well; that would make for a fine walking stick until she could get the two back to camp. The injured fellow's leg would be well enough by the next day, once she had the proper supplies.

The blond boy, who had been silent since she began, finally spoke. He gave her a broad smile, beaming as his companion became noticeably better. "Thank you, Mauria," he said, holding out his hand. "I'm Cal. That brute you helped is Garreck."

"Nice to meet you, though I'm sorry for the circumstances," Mauria replied, shaking his hand and returning the grin. "Why are you two so far from home?" It was clear that neither of them was Aelish. *She* was the only Aelemian she knew who wandered so deeply through the woods.

"We're travelling. I'm on a lesson break, and Garreck just needed some fresh air."

Interesting, Mauria thought to herself. *The rude one has a story.*

"Well, you're welcome at our camp," Mauria told them. "We have enough for both of you."

Mauria saw Garreck roll his eyes at this comment. It confirmed her suspicion about his prejudice. Well, he would soon learn that not all Aelemians were as soft as he believed.

She gave Garreck a rough pat on the back and forced a smile. "Follow me," she told them, before turning into the woods.

Garreck

What the hell did I get myself into? Garreck wondered as he sat beside a large fireplace, fully healed after almost breaking his ankle. *Well*, he thought dryly, *this would really anger Marten.* It was a small but comforting consolation for the mess he'd launched himself into.

Garreck leaned back in a sturdy Aelish chair and assessed his surroundings. A common quality resonated around the room. Was it satisfaction? Yes, that was the best word for it. These people seemed satisfied despite the hard lives they had chosen to live. Garreck was the only one in the vicinity lounging; everyone else seemed to have a job of some kind. Men and women were chopping meat and vegetables while some laid expanses of material out over ruddy tables. Others corralled the masses of children who ran in mad bursts every which way. It was chaotic, but controlled—everyone had a place. And they seemed to enjoy the work. No one seemed bitter or resentful that their job was any more complex or time consuming than the others. Garreck knew that if he had gotten the babysitting shift while someone else was boiling water, there'd be hell to pay.

As he scanned the area, Garreck saw Cal standing, arms crossed, on the other side of the room. He was nodding, deep in conversation with a few older members of Mauria's family. The kid was resilient, he'd give him that. Where Garreck sat, surly and grimacing off on his own, Cal was animated and glowing as he gained new friends and allies. For a moment, Garreck admired the younger boy, jealous of his easy nature. As he did, he realized that Cal wasn't the shaggy misfit he had originally pegged him to be. Between the post-penitentiary grime and the wear and tear of the road, Garreck had never seen him truly clean. Cal looked better now that he'd had a proper shower and been given a fresh set of clothing. He looked older, and less like the child he had seemed to be back in Cantor.

Cal caught his eye briefly, and Garreck was quick to look away. His gaze turned, instead, to the crackling fire.

Rasha

The streets of Rien were crowded, but calm. A tranquility passed between each citizen that Rasha had, for his whole life, tried to understand and emulate. Many of the passersby were moving with him, having just come from the large meeting house where twice daily services were held. Rasha let himself be carried along by the flow of multicolored cloaks, trying to remain composed as his stomach rebelled. It had been vocal since halfway through the last service, gurgling and churning away, and he was ready for the evening meal that his mother would be cooking at home. To keep his mind busy, Rasha instead thought back and analyzed the Shoam's teachings from earlier that day.

The services had been fine, he decided. They were words he had heard before, in one form or another, but they'd been delivered well by the Shoam. Indeed, for many it might have been an exemplary meeting. Perhaps he was the only one who found the messages overdone. Then again, Rasha doubted there were many people in Rien more consumed by religion than he currently was.

For the last year, he had been throwing himself into his faith, studying for many hours and going to services both morning and mid-day. It made his mother happy to see him so engrossed in the teachings, and it made him feel accomplished. Faith was everything in Rien.

As he neared his home, he saw his mother, Lira, waiting for him at the door. They looked similar, both with olive skin and deep umber eyes that matched their hair. Rasha's one distinctive trait was his scattering of light brown freckles. His father, Lira told him, had had them as well.

"How was mid-day?" she asked him, scuffing up his hair as she did.

"Well enough," he replied. "The Shoam added a few extra words on temperance that he left out this morning.

"I should have gone, Taklam knows I could use more of that," Lira laughed, popping a small piece of dark chocolate into her mouth as she did.

The two of them moved from the threshold to the warm kitchen within their tiny home. It smelled wonderful—of bread and roasted spice. Rasha savored every breath as he went to change for dinner.

While they ate, they chatted about the day, and Rasha noticed the beginnings of a new textile on Lira's loom.

"Did someone else ask about your work?" he questioned. His mother was a talented artist, and many people in Rien commissioned her to produce textiles and tapestries. She had even been known to hand paint pottery when asked. Because of this specialized line of work, Rasha and his mother had never had much in the way of money. He could see, however, how much joy her trade brought her. And anyway, the two of them had never needed much.

"It's actually for you," she beamed at him. "I found the thread while I

24

was out earlier, and I thought I would surprise you with it. Don't peek until it's finished!" The look she gave him was falsely stern and full of humor.

He closed his eyes and held his right hand up, placing his left over his heart. "I swear."

"Good," she said, reaching out fondly to touch his cheek. "Now that that's settled, there is something else I wanted to give you." She pulled out a folded piece of paper that had a large message inked across the front. "I saw this hanging in town and thought of you."

Rasha took the paper from his mother and read, eyes widening at the phrase "Summer Pilgrimage" that stood out among the smaller details.

"Why are you showing me this?" Rasha asked her.

Lira gave him a sad smile. "You are not happy, Rasha. You pray and you listen and you pray and you work, but that is no life for a fourteen-year-old boy. You need to do something that will set your mind at ease. I want to see you enjoy yourself for once."

Rasha looked over the sheet again. It *would* be exciting to go on a trip like this, but there were things holding him back that he could not ignore. "What about you?" he asked his mother. "Will you be all right by yourself?"

Lira laughed, "Of course, Rasha. I will miss you more than you know, but it will make me smile to think of you finding your happiness."

"All right then, maybe I will," he said, not wanting to voice a second, stronger fear.

Lira nodded and they fell back into normal conversation. After they'd eaten and cleaned and said their goodnights, it wasn't just Rasha's stomach that was full. His heart was, too. This, surely, was a life his god would approve of.

And yet, as he prepared for bed and recited the normal evening prayers, he did not feel Taklam's approval. He did not feel anything. Unlike the voice of the Shoam or his mother's comforting presence, that elusive deity went unheard. There had to be more that he could do—something to confirm that his devotion was more than a lifelong play at ritualistic theatrics. All at once he was thankful for the pilgrimage; perhaps it was the push he needed to finally connect with his god.

There must be more, he thought. *But, what if there isn't?* The unspoken fear from dinner surfaced just long enough to pique Rasha's anxiety before he sank slowly into sleep.

Cal

Aelemia was unlike anywhere Cal had been before. He and Garreck stayed for some time at Mauria's camp, and all the while he marveled at their way of life.

From his conversations with the many families in Marcan West, Cal came to understand that their worlds revolved around people. They lived and worked for one another, and as a result there was no hunger, no need, not even real sickness.

The lack of illness had taken Cal by surprise, but he shouldn't have been shocked after what he'd seen Mauria accomplish in the woods. He'd since learned that about half of the Aelish had a knack. They called them gifts, as Garreck had said. Unlike the Cantish, however, Mauria's people possessed the ability to heal, and Cal wondered at this extraordinary discovery. The Aelemians lead healthy lives until the end, succumbing only to the inevitability of age.

Despite the obvious attractions of this life, the lives of the Aelemians were filled with sacrifice. They never had more than they needed—no luxuries or surplus to be found. Because they shared everything and withheld nothing, ambition was never rewarded, and laziness never admonished.

Cal's Cratian need for balance and justice was challenged by this aspect of the Aelish ways, but it did not seem to bother those who had grown up practicing constant restraint. Any individual who did not agree with the Aelish customs had left long ago, and the families remaining taught communal values from early childhood.

Mauria seemed to enjoy it well enough. She worked with others, healed when needed, and joined in song and dance whenever the families got together. She had even dragged Garreck up for one upbeat, jaunty tune. Cal had cried out in delight at his companion's look of mingled horror and amusement as he moved with the others, reeds swaying in a vast field—every person just a piece of the whole.

It was not until their last day in Marcan West that Cal discovered Mauria might not be quite as content as she let on.

Cal was saddling the horses that their Aelish friends had lent them for their journey. They'd been given two powerful mares, each healthy enough to withstand the road ahead. It was too generous, but he had learned by then that their kindness knew no bounds. Just as he was testing the stirrups, he heard a knock on the stable doors. It was Mauria, and her expression was set.

"Did you enjoy this leg of your adventure?" It didn't seem like an actual question, but Cal decided to humor her small talk until he could discover the true purpose of her visit.

"Very much so! I almost think those guards in Cantor deserve my thanks. If they hadn't arrested me, I'd probably still be roaming around a city full of bigots, instead of getting to know the nicest people in Colliptia."

Mauria rolled her eyes but didn't protest. They both knew he wasn't exaggerating.

"Where will you go next?" She was still stalling, but Cal could tell they were getting closer to whatever she was building towards.

"We're not sure," Cal told her. "Technically we could head back home, but something tells me Garreck isn't ready for that yet. And I've never been one to say no to an adventure."

"I'm coming with you,"

There it was. She said the words as fast as she could, cutting in and continuing on before Cal could respond, her speech clearly premeditated.

"You need me. You need someone who can heal, and someone who knows these woods. I know the other communities in this country well, and I know how to fight. You have none of these things. So, I'm coming."

Cal raised an eyebrow. "You can fight?" This, more than anything else she'd mentioned, stood out as strange. Of course, she would be useful, Cal didn't doubt it for a second. But where had she learned to defend herself? The Aelish had no need for it in their world.

Mauria only nodded at his question, still looking him straight in the eye. For a moment, Cal considered making her wait for an answer. He could see, however, that there was more to this request than Aelish generosity. They might need her, but he had a hunch she needed them just as badly.

"Sure, you can come," he said, holding out his hand. She shook it and smiled at him, eyes glossy but set.

I'm collecting quite the group, Cal silently mused. The moment might have been humorous, if not for the look of unadulterated joy that had settled over Mauria's features.

Mauria

Mauria stood on the earthen road that led away from her camp. She looked out on the green gardens, the bubbling streams, and the toiling men and women. All were safe—sturdy and unvarying. She turned away, beaming. *This is my time.*

Garreck

To be honest, Garreck was grateful that Mauria had joined their crew. With three, there may have been more bodies, but somehow there was also more room to breathe.

They spent most of their time in the woods, working their way through trails that varied in size. Sometimes they travelled along wide, expansive paths of worn, trodden earth. Other days the roads were barely broad enough for their horses to squeeze through, and the ground lay hidden beneath dense layers of vines and weeds. Mauria said the trip was preferable to the way north. In Marcan South the Aelemian customs intermixed with Rie architecture; she swore that once they reached more populated areas it was worth a look.

With each mention of Rien, Garreck buried his disdain. Though he kept it to himself, he couldn't help thinking of the Cantic papers reporting on Rie rebels who preyed on roads like this. Garreck knew the evil that the Rie were capable of. Not wanting to appear weak, however, he resigned himself to keeping his mouth shut and his eyes open.

Cal, on the other hand, couldn't help but speak. He jabbered on and on about the differences between Cratos and the many places they visited. To Garreck's utter dismay, Cal seemed fascinated by the different types of flora and fauna, and damn if that wasn't their whole trip. They were in the *woods* for God's sake.

He couldn't help but grin a bit, though, as Cal prattled on. Garreck envied Cal's comfort in himself and his world. Cal knew that at the end of their travels he would return to a loving family, surrounded by support and understanding. Garreck had no such promise. At this point, Marten might very well have burned all of Garreck's possessions just to spite his rebel son.

For now, and for as long as humanly possible, he would live this new life and forget about the old one. Maybe someday he'd find somewhere he wanted to stay, or someone who didn't want to see him leave. Neither Cantor nor Aelemia had filled either desire so far.

There was only one other country in the known world apart from Cratos, Cantor, Aelemia and Rien. Devoran, unfortunately, was not a typical vacation spot. Not that they were exactly taking a typical vacation. Even using that word seemed a bit of a stretch in Garreck's opinion. Barring a suicide mission across the Western Sea, however, Devoran was the farthest he could venture in his personal pursuit to escape his family.

Garreck decided he would not be the first to bring up the idea of exploring Devoran. Then again, if someone else were to mention it, he would not stand in the way.

Cal

Cal could tell that Garreck was annoyed with him, but he found it hard to care. The land was vast and they were free to roam with tremendous abandon. Never in his life had Cal had so much ownership over his own experiences, and he savored every second of it.

Once he became acquainted with Aelemia, however, Cal began to crave more. The area's verdant vegetation fed him clean air that kept his spirits high and his energy up, but the moment Cal felt that he had conquered this new world, its vibrancy became quite stale.

29

What was wrong with him? Had his life in Cratos been so formulaic that the unknown was all that would do? He hoped not. An unquenchable existence sounded horrid and tiring. Even so, he itched to move on.

Mauria had taken them to Marcan South, and from there it would be easy to move into Rien. That country, however, did not particularly appeal to Cal. Cratos was a civilization with an immovable center; logic and reason reigned supreme. The faith of Rien sounded too similar. Their god governed them much the same as the order he submitted to back home, and Cal wanted more.

He thought about this for some time, playing with an idea he knew the others would not like. However, after a while the pressure within him became too much, and he made his proposition.

His restlessness peaked on a clear, perfect night. The fire they made danced and flickered and cast shadows on the woods around them. Garreck sat with his back inclined, head tipped toward the stars that peaked through the canopy overhead. Mauria had gone to get more firewood. When she returned, Cal spoke up.

"So," he began, his eyes on the flames in front of him. "What would you say to a trip to Devoran?"

From the corner of his eye he thought he saw Garreck's mouth turn up a bit at the edges, but apart from that he said nothing. Mauria had the opposite reaction, and seemed to stiffen as Cal said the country's name.

"There are many stories about Devoran," she said in a low voice. Cal could tell she didn't want to admit to believing these tales, but they must have left an impression on her.

"And I've heard some," Cal replied, "but I always took them to be cautionary: tales for children to enjoy and learn from."

Mauria glared at him, and he could tell he had offended her. *Good*, he thought. If he couldn't get to Devoran with their blessing, he would use their stubborness.

"The stories have merit," she told him in an icy voice. "Aelemians have attempted to trade with the Devora for many years. Not everyone returns, and those who do come with stories of powerful magic." Her voice grew quieter as she continued. "My grandmother used to tell us a story of her brother, Willem, who got lost in the forests of Devoran. Willem had been out near the border and, without knowing, strayed off—away from Aelemia. He came home with stories of wind that spoke to him, screaming and chasing him about. He told her of mountains that came crashing down around him and even fire that fed on his fears."

Mauria's face was ashen, but from the other side of their circle, Garreck snorted. "And you believe these ramblings? Please. We know magic exists in small forms because of our gifts." Cal opened his mouth to argue, but Garreck held up a hand and continued, "True magic has not existed for centuries."

"If it even existed at all," Cal said, unable to control himself. "Magic itself is most likely imagined for the sake of good storytelling. Your knacks," he looked from Garreck to Mauria, "are simply heightened abilities."

"I don't care what they are." Mauria cut in, testily. "But for the record Cal, you're wrong," she said with a haughty shrug. "And I am not *afraid* to go to Devoran, I'm just relaying what I know. I'll face whatever truth lies in those stories just as bravely as you will."

Garreck smirked, "Well that's settled then. If no one here protests, we will venture within the bowels of that country which spooked poor Willem Hoan."

"That's settled then," Cal returned quickly, hoping to cut off any retort from Mauria. He was quite pleased with himself and felt the tingle of a new objective building within him. Satisfied, he turned back to the fire which seemed to have picked up its dance.

Rasha

Rasha woke to the rumbling of the pilgrimage wagon and the smell of dry heat. The way was long, and although he was surrounded by fellow travelers, the journey left him with excess time to think. Every now and then those thoughts drifted to his mother, and Rasha felt a pang of guilt for leaving her alone. Yes, his mother had first suggested the excursion, but that did not make it feel like less of a betrayal on his part. Rasha's father had been gone long enough that memories of him were only the recollection of stories, and wife and son had spent the last fourteen years as one steadfast unit. Being separated now was an absence Rasha felt with every breath.

And yet, although his guilt ran deep, he had not hesitated before signing up for the journey the day after he'd first read the flyer. He comforted himself with the knowledge that his was not a trivial diversion; it was something that his mother could be proud of, and something that he would return better because of.

Rasha had to admit, however, that the trip was a bit less seductive now that it was actually underway. There were about fifteen others traveling with him, and with only two wagons the space was beginning to smell. This was part of the pilgrimage—that sacrifice of comfort. Still, he needed some air.

When the wagon finally stopped, he got out to stretch. They were somewhere in Southern Cantor, and the thin forest hinted that they might be nearing the Aelemian border.

His group ate a simple breakfast, and spent the rest of the day gathering supplies they would need for the remainder of the trip. Their stops would be less frequent once they went deeper into the forest. First the pilgrimage would cross through Marcan South, and eventually they would make their way through Marcan North to the Sea of Torp. There was an island not far off the shore that was said to clear the mind and refresh the soul; Rasha hungered for it.

At night the group came together again for a small meal, and one man volunteered to lead them in an evening prayer. It was during a moment of silence that Rasha felt a shift in the brush around them. Everyone in the circle sat without making a sound, but outside the glow of their firelight Rasha thought he heard movement. He opened his eyes and peered out into the night, squinting through splotches as his eyes adjusted to the dark. When he was finally able to make out the onyx outlines of bushes and trees, he saw nothing out of the ordinary. Blushing, embarrassed at his own cowardice, he turned back and closed his eyes in an attempt to rejoin the service. With effort, he pushed away all thoughts of the outside world and prayed.

This exercise would prove impossible a few hours later, but not because of silly superstitions. No, as Rasha lay in his wagon, his eyes wide and staring at the ceiling above him, it was the smell and heat of the bodies around him that had him begging for peace. He willed his mind to close down—for sleep to come—if only for a few hours.

"Restless?" a voice asked from behind him. He shifted in the cramped space to find a girl looking at him, her eyes shining in the small bit of moonlight that leaked in from cracks in the wagon walls.

"A bit," Rasha answered. "It's hard to breathe here."

She nodded. "In a few ways, I think. I didn't know how crowded this would be."

"I couldn't agree more, but right now it's the smell."

She laughed at that. "I'm Abi," she told him. "You're Rasha, right?"

Rasha's brows crinkled in confusion, and Abi noticed. "I heard you chatting with the others while we were gathering," she explained.

"Oh," Rasha said, rather lamely.

Abi didn't seem to mind. "Would you want to take a walk outside? I don't think I can spend another second in here."

Rasha was tempted. Not only could he do with air that was crisp and fresh, but he also thrilled at the idea of a walk alone with this girl. The purpose of his travels was selflessness and sacrifice, though, and what more of a distraction could he find? All he could focus on right now was Abi's long dark hair, and how small and sweet her smile was.

This inner struggle was short lived, however, as it was soon interrupted by a faint smell of smoke, which only grew stronger as Rasha tried to identify it. In the end, the source of the fumes didn't quite matter; the piercing screams were far more disturbing.

"What is that?" Abi asked, her voice shaking.

Rasha rushed to the door of his wagon, only to see the other ablaze. Strangers ran, chasing Rie men and women, yelling and killing with abandon. Rasha froze, unsure of what to do next. He knew there was a Cantic fear of his people, but such prejudices could not be strong enough to cause *this*? These men must have been bandits or criminals. Whatever the source, Rasha saw no way out.

"Abi, come on!" Rasha yelled, pulling her away. They wove in and out of the madness, dodging as much of the violence as they could.

"Rasha!" The yell accompanied a wrenching of his arm as Abi was torn from him. He turned and saw another woman, her face partially obscured, throwing Abi back into the chaos. Rasha whirled around and ran towards them, only to be hit hard in the face by an unknown assailant. Dazed, Rasha saw the shadow of a man coming towards him, his features flitting in and out of view as the fires raged around him.

Rasha couldn't think. He took in the horrific, blazing scape in front of him, and acted.

He ran.

Later, this moment of indecision would haunt him—to do nothing as his companions were slain. But Rasha was no match for the rage that burned through the camp like venom, and he lost control of all honor and sense. He stole into the safety of the woods, confused, and more afraid than he could ever remember being.

He ran and ran until he could no longer hear the hell he'd left behind, and did not stop until the sun began to rise. He fled through the dimly lit forest until he saw a small camp. There, three people were sleeping around a fire that had been reduced to white coals. Not caring who these travelers were, Rasha broke into their clearing. Exhausted by his escape and the slow drain of adrenaline, he stumbled and grasped at the air. His vision failed, and then his mind went dark.

Mauria

"Who the hell is that?" As Garreck's voice rang out, Mauria's eyes flew open.

What had happened while they slept?

She turned toward Garreck and then to the figure he was pointing at. It was a boy lying flat on his face, his green cloak splayed haphazardly out on the ground. He was clearly unconscious.

Cal got up and nudged the body a bit, trying to wake him. "Did you see him come last night?" he asked her, perplexed.

"And just fall back to sleep without saying anything? Not likely," she retorted, her voice sour. But, as she spoke Mauria got up to join Cal next to the boy. He was at least two years younger than she, with tan skin and freckles. Just looking at him softened her a bit; something about the roundness in his face reminded her of Kent.

"We should let him sleep," Mauria said, but she could tell by the look on Garreck's face that he was not going to comply. Sighing, she took the boy's shoulders and gave him a light pull, turning him upwards so that he was flat on his back.

He was awake in an instant, his eyes opened wide from the movement. He sat up quickly, studying them with nervous apprehension. "Who are you?" When he spoke it was in a Rie accent. If it hadn't been clear from his cloak, the stranger's voice confirmed his nationality.

"We'll ask the questions," Garreck interjected. As much as Garreck had grown on her, there were times when it was all too clear that he had been raised in Cantor.

"My name is Rasha," the boy answered. "I was on a pilgrimage to Torp, and we were attacked." Mauria saw fear flash across Rasha's face, and reflected in that fear were the unknown horrors he'd encountered in the night.

"You're safe with us," Mauria told him. "Where were you when you were attacked?"

"We were almost to Marcan South," he replied. "I think we were still in Cantor. We had stopped for the night and when I woke, people were all around us. There was fire, and I saw them..." he cut off, unable to continue.

"I've only ever heard of Rie rebels in those parts," Garreck said, a bit defensive. "Seems like you people will even go after yourselves now."

"They weren't from *Rien*," Rasha said, startled by the accusation.

Garreck just shrugged and shook his head, unconvinced. "Whatever. I need to take a walk," he told them, before setting off into the woods.

Mauria watched Cal's eyes follow Garreck before he turned to take Rasha's hand. "Go back to sleep," Cal said with a soft tone. "You're safe here, truly. We'll have breakfast for you when you're ready."

Mauria appreciated Cal's charisma now more than ever before. Cal's voice was soothing, and she watched as Rasha's terror shifted into something like relief. After seeing the sincerity in Cal's eyes, Rasha lay back down, his own eyes closing almost immediately.

Smiling at Cal, Mauria went to make a fire out of the still sizzling remnants from last night's blaze. She was not surprised that Cal had won over Rasha so quickly; she knew all too well how compelling that boy could be when he put his mind to it. Not personally, of course.

She was far from Cal's typical conquest. Many a man from her camp, however, had become familiar with Cal during their stay in Marcan West. She had seen a few girls try to coax a bit of the same from Garreck at first, but they had about as much luck with him as they would have with Cal. They were better off, though, in Mauria's opinion.

She wondered where Garreck's anger had come from. His resentment of Rasha had been immediate and persisting. Either Garreck had a particular reason to hate the Rie, or intolerances in Cantor were strong and fierce.

As the fire shifted from smoke to sizzling coals, Mauria took some of the meat they had salted and prepared to roast it for Rasha. She had felt like the newcomer up until this moment, and she would make sure he was welcomed when he awoke.

Cal

While Mauria cooked and Rasha rested, Cal wandered away from the site, searching for Garreck. It did not take him long— Garreck had settled at the base of a large oak tree not far from their camp. His face was still grumpy and grim, and when he saw Cal approaching he scowled. Cal ignored this, and walked briskly over to where Garreck brooded. He plopped down against the oak tree's wide base, but Garreck did not speak. He just raised an eyebrow, daring Cal to question him. Cal loved it when Garreck did that, though he would never admit it.

"It's about Rasha." His voice was serious. There were times when Cal enjoyed bickering with Garreck. During those times his voice was animated and challenging, but this was not the same. In level tones he said, "Promise me that you'll leave him alone."

"I won't tolerate a Rie long, Cal," Garreck replied, and Cal knew he was serious. In Cal's world the Rie were laughable, for religion was not highly thought of in Cratos. But in Cantor, it was something much more. Cantics believed that the Rie were dangerous extremists, bent on spreading their ways through the North. Garreck was certainly not immune to Cantic assumptions, Cal knew this firsthand, but he needed his leniency here.

"I don't often comment on the ways of Cantor," Cal said, eyes locked on Garreck's. "But it seems necessary now. You need to understand that not all Rie are radicals, just as not all Aelemians are peaceful." For good measure he added, "And not everyone from Cantor is a mindless soldier." Garreck glared, but he continued. "I don't know what will happen to poor Rasha, or where he will choose to go, but while he is here you must treat him well. He has earned nothing less."

Garreck turned slowly toward Cal until his face was only inches away. He was so close, in fact, that Cal could feel the heat of his breath as he murmured, "No promises."

After a long pause, Garreck got up, brushed himself off, and went back to the camp.

Rasha

Rasha stirred once again when he heard footsteps approaching. When the two men came back to the fire, both looked a bit affected. Rasha didn't know what to make of it, but at least the older one wasn't mad anymore.

The woman had identified herself as Mauria. She was pretty, with auburn hair that cascaded around her pale face and resin-colored eyes. She made Rasha feel safe, although after the events of the previous night, he doubted he would ever again feel truly safe.

Rasha took his time sitting up, taking in his surroundings for the first time since his collapse the night before. The most obvious detail about the camp was its scarcity. The trio he'd stumbled upon seemed to own very few possessions. In total, they each had a horse and about a week's supply of provisions, meaning they stopped frequently to restock and refresh.

This left Rasha with several different options. The most logical course of action would be to find a shop the next time they rested, and either begin again with a new Rie cohort headed north or buy passage back to Rien. If it had just been a matter of him getting lost in the woods, these would have been his only two options. If he had not just been subjected to blood and pain and carnage, the choice would have been simple. And yet, this was not the case.

He had endured all of it. He had listened in agony to unanswered cries for help as he ran from a meaningless death. Each shout still echoed in his ears. Rasha had assumed that Taklam spoke to his fellow Rie worshippers. He'd believed that if he was good and kind and reverent enough that Taklam would speak to him, too. And yet his god had watched his subjects—all those men and women—die, and there had been no divine intervention. Rasha prayed that Abi had somehow escaped, but he knew his prayers were empty; he was empty.

And because of this, for the first time in his life, Rasha did not want to do what was logical. For the first time, Rasha did not know where his path was going to take him. And with a sadness that sank deep to the marrow of his bones, he wasn't sure if there was anyone else who did, either. His body ached to rebel, to lash out against the crippling fear that there was either a vindictive god—or no god at all.

Whether it was from bitterness or frustration, Rasha closed his eyes, and let sleep take him.

It was dusk when he opened his eyes again. He had been out for most of the day, and by now the air was muted as the last bits of daylight fought against the incoming stars. Mauria smiled at him as he sat up, and offered him a stick full of venison. It smelled wonderful. With a returning smile, he accepted it and began to eat, only then realizing how hungry he was.

"Where are the other two?" Rasha asked Mauria when he came up for air.

"Out for a walk," she replied. "They wanted to go for one final scavenge before we head out. Any berries and mushrooms we can save along the way will make a difference once we are more remote."

This news made Rasha pause. He had assumed they'd be going toward a camp or community in the area. Where could they be heading that was so secluded they needed hoards of provisions?

Mauria must have seen the question on his face, for she added, "We're on our way to Devoran." Her voice was steady, but there was a note of something hidden behind the even tone. Was it fear?

"I see," Rasha answered, chewing his venison, careful to keep his expression neutral. While Cantic murderers may have been the more practical foes, the Devora were worse in the minds of most of the Rie. This was due primarily to the religion they practiced. Rien was a land of staunch piety. They gave themselves entirely over to the one true god. Their culture was crafted to fit the needs of their monotheistic center, and their faith was the origin of every code and law. In contrast, Devoran was a wild place, lacking focused faith and preaching devotion to the earth, but not to any god. Rasha might have been angry, but he was not ready to give up on his religion entirely. Maybe, such a place would provide him with some space to think. If the Devora had given up on Taklam, maybe he would not follow Rasha there.

"I think," Rasha began slowly, looking down at his meal as he spoke, "I might like to join you, if it is not an imposition."

Mauria paused for the briefest of moments before fixing her mouth into a kind smile. "You'll have to manage to live with Garreck," she said to him. "I don't know if you were able to read his subtle cues when you first arrived, but he's not too fond of the Rie."

"Yeah, I got that," Rasha told her, his voice apologetic. Mauria waved her hand dismissively.

"If you are tough enough to stay, he will be tough enough to have you here," she told him. "But I must warn you that we're quite the mangey crew. Cal's all right, but Garreck and I each have our baggage. Garreck especially," she rolled her eyes, "but I've got it, too. I'm stubborn, and not much of a lady."

Rasha laughed at this. "I'll take my chances."

Garreck

Of course, *he* was coming. Garreck's hands were clenched as he watched the back of the Rie's head bob in front of him. He had grown up hating Rien. And for good reason. His father came home everyday with news of another Rie attack. Newspapers were filled with their terrorism and malicious plots. One of Garreck's good friends growing up had died from a Rie ambush on a Western Canitic road. They were heretics and villains, and now there was one travelling with him.

The boy seemed docile. Garreck could not deny that there'd been no outward animosity from Rasha. At least, not yet. But he was patient, and knew that with time the Rie would show his true colors.

Feeling his temper and anxiety flare as he thought of the evil plots that Rasha might have planned, Garreck took a deep breath, and let his mind wander to other things. He had begun to compartmentalize his familial strife, stowing it away in the dark corners of his mind. It stayed there, for the time being, as Garreck knew there was nothing worth exploring. His father was an angry man, and Garreck would have to face him once he returned home. Those were simply facts; they could not be denied, but they could be ignored. And since he did not plan to return to Cantor for some time, he would let those dormant problems rot until he was forced to face them. Devoran didn't care about his failings, after all.

Garreck smiled inwardly at the ridiculousness of their venture. True, he didn't believe the ludicrous stories that Mauria told, but he also knew better than to disregard myth altogether. Most likely there was something dangerous enough lying in Devoran that kept wandering Aelemians on edge, but he was sure it was far less threatening than the Aelish imagined it to be.

That anonymous threat tugged at his senses, but his eagerness to continue was far stronger than any misgivings he had about their destination. His heart felt lighter with every eastward step. He was glad Cal had suggested it.

Cal, the man in question, was currently riding ahead, scouting about for a place to rest. He couldn't believe he had once thought Cal weak; Cal had shown his worth since their first exploits in Cantor. What Garreck had mistaken for fragility had ended up being valuable charm and sense of self. Though Garreck himself had always acted before thinking, Cal was thoughtful in all that he did.

Conflict rolled around Garreck's face, though no one was around to see. If they had been back in Cantor, Cal would not be on his mind. The man would probably be dead, honesty, at the hands of some street gang or rebellious bar men. For all his presence of mind, Cal was no match for the biases of Cantor.

It hurt him, he realized, to think of someone harming Cal. Sure, he was a cank, but he was turning out to be a better man than most he had known back home.

Damn it, Garreck thought, simultaneously annoyed and amused by this new revelation. All this compassion, maybe *he* was the cank.

Cal

It took another week for them to reach the border of Devoran. During that time, Cal made every possible effort to bring his group together. The tension between Garreck and Rasha was tangible and infected their troupe, saturating everything around them with the disease of distrust. He didn't blame Rasha for any of his negativity; it must have been impossible for the kid to ignore the open dislike that constantly emanated from Garreck.

There were times, though, as they sat around the fire—listening to katydids and crickets humming subtle chaos—that the four travelers seemed to find some peace. These moments were fueled by nothing other than reflection, a deep sigh at the end of each quietly contentious day.

To Cal, these instances seemed as good as any to introduce some bonding time. In Cratos they believed very much in the power of words and stories. It was how they kept their history alive. First it had been word of mouth, but even after they'd learned how to produce written tales, verbal storytelling remained an essential part of Cratian community. So, one night, he just began to speak.

They were all sitting around the fire, lost in their own recollections. For whatever reason, Cal's own thoughts drifted to a time when he was young, and he had watched Caroline prosecute a woman for gambling.

"Rasha, what are Rien's policies on gambling?" The words were the first that had been said in some time, and Rasha jumped at the sound of Cal's voice.

"We have strict laws against it," Rasha told him once he had regained his composure. "But ours is a faith-based ban. I don't understand why Cratos wouldn't allow it."

"What was the situation, Cal?" Mauria asked. "Did they find out she was cheating people, or something?"

"Well, first of all, gambling is always cheating people." Cal could tell Garreck was about to interrupt so he spoke quickly, "She wasn't purposely trying to take people's money though, no."

Encouraged by their interest, Cal told them the story. The trial was not so long ago that he could not remember its details. He described a simple oak room, pristine but unadorned, and recalled the dyes of charcoal, ash, and oatmeal that dressed every man and woman of the court. Cal lingered on the details of the defendant's face, on the shadows from sleepless nights and early withdrawal that etched her features. He paused after relaying the verdict—guilty. Each jury member had agreed wholeheartedly that she needed help.

Garreck was the first to respond. "Unanimously guilty. For gambling? Just gambling?" He seemed shocked, skeptical.

"Of course," said Cal. "We take our health very seriously in Cratos. Gambling is addictive, and as such she was endangering not just herself, but those around her. It was reckless."

"But that's her choice!" Garreck retorted, "I get that you don't want her screwing with everyone else's lives, but she should be able to play cards or dice in her own home!"

"The court saved her from herself that day," Cal explained. "Our prisons are not as superfluous as those of Cantor, Garreck." A smile played across his face as he said it, and Cal shot Garreck a playful wink before continuing. "She was sent to a rehabilitation facility to help her with her problem."

"It still seems like a load of crap to me," Garreck said, disgusted.

"I agree with Garreck," Rasha said quietly, and everyone turned, surprised. "If Cratos does not object to gambling on a moral basis, then that woman has a right to her own methods of enjoyment. Everybody does. Who are your people to take that from her?"

A small pause followed his words, broken by a simple, rather lame "yeah" from Garreck.

"Well, at least you all have something to gamble *with*, if you wanted to give it a try," Mauria told them. "We don't have money in Aelemia, remember? So we'd just be gambling with turnips or snap peas."

Garreck barked a laugh, and Cal was thrilled to realize that it was not the condescending sound he had expected, but an actual, genuine chuckle. "Man, I could give you guys some wild stories about gambling in Cantor," Garreck told them, chest still shaking from Mauria's joke.

They continued like this all night, and for their last few nights in Aelemia, the fire was a place of stories. It was there that Cal learned of Mauria's fear of owls, though she didn't elaborate on the inciting incident, claiming that it was too traumatic to relive. And it was during a fireside story that they learned of Garreck's favorite holiday as a child.

"It was about nine years ago, so I had just turned nine myself," Garreck told them with unusual enthusiasm. "My father had gone off on business, and while he was away my mother brought us to the ocean. My brothers and I fished and swam, and Mum made us a picnic that we ate on a blanket." After a quiet pause he added, "That's the only time I've ever really seen my mom happy, come to think of it."

Moments like these brought them together, and Cal was grateful to learn so much about his new friends. One night, Rasha was even kind enough to explain the Rie religion when Cal asked. Rasha went through the mechanics of his faith, which included complete submission to their god and continued prayer and dedication to peace. Cal had been hoping for Rasha's opinions as well as the facts, but did not push him when they were not provided. Garreck, however, noticed Rasha's vagueness and was not as tactful as Cal.

"Yeah, but what do you believe?" he asked when Rasha had finished.

"I ... I am confused," admitted Rasha, and his eyes burned as he said it. Cal could almost feel the heat that emanated from their youngest traveler, even near the warm fire. "You know what I saw in those woods," Rasha continued. "But what troubles me isn't just what hate can do to a man—it's also what *fear* can do. Those murders were evil, but am I any better for fleeing?"

"You saved yourself, kid." Garreck's comment was soft, almost sympathetic.

Rasha shook his head. "I condemned myself to a lifetime of shame and questioning." He paused before looking up, his eyes searching. "How can a god exist who allows for such violence and cowardice? I have prayed to an idea my whole life that I failed and was also failed by. How do I move on from that?"

Cal saw Mauria stir to his left, though she said nothing. Cal supposed she was trying to decide whether or not to embrace Rasha. Cal had never been much of a hugger, so he offered Rasha what he could. It was not much, but perhaps a small distraction would temporarily relieve this boy's torment.

"Cratians have no religion," he admitted. "We see life as ours to lead well, but we don't think it's dictated by anything other than our minds and our free will."

He looked at Garreck, "Does Cantor have a place of worship?"

"We have one," he said, shrugging as he did. "I go once in a while, with my whole family. They look like they buy into it, but they're also fake as shit." He blushed a little before he added, "Sometimes I believe, though. I don't know what or who I believe in, but I think there's something there—something keeping me from going completely off the rails." He laughed. "Not doing a great job of that though."

They all laughed, even Rasha. "What about you, Mauria?" Cal asked.

"The Aelish have a slightly different take on religion. We believe in community. It's not the same thing, I know, but the devout quality lines up with how Rasha talks about his god. We worship each other, live for each other. I think it's what keeps our way of life afloat."

"That sounds exhausting," Garreck muttered.

"Tell me about it," Mauria said, a bit sadly.

Rasha

The morning after their particularly intimate discussion about belief, Rasha caught up with Mauria. The forests had grown thicker as they neared Devoran, making it difficult to ride on horseback. Though it slowed their pace, they had been forced to walk the animals as they forged their way along the easternmost edge of Aelemia. With difficulty, however, Rasha was able to squeeze himself between Mauria and the thick brush to the right of the trail.

"Mauria, may I ask you something?" Her fireside statement about the Aelish had raised several questions for which he was hoping to get answers.

Mauria turned to him and smiled. "Of course, what's on your mind?"

Rasha paused, wanting to frame the question correctly. "You know I'm glad you're here. If it weren't for you, I might still be lost in the woods of Marcan South. But, I guess I don't understand why *you* are here?" She didn't immediately respond, but she did not look mad, so Rasha continued. "What made you leave your family? It sounds like everyone is so happy and kind in Aelemia."

Mauria shrugged, "I think you know the answer better than most, actually. Tell me, why did you first go on your pilgrimage?"

Rasha grimaced, and took care to choose the right words before he answered. "I didn't feel complete back home. No matter what I did, something seemed to be missing."

Mauria nodded, "That's exactly how I felt every day in my community. My family is loving, and I miss my brother dearly. You actually remind me of my brother a bit. Kent is as sweet as you are … and as kind. But I've breathed better ever since I left." She paused, as though wondering how honest she wanted to be, but seemed to decide she could trust Rasha. "It might sound braggish to say it, but I felt held back while I was there."

"I know exactly what you mean!" Rasha told her fervently. The tips of his ears were still slightly pink from Mauria calling him "sweet," but he persevered. "Whether it's Taklam or fate or destiny, I've always felt like there must be some larger plan for me."

A grin spread across Mauria's face. "Well, I hope we're together when we each discover our callings," she told him.

"Oy! Can you two pick it up? We've found something!" Garreck's voice came at them from somewhere ahead.

"Come on," Mauria grinned conspiratorially at Rasha as she nudged her horse along. "Apparently there's something that can't wait five extra minutes."

Garreck

When Mauria and Rasha finally made their way to the front of the group, Garreck gave them a reproachful glare. "What took you so long?"

he demanded, immediately regretting his words at the look he got from Mauria.

"Oh, I don't know, Garreck. It's not like we're on a meandering quest with no timeline whatsoever." Her eye roll was so pronounced that Garreck dared not go head to head with her.

"Fine, well, now that you're here," he muttered, "Cal and I have found something that you need to see." He moved aside to reveal an enormous tree. The trunk was thick and vast, with bark growing around the outer edges of an old wooden sign that looked to have been nailed there long ago. Garreck felt vindicated when he saw the others move forward, eyes wide as they took in the faded lettering on the face of the wooden board. Though muted and dull, the message was still discernible:

Should you move forward, travelers, beware what lies beyond.
Great danger lurks 'round every bend, as other souls have found.
Turn back and find your happiness in places close to home,
For all who venture past this point risk pain and certain doom.

"Boo!" Garreck yelled. Rasha jumped, so startled that he fell forwards, just beyond the base of the tree. Horrified and embarrassed, the boy scrambled to his feet, not meeting Garreck's eyes as he did.

Garreck roared with laughter. "Are you joking? You aren't actually afraid of this foolishness, are you?"

"That's not funny, Garreck," Mauria scolded, casting an apologetic glance towards Rasha. "So what if he is? I told you all about the terrible stories I've heard. Shouldn't we all be frightened that there's a menacing sign confirming all our worst fears?"

"It reads like a fairy tale," Garreck told her, in disbelief. "I mean, the thing rhymes! It seems like the sort of joke the Devora put up to turn away annoying little scoundrels like ourselves."

"What do you think, Cal?" Mauria asked, pretending as though she had not heard what Garreck said.

Cal looked back at the sign and read it through again before he answered. "I agree with Garreck," he told her.

Garreck gave a triumphant, "Whoop!" But Cal shot him an "I-don't-think-is-the-time-for-you-to-be-an-ass" look, and Garreck acquiesced. He settled for a smug, raised eyebrow that colored Mauria's face a deep shade of plum.

"Listen," Cal continued. Garreck knew Cal sensed the burgeoning explosion in Mauria as well as he did. "We've come all this way, and I think there's something to be said for such an obvious sign. If they were malicious, they wouldn't be this polite about explaining the danger, would they? They'd try to draw us in. I think this is just to keep prying eyes away from whatever's back there."

The longing in Cal's voice was not a healthy thing, but Garreck was not about to address whatever hero complex was urging Cal to move forward—not while he was getting his way, at least.

Mauria looked beseechingly between Cal and Garreck, but in the end it was Rasha who decided their fate.

"We should do it, Maur," he said. "They're right. We've come all this way. If we go back now, we return to the exact same lives we had before."

Mauria whirled to face him, but did not respond. Her expression changed from frustration to resignation, and after a moment of thought she threw her hands up and said, "Fine, then."

It was not necessarily a ringing endorsement, but Garreck didn't care. With confidence, he strode to the front of the group and took the first steps into Devoran.

PART TWO

Beware the curious mind that plucks
its valiant songs on harp and crwth.
-noble,
foolish,
probing
airs of sound, fast searching for some truth.
Take heed, that pluming melody!
Take care, that wandering sound!
Once fact is filtered from the rest
it cannot be unfound.

Rasha

*T*he first few steps into Devoran were disruptive. Rasha felt as though they had been swaddled in a heavy blanket the last few days of their trip, only to be roughly shaken out of it. Within moments of crossing the border, Rasha felt a change in the atmosphere so pronounced that skinridges peppered his arms and neck, each small hair standing on edge as though an electric current were passing through him.

The most pronounced difference between Devoran and the rest of Colliptia was its shocking beauty. Rasha's first glimpse of the wild country reminded him of an immense, patterned quilt. His eyes ran over patches of rolling hills and rocky crevices, fields of wildflowers, and a vast body of water, the surface of which refracted rainbow sunbeams of light. There was light *everywhere*. Devoran glittered around him, every surface brushed by glorious, penetrating sunshine.

There was a strange familiarity to it all, but Rasha sensed some vital connection was still missing. He did not know how to exist in this place. Not yet.

This feeling continued as they plodded their way deeper into Devoran. Eventually, as it grew dark they were forced to stop. They made camp under the trees on the edge of a small meadow. Mauria insisted on it, even when Rasha begged to sleep under the clear night sky, arguing that the stars were too beautiful to ignore. She fought him on it, though. Hard. They were in an unknown land with a dangerous reputation, and she demanded the cover of the forest.

Rasha conceded, but set up his things as close to the clearing as he could get. His arms sprawled out through the shadows of the trees around them so that his hand glowed with moonlight.

He watched Mauria over by the fire. She had agreed to wait with it until the embers dulled, and she seemed not to mind this task. Rasha understood. This chore gained Mauria a few precious hours of privacy while the others gave in to sleepy eyes and greedy yawns.

But Rasha could not sleep. The exhilaration of this place kept his heart racing, and, though he arranged and rearranged himself, neither his body nor his mind could rest.

So, although it meant intruding on her quiet moments, Rasha eventually crept over to join Mauria at the fire, having given up on going to bed.

As he made his way over, he could hear quiet whispers coming from where Garreck and Cal were lying. They had been bickering quietly each night for a while now, though Rasha sensed it was all in good fun. When Garreck was angry, everyone knew it.

"I guess none of us can sleep," Rasha said to Mauria as he approached.

Mauria looked first at him, and then toward the silhouettes of their companions.

"When do you think they'll realize it, Rasha?" she said, and Rasha understood the implication without her having to state it.

"Who knows. I don't think Garreck would ever admit it, even if he did somehow figure it out." Rasha shrugged and edged closer to the fire as he spoke. The Devoran summers were relatively mild, but a crispness hung in the night air that kept him searching for warmth.

Mauria took a long branch and prodded at the dying flames in front of them. Rasha watched her eyes follow the tiny lines of smoke as they swirled from the burning remains, almost imperceptible in their delicacy.

"My mother used to ask me what I saw in the smoke," Mauria told him.

Rasha looked at her. "And what did you say?" he asked.

"Back when I was small enough to fit in her lap, she'd hold me to her. I can still remember the heat from the fire and feel that sense of closeness you have with a parent. When she asked, I always made something up. Sometimes is was a stallion galloping through fields of swaying stalks of wheat. Other times it was an approaching mob, and occasionally it was a jungle animal swinging from branch to branch. It was never what she expected, but rather than chastise her fantastical daughter, my mother would just smile." Mauria grinned as she said this, and Rasha could see the affection she had for her mother.

"What do you see, Rasha?" She directed the question to him quickly, and Rasha scrambled to think of an answer.

"I'm not sure," he said truthfully.

"Once I started really looking, I began seeing a river—one that was carving away at the shoreline, creating something new and wild." Her eyes were bright as she added, "I don't know if I have ever connected to anything in our world more than that imagined stream."

"That fits you perfectly, Maur," Rasha said, and he meant it. She was made to cut through their world, carving it to fit her desires.

Mauria smiled, "Looking back, I think my mother knew that, too. Even when I was seeing jungle animals, I was really just seeing *change*.

Rasha gazed upon Mauria and saw that she had fallen deep into her own thoughts. He picked himself up, gave her a quick hug, and started to make his way back to bed.

As he walked, however, Rasha was sure he heard the sounds of footsteps crunching over branches in the darkness just in front of him.

"Is that you, Rasha?" The call came from the opposite direction.

"No, I think there's someone over there," Rasha whispered as loudly as he could, hoping that Cal could hear what the intruder couldn't.

"It's probably just an animal," Garreck's voice insisted. "Settle down, the both of you."

Rasha felt a tap on his shoulder, and he swung around, his heart beating madly and his hands pulling quickly into fists.

"Easy there, soldier." It was only Cal. "Come on over with us, Rasha," he insisted. "Just for a bit; it will make me feel better. If it's a robber or a murder, Mauria has the best chance of fighting them off."

Rahsa didn't necessarily agree with Cal. Yes, Mauria was a force to be reckoned with, but Garreck was the one with the muscle. All the same, being with the other boys was more favorable than being alone until his nerves calmed.

Rasha walked with Cal over to where he and Garreck were situated. "What were you guys talking about before whatever that was interrupted?" he asked, sinking down to the ground, his head resting on his knees.

"Cal was being an idiot, actually," said Garreck, "So, same old thing, really."

"It's not idiotic to be afraid of weapons!" protested Cal, his hands flying in annoyance. "You really don't need a permit in Cantor? No Papers?" Rasha had a feeling Cal had asked variations of this question before as Garreck did not even indulge him with an answer.

Unfazed, Cal continued to prattle on. "I could walk into a shop, buy a battle axe, and then carry it out onto the street? What if I was an aggressive, deranged killer?"

"Then you kill a few people and eventually get caught and punished," Garreck chuckled. "Why? Are you planning on it now that you know it's possible?"

Rasha laughed, but Cal only smiled at the joke. "It seems so irresponsible," he said, shaking his head. "If you have the power to stop it, why not stop it?"

Gareck sighed. "Because it's not our place to deny someone the chance to defend themselves. What if someone assaulted you on the street? You'd be happy to have that battle axe, huh?"

There was a pause as Cal took that in, and Rasha could see that Garreck had won. As if in confirmation of this assumption, Cal just shrugged and said, "Fine, but if the Cantics are so against denying citizens their rights, why are they so against people like me?"

Rasha's head whipped towards Garreck, who clearly hadn't expected the question. It was the first time Cal had referenced who he was in such a direct way. Rasha had heard from Mauria of Cal's exploits with the Aelish, but they had never discussed it so casually before. By the look on his face, it made Garreck uncomfortable—embarrassed.

"Honestly," Garreck said slowly, "because it isn't natural."

Cal thought about that before he responded. "I think the reason the Cantics don't like people like me," he said thoughtfully, "is because they do not understand people like me. It's the same reason they hate the Rie. They don't take the time to comprehend the unknown, and so they just fear it."

Cal looked at Rasha as he said this last bit, and Rasha nodded, his eyes moving to the ground as he did. He agreed, of course, that this was the root of Garreck's prejudice, but it felt odd to speak candidly about a topic this sensitive.

"Tell me something," Cal continued. "Have you ever had a reason to hate somebody like me? Like Rasha? Back in Cantor, you would have called me a cank, and we never would have spoken. But would there have been any real reason for your disdain?"

Rasha wondered if this was the first time Garreck had been forced to confront the origin of his own prejudice. If it was, his ability to give honest thought to the subject was honorable, particularly when the two objects of his derision sat looking at him.

"I guess not," Garreck admitted quietly. "It's what my family believes—what my people believe. It's just a part of who I was."

The last word caused Cal to look up, and Rasha saw a happiness so pure it was almost intimate.

"Was?" Cal questioned.

"I think so," Garreck said. "Things have clearly changed since the first time we met, Cal, and as irritating as you can be, I don't hate you. Either of you." He shot Cal a smirk when he mentioned him, but the last part was directed to Rasha, who nodded back.

"Thank you, Garreck," Rasha told him as he got up. Although there was nothing private about their conversation, Rasha was beginning to feel as though he were intruding. He walked slowly over to his things and curled tightly into his blankets, knowing the sleep he craved would finally come.

Before he surrendered to unconsciousness, Rasha heard a few last words as they came drifting over to him in the clear night.

"Garreck?" Cal's voice was so low in the darkness that it could have been the wind.

"Yeah?" Garreck responded, just as quietly.

"I'm glad that you don't hate me."

Cal

Cal's excitement as they entered Devoran was incomparable to anything he had ever felt before. From their first night and on, the world was his to conquer. *This* is what Cal had been longing for; whatever void their other destinations had failed to fill, this satiated. In the more wooded areas, the light from the sun was almost completely obscured by thick, expansive vegetation. Leaves of purple and pistachio colors reached out with thin, curling finger-like fronds, and elusive creatures chirped from the protection of the trees. In the open valleys and plains, golden tufts of mossy leaves crackled quietly under their feet, and the horses hooves sent swirls of dust rising from faded cracks in dried mud.

For most of their journey, the terrain was so diverse that the group struggled to follow the main road. At times they lost the path all together and had to hope that their instincts would keep them on course until it became clear again. Cal noticed the others were nervous as they worked to stay as on-route as possible, but he lived for the challenge. He was Mendolin Vassar braving the Sea of Torp or Barny Comeel who went over the Western Sea in search of greatness. To be fair, Cal hoped for a bit more success than Barney, who had not been heard of in some eighty years.

But it mattered not. They had numbers and bravery on their side, and his gut told him that something bigger than himself was beginning to form.

A separate part of Cal's instinct *did* manage to put him slightly on edge. Every once in a while, when they had stopped to rest for the night, Cal thought he heard a patter of movement nearby. He was sure he could feel eyes upon him in those eerie moments, and he would lie awake for hours, trying to catch a peek of their elusive guest. However, Cal also knew that any number of animals could be at the root of these happenings, so he managed to push these forebodings away, and instead enjoyed their grand adventure.

Every once in a while, though, uneasy thoughts would bubble to the surface. When they did, his thoughts strayed to their defenses, which were few. Garreck had a bow, and Mauria claimed to be proficient in combat though Cal had never seen it demonstrated.

"Hey, Mauria," Cal asked during one such tangent. "How did you learn how to fight?" She hadn't seemed too keen to talk about it back in Aelemia, so he'd let it drop. If he were honest, a small part of Cal was suspicious that she had made the skill up in an attempt to seem valuable. He didn't think this likely though, and he'd been itching to learn more.

Garreck looked over, "I didn't know you could fight, Mauria." Cal looked to see a tinge of curiosity on Rasha's face as well. They seemed as surprised as he had been when Mauria first mentioned it.

Her eyebrows came together slightly, and she turned away from them. It wasn't a denial; she talked as she made her way more slowly down the path. They were travelling a particularly beautiful stretch, a meadow filled with fireweed that ran parallel to a beach of onyx-black sand.

"I learned by watching Cantic troops," she said. Cal had not expected this, but it made sense. Aelemia was a staunchly pacifist community. He didn't imagine they gave many lessons in self-defense.

"Have you been to Cantor?" Garreck asked.

"No, I used to watch the practice drills when they came out to use some of the green space near our community. It was far enough away that no one noticed. But I always liked to explore, and one day I came upon one of the companies."

Her eyes were glossy, but her voice did not waiver as she added, "I had never seen anything like it."

"Ugh, I used to hate trips like that," Garreck complained. Cal started to shush him, but Mauria's glare achieved the desired result.

"You take such things for granted," she chastised. "Imagine growing up knowing there were parts of you that were not wanted—not acceptable. My family is loving and nurturing, but they never would have allowed me to learn something so inherently aggressive."

She smiled a bit as she added, "So I kept it from them. And I watched and practiced for years, and eventually it stuck. I adapted pieces of it, of course; you Cantics are a bit too graceless for my taste."

She threw a playful grin at Garreck, and he laughed. "There's nothing graceful about combat, Mauria, surely you picked that up."

Cal saw the same look of determination cross Mauria's face that he had witnessed in the barn on their last day in Aelemia. She raised an eyebrow at Garreck and said, "Oh, isn't there?"

The boys watched as Mauria moved to a place in the meadow where the wild flowers grew less densely. She seemed nervous as she fussed with her footing and positioning. However, Cal saw her take one long, deep breath that grew from the depths of her torso—and then she began.

Cal had never seen anything more entrancing. Coupled with the alien-like quality that Devoran possessed, Mauria's movements took on a similar, otherworldly appearance.

She flowed through every punch and kick with a self-possession that was startling in its assurance. One high thrust of a leg left her at a 130 degree angle, and yet her muscles held the position until she was ready to transition to the next.

Cal might not have noticed any of this, however, for her face revealed the true import of Mauria's skill. She glowed. There was a joy within her that Cal had not yet seen. Perhaps there had been glimmers of it along the road, but it shone out of her now, untainted by the baggage she claimed to carry.

When Mauria had spoken of the Aelish religion, she had told them that her people believed in each other—that their conviction lay in community. What Cal witnessed now was not a faith in others. It was a total and immovable faith in self. Had Rasha and Garreck noticed, too?

Mauria finished her exhibition with a controlled spin, one leg up and tight against her chest, before coming down on one knee. She looked up, smiling up at them with an unrelenting brilliance.

"Well?" She aimed the question at Garreck, breathing heavily as she did.

For once, Garreck was speechless. Cal simply let out a low whistle.

"Beautiful," Rasha told her, smiling.

Garreck

Having Mauria put him in his place would normally have sent Garreck reeling. This time, however, he was more impressed than upset. Mauria's show of vulnerability introduced a new side of her that was both raw and strong, and Garreck saw many pieces of who he was reflected within her. He knew what it felt like to have to hide who he was.

Thoughts like this carried him through to the next day—another winding walk filled with beauty but very little action. Cal and Mauria were ahead of him, bickering about one of the many differences between Aelemia and Cratos, but it was not hard to hear the arguments being hurled back and forth.

"Childhood isn't about having total control over your surroundings," Cal protested. "It's about learning how to be an active citizen. If I didn't learn how to follow the rules my parents gave me, I'd probably be in prison."

Garreck coughed pointedly at this. They had, in fact, met in prison. But Cal either did not hear him or did not want to indulge him.

"Kids need to be able to test themselves!" Mauria trilled. "They need to learn their limits. Honestly, they'd hardly need parents if they could make a living without them."

"I'm with Mauria," Rasha said.

"Of course, you are," Cal said, his hands going up to massage his temples, as if the conversation was giving him a headache.

"I'm not just on her side for the hell of it," Rasha said, shocking everyone with a rare moment of forcefulness. "It's how I grew up, too. My mother always gave me free reign when I wanted to leave. That trust made me feel mature and responsible, and it helped me to grow."

"What about—" began Cal, but Garreck cut him off.

"You're all wrong," Garreck said, quickening his steps to catch up with them. The others glared at him, obviously annoyed that he wasn't siding with either of them.

"I'm all kinds of messed up, and a lot of it had to do with how controlling my parents were. Well, *are*," Garreck amended. "I guess they're still like that when I deign to be in the same country as them."

"Yes, but Mauria and Rasha are talking about the other end of the spectrum. You can't possibly believe children would be fine wandering about on their own?"

"I guess not," Garreck admitted. "Kids need to feel supported, but they also need to make mistakes."

Mauria seemed placated, but Cal was unable to forgo a good debate. "Tell us then, Garreck," he said. "What is one rule your parents had that was so terrible it caused you to give up on order altogether?"

"Not what I said, Cal, but fine." Garreck thought for a moment. He could have gone with any of the smaller examples, but instead he chose the first that came to mind.

"All right. One rule growing up was that we weren't allowed pets," Garreck told them. "My father hates animals and never would have tolerated having to care for one. We had all these rabbits in our yard, though, and I would pretend that they were ours. I'd chase them around for hours until my mother called for me to come in."

"Not being able to have a pet hardly seems like cause for disownment, Garreck," Cal said in a slightly bemused tone.

"No," Garreck agreed. "You're absolutely right. But I let a rabbit into the house one day, and my father caught me playing with it. Marten

Landsing is not a man to mess with. He grabbed it by its ears and took it outside. I thought he was going to put it down and let it run away, but instead he held it out. The entire time it screamed and kicked." Garreck looked at Cal and Mauria in turn before he added, "He made me get my bow and shoot it. Just like that." Cal gasped and Mauria's face lost a bit of its color. "From then on the rule in our house was that any unwanted animals would be dealt with just like that rabbit."

Garreck sighed before adding, "Kids need loving parents."

The others didn't know what to say, and Garreck wasn't sure either. He walked ahead of them, feeling embarrassed. When Mauria bared her soul, it was beautiful and moving. When Garreck shared his own rough edges, there was silence and a large, heaping pile of pity. In fact, the moment the memory came out Garreck resolved not to fall victim to such honesty ever again. That is, until Cal caught up with him.

"I'm sorry that you grew up in a home like that, Garreck," he said. The depth of emotion in Cal's eyes was overwhelming. Garreck did not want to return that look.

"It's all right," Garreck shrugged. "Sorry for laying it all out like that. It was stupid to take your conversation and bring it down to my level."

Cal shook his head vigorously. "No, it's nice to hear something real about you. It's nice to know you." He smiled at Garreck and then turned back to fall into step with the others. Watching him, Garreck still didn't feel as though his vulnerability had had quite the same impact as Mauria's. Maybe though, something good came out of it.

Cal

Garreck's admission moved Cal in an entirely unexpected way. He was so affected that if Garreck had told his story on their seventh day in Devoran, it would have been the most important thing that happened to Cal all day. But instead, Garreck bared his soul on the eighth day, which was also the day they reached the site. On that day, everything else was minimized.

A site for what? They were not sure. However, after over a week of listening to a delicate balance of nature, self, and silence, they *heard* the commotion before they saw it.

The low bass of heavy objects falling came first. Cal felt the sonorous boom in his stomach just as much as he heard it through the trees. Next came the clanking of tools, followed by the unmistakable tones of men.

Cal and the rest made their way carefully to the edge of the clearing, peering behind large strangler figs that grew like a shield where the forest met the desert beyond. While the air a few feet from them seemed dry and hot, the forest was damp and humid, and Cal had to resist the urge to swat at the many insects that swarmed them as they hid, immobile.

Before him was a short stretch of sand the color of clay, which gave way to a vast depression. From where he was, Cal could see layers of stone and earth sparkling in the afternoon sun—the different colors stacked on top of each other, revealing the age of the land.

In addition to its incredible beauty, the pit was also filled with workers. Some seemed to be miners, covered in the debris of the underground. Others were fresh and businesslike, conversing closer to the top of the cavernous summit. They did not fit with the Devoran that Cal had come to know. And while he certainly had much to learn about the place, the clothing and mannerisms seemed more familiar to him than he would have expected.

"Shit," Garreck said from somewhere behind Cal's head. "*That*, my friends, is Marten."

Cal followed the hand that had appeared to his right and saw it pointing toward a tall, well-dressed man about a hundred paces below them. He was handsome, with the same dark skin as Garreck. His hair was cropped short, however, and his face seemed fixed in a permanent scowl. What bothered Cal most, however, was the way he was treating the woman in front of him. She was talking quickly and seemed apologetic, her hands gesturing wildly at times. Marten just stared, hands clasped casually but resolutely behind his back, conveying so much contempt that Cal could feel it from where he crouched.

"That's your *dad*?" Mauria said, the disgust in her voice told Cal she had also noticed his hostile manner. "I guess that fits your story, huh?"

"No wonder you have issues," Cal tried to joke, but Garreck had gone pale.

"We need to go." Garreck was already turning as he said it.

No one argued. Something felt off about the site. If Devoran was so mysterious, why was a group of Cantic miners working diligently on an operation that seemed years underway?

Cal's head spun with unanswered questions as they retreated. Was it just the Cantics, or were other countries represented among the many individuals they had seen? Perhaps most importantly—what were they looking for?

Mauria

They walked for a long while before anyone began to talk. Mauria was not so bold as to break the stretch of silence that followed their quick encounter at the Cantic site. She kept looking ahead at Garreck, who marched, quick and resolute, at the front of their procession. Mauria thought this was not only to get them as far away from Marten as humanly possible, but also to hide whatever range of emotion was plaguing Garreck's features.

After some time, his pace slowed, and they came to rest in a damp but guarded space against a small, rocky shelf.

"What on earth was that?" Mauria cringed as Cal spoke, fearing an end to their silence.

Thankfully, Garreck's temper remained neutral, and he ran both hands through his hair before glancing up. "I don't know."

"It looked like an excavation site of some kind," Mauria volunteered, "but I couldn't see what material they were mining."

"We aren't lacking in anything vital that I can think of," Garreck said, eyebrows pressed together with the effort of remembering. "Like I told you, I've worked in Marten's office, and our government is doing fine. We're not short on iron or lumber or anything like that."

Cal's eyes lit up. "Maybe it's something specific to Devoran. There's so much we don't know about this place. Maybe it's something valuable."

Mauria laughed a bit at this. At Cal's questioning look, she just shook her head. "You're always ready for a new intrigue, aren't you?"

Cal had the grace to look sheepish but nodded, adding, "It's exciting to think about. What if they found land filled with gold or gems or something fantastic like that?"

"It's nothing like that, I'm afraid."

A cold chill ran through Mauria when she realized the statement had been made by an unfamiliar, distinctly adult voice. She immediately jumped to her feet, ignoring the urge to flee and saw the man who'd spoken emerge from the brush on the far end of their enclosure.

He was tall and well-built, with more hair than she had ever seen on a man before. He was not wild, and yet there was something distinctly *other* about him. He wore clothes similar to those of Aelemia, simple and functional, designed for both comfort and toil. She saw nothing manufactured on his person, and more importantly, she saw no weapon.

She relaxed upon this realization and felt her posture ease as she took a step toward the stranger.

"Who are you?" she asked.

"I'm Damean." His voice was neutral, but his eyes flashed. The combination made Mauria even more uncomfortable.

"Why have you been following us, Damean?" This came from Rasha. "We've heard noises ever since we came to Devoran. That was you, wasn't it?" His words seemed to summon the many crunching leaves they'd dismissed as wind or animals, and she shivered, uneasy with how vulnerable they'd been.

Damean did not look apologetic. Instead, he shrugged and said, "I had to be sure of you four. I've been deciding."

"Deciding what?" Mauria's voice was a bit higher than normal as she eyed the stranger.

"If you could help," he said simply, giving them a quick grin that was more of a challenge than an actual smile.

They all stared at him, but it was Garreck who said, "Sorry, Damean, but we obviously don't know what you mean, given that you've provided us with absolutely no information whatsoever. What do you need our help *with*."

Damean's eyes trailed back in the direction of the Cantic excavation. "I'd rather not explain here," he told them. "They have scouts that patrol the forest occasionally, and you would certainly be no help if you were found. Would you be willing to come with me?" He must have sensed their hesitation for he added, "I promise you'll be safe."

"Of course, we'll come with you," Cal said, automatically. Mauria shot him a wide-eyed look. Cal seemed to be the unspoken leader of their group, that much was clear, but that did not mean they would aquiesce to every idiotic scheme he put his heart to.

"I don't think that's such a good idea," Mauria said, her voice heavy with implication.

She expected the other two to agree, but instead of jumping to Mauria's defense, Garreck put his hand on her shoulder. "I know it's not ideal, Mauria, but I'm telling you right now, it's better than going back to Marten." The earnestness in his voice stayed the retort that waited poised on her lips.

After a deep breath and several unkind thoughts, she said, "Fine." Though she could not keep her teeth from grinding with frustration. "But if you kill us, Damean, kill that one," she pointed at Cal, "first."

Mauria thought she heard a quiet laugh from over by Rasha, but she ignored it. Their already precarious journey had become even more of a risk in a matter of moments, and she didn't care for it.

Garreck

Damean led them farther away from Marten and deeper into the heart of Devoran. The landscape continued to shift and vary as they traveled, and although its splendor was undeniable, an ominous cloud had settled around their troup.

This stranger didn't seem threatening, but Garreck was sure that Damean could have killed them all if he had wanted to. That they were alive was proof that Damean did, in fact, need them. But Garreck also had a hunch that whatever it was the man sought their help with, probably wasn't an easy feat. They would just have to leverage something for themselves when the favor was eventually asked. Hopefully, they'd be in a position to ask for more than just safe travels.

In addition to a nagging fear of what was to come, Garreck was lost in a sea of questions regarding the Cantic excavation. His father had never spoken of Devoran. Not in all the years that they had worked and lived together had Marten so much as spread one fairytale of magic or mystery. Not that it was his style to do so, of course, but it had always been Rien that Marten focused so specifically on. *Murderers, terrorists, extremists*—the Rie were hellish and cruel in every mental image his father painted for his children. But Devoran never came up.

What could be so secret that it wouldn't cross Garreck's desk at the office or be whispered about in the safety of their home?

Cal

After a few hours, they came upon a cottage that had been built at the mouth of a large cave. The sturdy, wooden structure grew out of moss-covered walls of weathered rock, and a stable filled with animals could be seen in the wide yard that stretched around the house in a sizeable crescent.

Damean gestured for them to follow as he made his way through the thick wooden door of his home, and the four conceded with only mild trepidation. Even Mauria's attitude seemed to have mellowed to a quiet discomfort. If Damean had some sinister plan, he surely would have executed it by now. They were travelers far from home, in a strange land, away from any form of aid. Cal was certain that while Damean lacked a degree of social grace, he meant them no harm.

If they were about to be slaughtered, Cal was at least glad they had been able to catch a glimpse of the inside of Damean's house before it happened; it was spectacular. Cal thought of the modern comfort that radiated from his parents' house in Cratos, and smiled at how two such dissimilar places could be simultaneously inviting. Damean's house was not clean, but something about the imperfections only worked to enhance its charm. Dust and cobwebs glinted in the sun's rays, and stacks of well-worn books were scattered all about. The air was saturated with scents of pine and pipe smoke, and the entryway was cloyingly warm. Deeper inside, the pieces of the house where the cave began were masterful. Cloth hangings fell in folds from high ceilings, and bits of stalactites sent prisms of light dancing across limestone and calcite crevices.

Cal was dazzled by it, and only begrudgingly looked away as he sat down at the small kitchen table.

Damean brought over cups of water that he scooped from a large barrel. Cal took it gratefully, not realizing how thirsty he was until it was offered. He saw Mauria eyeing it suspiciously. In a show of either bravery or stupidity, Cal took a deep sip of his own, hoping to prove through example that it wasn't tainted.

Or, this is how I die, Cal thought ruefully. *How dreadfully boring a death that would be.*

When they were all settled, Damean spoke. His voice was not smug, but there was a hint of rye amusement in his tone that Cal did not understand. "You seem confused by what you saw back there." He addressed the group as a whole, though his eyes lingered particularly on Garreck. "As I'm sure you can tell, it is not new. The Cantics have been digging through this country for about eight years now. Devoran is vast, and so it has not affected our lives here significantly, but I believe the outlook is grimmer for the worlds outside this place."

"What do you mean?" Cal asked. "Do you know what they were collecting?"

"It doesn't make sense for them to be collecting anything," Garreck cut in. "Cantor has all that it needs. More, in some cases."

Damean grimaced. "It isn't something they are running out of. It's something they never had."

He reached across to one of the stacks of ancient books and pulled out a large almanac. Without pausing to wipe the thick coat of dust from the cover, he thumbed through the pages, stopping when he'd found the one he was searching for. Tilting it back, Damean shifted the book so that the others could see it. Cal leaned forward to get a better view and felt Mauria nudge him back out of the way.

"Will you relax?" she hissed at him.

Cal shot her a skeptical glare, "Hark, who's talking?"

"What do you think this is?" Damean asked, ignoring their whispers.

Cal turned away from Mauria and refocused on the page. It was filled with simple symbols that Cal recognized. There were stalks of wheat, corn, and little mounds of stone all over a rough map of Devoran. Some areas were marked with tiny trees, others contained chunks of flowing river.

"Is this a map of Devoran's resources?" Cal asked curiously.

"It is."

"What do the little suns represent?" Mauria inquired, her interest temporarily outweighing her disdain.

"Long ago the Devora found a way to use the sun for energy."

Cal was enchanted by this idea. His Cratian brain couldn't help but marvel at its efficiency. His excitement slipped as he noticed a mark he'd overlooked at first glance.

"And the green flame, Damean?" he asked.

"That is moridium. It's a resource unique to Devoran, and the one the Cantics are collecting." His face conveyed little emotion, but Cal saw Damean's hand grasped the book more firmly as he told them of this unknown element, his knuckles momentarily taut and white.

"What is it for?" Rasha asked quietly.

"Destruction," he said. Realizing that he had once again given them a deficient explanation, he added, "Did you know that your countries were once part of Devoran?"

Their only response was a palpable silence, which Damean correctly interpreted as a "no."

"It was long ago, but our oldest texts confirm that there was a time when our countries were united. There were differences between the people, as there always are, but they lived in relative harmony. Because of their magic, some were better suited for different positions within that great nation. There were mathematicians and philosophers dedicated to intellectual progress, politicians who made difficult decisions when others could not, and theologians who searched diligently for their purpose on this earth. There were healers and humanitarians, and there were sorcerers."

Damean paused, letting the information sink in. Cal felt skinridges popping up as this secret history was revealed. It was obvious what the different sections had gone on to become, but he worried over the the last grouping that Damean had named.

Damean must have seen the question in Cal's eyes.

"These sorcerers were peaceful and made it their duty to protect the earth. They allocated resources, replenished and monitored all that Devoran consumed, and discovered Magic in its truest, purest form."

Looking at his friends, Cal was surprised to find that their reactions did not all match the wonder that he himself felt. Garreck rolled his eyes, Mauria stiffened, and Rasha's jaw slackened.

"This structure suited Devoran for many years," Damean continued, ignoring the mixed response to his words. "However, as it is with most great events, an accident led to the discovery of moridium, as well as its potential for evil."

Damean's bright eyes clouded when he said this, and his tone shifted—darkening quickly.

"The sorcerers guarded against those who would misuse moridium, but men are greedy, and their greed eventually became too much. They were forced to use their Magic against their fellow Devora, and the idyllic nature of their land came to an end. Vengeful and afraid of what the sorcerers were capable of, factions within Devoran broke off. They became the countries we have today, and while there is still no true Magic in those parts, strands of power remain from when we were one people—your knacks and gifts, as you call them."

Cal gawked at Damean, the many facets of his personality warring within him. When he first met Garreck, he had scoffed at the term "gift," as it implied more meaning than their knacks deserved. But now, Damean claimed that the abilities possessed by normal people like his mothers were not only special, but *magic*?

Cal's mind was far away, but somewhere in the room Rasha let out a low whistle, and he heard Garreck mutter, "You've got to be kidding me."

Garreck

Garreck considered Damean's words, but had trouble digesting the new information. He had always suspected some amount of Magic to be at the root of his gift, so this piece of news was not necessarily difficult to take in. Everything else seemed like absolute nonsense. However, for the sake of the group, Garreck decided to forgo his deep skepticism concerning sorcerers and ancient lands and focus on the more important details that Damean had provided.

This dangerous element, for starters, was deeply troubling. "What exactly does moridium do?" he asked.

"It is the most volatile substance in our world." Damean's grimanced, his forehead coming together. "For some time it was harmless—a pretty stone that was used only for its unique color and sheen. At some point, however, the ancient Colliptians found other, more fearsome ways to manipulate it. They discovered that when moridium comes into contact with fire, the consequences are catastrophic. Very quickly, it became a popular way to gain power and spread fear. There was a time where cities were destroyed by moridium—engulfed in flame and dimished to ash."

Garreck listened, and didn't doubt that moridium was something Cantor would seek. The Cantics maintained a powerful military force, and such a weapon could be extremely useful. Their leaders valued power and were imbued with a "more is better" mentality.

What worried him most was how sure Damean was that the moridium would be used against another country in Colliptia. *The outlook is grimmer for the worlds outside this place.* That is what he had told them. And although the Cantics had always had tensions with other lands, they were not at war with anyone. Instinctively, Garreck glanced at Rasha, and though he willed it away, he could not stop his mind from adding, *yet.*

"Have you heard of their plans for the moridium?" Garreck asked Damean, hoping to squash the dark thoughts that had begun seeping into his mind, percolating in a swirl of apprehension.

Damean nodded. "They have been weaponizing for about a year now and began transporting large quantities out of Devoran last month. I haven't heard who it will be used against, if that is what you're asking."

Garreck said nothing, but his expression was grim. In that moment, Garreck was filled with an uncomfortable combination of obsidian anger and shame. It was not just because of the betrayal he felt, for after the many hours he'd dedicated to resenting Marten, Garreck had always known the evil of which his father was capable. No, his fears were selfish ones, for he was more concerned with his own role in all of this. For years he had unknowingly been part of this problem—a cog in a machine much larger and crueler than he had known.

Garreck looked down before his face could betray him and heard rather than saw Cal ask, "What do you want from *us*, Damean?"

When there was no immediate response, Garreck raised his eyes to look at Damean, who was staring intently at them. It was as if he could see deep into each of their beings, silently measuring their merit and value.

"I'd like you to try to stop them," he told them after a moment. "As this young man noticed, I've been following you for some time. From what I can gather, you seem to represent most, if not all of the countries in Colliptia. It's going to take many different voices to stop whatever Cantor is planning."

"No offense," Garreck interrupted, "but you're out of your damn mind." Damean seemed to have good intentions, but this whole thing was getting a bit ridiculous. "You see four kids a third of your age wandering around in the woods and decide they're the ones that you'll put in charge of stopping a war? You're insane. Why don't any of your sorcerers fix it like they did last time?"

Mauria nodded in agreement with Garreck's words, and even Cal's expression of elation dimmed a bit. Rasha looked at Damean, however, and it was he that answered Garreck's question.

"They already helped once, didn't they? And this war doesn't seem like it's going to effect Devoran. They haven't tried to stop the Cantics from digging; I think they're sitting this one out."

Damean's small smile came as confirmation, and Garreck couldn't control himself. "Let me get this straight; they're too apathetic to care that there's a country about to get obliterated, even when they could do something to stop it?"

"We *have* intervened before … and at great personal cost." Damean's voice was as even as ever, but something flashed briefly behind his eyes. Was it anger? "What my predecessors did to ensure humanity's survival took all that they had. If humankind is doomed to repeat its cycle of greed and violence, we will let them. We can't resolve their follies each time they lose their way." It was during this last statement that Damean's patience slipped, and Garreck felt the chill of his now icy tone.

"So you're one of them? A sorcerer?" Cal couldn't hide the wonder from his voice. Garreck would have laughed if he wasn't fuming at the idea of a powerful race of whatevers simply watching the world around them burn.

"I am," Damean answered, "and I am simply asking and educating. I can't make you intercede; I can't even make you care. But from what I saw all those nights in the woods, you all have a stake in this. I thought you should at least be warned."

The energy around the table fluctuated between such extremes that it was hard to know what anyone was thinking. Garreck would have happily continued to berate his host, but Damean seemed to sense how unsettled they all were.

"I think that's enough for today," he told them. "The sun is going down, and you've had to absorb quite a bit. If you'd like to stay here, I can lend you a few rooms."

"That would be amazing," Cal answered so fast the others didn't have a chance. Garreck had a feeling that for all his resilience, Cal had missed his creature comforts over the last few months. Either that or Cal was afraid to leave this new leg of their trip unexplored.

Damean brought them to the second floor and directed Mauria into a guest room down the hall. Mauria's face revealed an internal battle between not wanting to be alone and not wanting to pass up a rare opportunity for some privacy. In the end, the latter won, and the boys climbed their way to the third floor while she headed off on her own. Garreck was happy for her; she could defend herself if she needed to, but he was certain that the only thing she'd have to worry about was of falling asleep too quickly. It *had* been a while since any of them had slept in a bed.

When they reached the top of a set of narrow stairs, Garreck was glad to discover that their room upstairs was large, a dusty attic filled with natural light cast by the setting sun. Candle stubs were scattered about and several thick, straw mattresses were tucked away in warm corners.

"Relax and get some rest," Damean said as he bid them goodnight. "We'll talk more in the morning." Garreck watched him close the door and heard his footsteps fade as he walked back down the steep wooden staircase.

Garreck had planned on debriefing with the others, but as he sat down he was hit with a sudden wave of intense exhaustion. He was able to grumble a quick "g'night" before dipping into unconsciousness. He didn't know what to expect from his dreams that night. He was sure, however, that each would be plagued by fire.

Rasha

Rasha woke before the sun had arisen and crept quietly outside. Back in Rien, Rasha had prayed every morning at just this time. After the pilgrimage massacre, however, he'd no longer felt the urge to talk to his deity and had attempted to give the ritual up completely. To his irritation, Rasha quickly discovered that morning prayer was such an entrenched routine that his body rebelled against its dismissal. Unwilling to pray, but also unable to fall back to sleep, Rasha instead began using these quiet moments to meditate.

He found a small spot in the clearing outside of Damean's house and knelt, bowing his head and stretching his arms in front of him. Rasha felt a few pops as the knots in his back worked their way out, and he relaxed for a moment, absorbing the silence and stillness of the world around him. He sank into his surroundings, letting himself be taken over by the gentle hums of waking life and did not move for a very long time.

When the sun burst over the barrier horizon, Rasha brushed himself off and made his way inside. Not wanting to wake the others, he gravitated toward one of Damean's many piles of books, sliding his fingers over some of the grime to read the titles written sideways on the bindings.

"Quite the collection, yes?" The voice made Rasha jump so violently that he dropped the book he'd been leafing through. Damean smiled, picked up the book, and held it out to Rasha, taking a quick glance at the title. "Which did you choose?"

Rasha gave him a small grimace and reached for the text, still collecting himself. "*Honeybee and Wasp.* We tell the story in Rien as well, but I've never seen it written down. It's something we use with Rie children."

"Ah yes, it originated in Devoran—like most things. A single wasp makes its way into a beehive, chaos ensues, and an entire community is destroyed. I wonder what the story's message is in Rien?"

"It's about trusting in divine intervention to save you." Rasha said at once. Rien was built on the foundation of religious piety, after all. "If they had remained calm and believed in the goodness of their god, they would have lived. Instead they let personal concern for safety reign, and they felt the consequences of their selfishness."

Damean nodded. It wasn't in agreement, rather it was as if Rasha had confirmed a private suspicion.

"Why, what do you think it's about?" Rasha challenged.

After considering his words, Damean asked, "Did you know that some wasps are harmless? There are variations that infest hives, and there are others that pass by—curious rather than menacing."

"I'm not sure I follow," Rasha said. "If the Devora don't believe in trusting Taklam to know the difference, wouldn't pausing to find out still lead to destruction?"

Damean shrugged, "Or prosperity. More often than not you benefit from embracing the new and unknown. You just have to believe that it's worth the risk.

Rasha began to respond, but was cut off as Mauria came out of her room, stretching opulently as she did.

"Sorry, I don't mean to interrupt," she said as she sat down near then, stifling a yawn. "How did you sleep, Rasha?"

Rasha gave her a light shrug, eyes still on Damean who had gotten up wordlessly. The sorcerer began puttering in the kitchen with the beginnings of breakfast as if their conversation had never occurred.

Mauria

They decided to stay with Damean while they worked through the information with which they'd been presented. Damean didn't seem to mind the company, and it did them all some good to rest after so many weeks of constant movement.

Mauria quickly found that, although Devoran was foreign to them,

Damean's life was comfortably similar to what she had known in Aelemia. He was a solitary character, but hardworking, and for the first few days of their stay, Mauria and the boys attempted to help with Damean's different chores and tasks.

Mornings consisted of a few luxurious hours of reading and eating, while the rest of the day was spent tending animals, fixing broken items around the property, and harvesting crops. Some of these yields—carrots, sprouts, and pumpkins—she knew well enough, although in her experience they were typically picked at separate times throughout the year. Others were completely new. There were fields of trees with bulbous, pale-yellow fruits that smelled of citrus, and one ficus so dense and expansive it took Mauria's breathe away; Damean called them Banyans. Vines of vibrant grapes wove themselves through the top edges of wooden fences, and the smell of manure mixed pungently with the otherwise sweetened air.

Surrounded by all of this beauty and quiet comfort, Mauria's disappointment seemed a bit selfish. Damean posed no threat to their company, and the diversion provided them with necessary moments for reflection. She was, however, disappointed all the same. From the moment Damean had spoken of his relationship with magic, she had longed to know more about a world with actual power. Her gift, which along with slight stress had always provided her a source of pride, seemed minute compared to the kind of abilities that Damean had spoken of.

He hadn't said it outright, but it sounded to her as if sorcerers could control the elements; *monitor* had been Damean's word. As she looked back on the spectacles they had witnessed in the last few weeks, she knew that this hunch was right. Devoran had *more* of everything: light, vegetation, color. It even had more air. Whoever lived here had cultivated a world with more life than anything they had in the west.

Somewhere, in a time to which Mauria didn't belong, her people had left this world of wonder. What bit of magic they took with them pulsed within her, and through that small degree of knowledge she began to feel a part of this land. At times this sense of connection was so strong that it unnerved her. Occasionally, her skin would tingle as she made her way through Damean's property, and each time she felt whole when she returned to the cottage; more complete than she had ever been in her entire life.

Rasha

Rasha would have been content to stay at Damean's forever. He felt completely at peace in the quiet repetitiveness of this life. After a few days, Damean asked the group if they wanted to accompany him to town. Rasha was shocked by this suggestion. Even though Damean had explained that there were other Devora in this world, the atmosphere around the sorcerer's home was so intimate and so personal that Rasha couldn't imagine an area in Devoran that belonged to a community, rather than an individual.

"What's in town?" Rasha asked him.

"Gaian is our capital, but it's more akin to a western bazaar or market. There aren't many people who *live* in town, but everyone gathers to trade. If you haven't noticed, Devoran is an eclectic place, and while I have most of what I need right here, there are some things I depend on others for."

"Will it be okay that we are with you?" Mauria asked carefully.

"Oh yes, you'll be perfectly safe," replied Damean. "No one will mind. They will notice, of course, but we welcome outsiders in Devoran, despite all that our history might imply."

"Now that you mention it," Mauria said, "my people tell stories of great danger here. Where do those come from?" The question was direct and slightly accusatory. Rasha was thankful that Damean did not seem offended. If anything, Rasha thought that their host seemed a bit bored by the comment.

Mauria seemed to notice his lack of enthusiasm, for she added, "It's a reasonable concern, Damean. I'd like to know before we go walking into the fox's den."

"Yeah." Garreck chimed in. "What was the thought process behind that hokey sign at the border?"

"Like any place, we have those who fear outsiders," Rasha's eyes unconsciously flitted toward Garreck at Damean's words, "but we preach tolerance here. On our borders there are sometimes Devora who wait for unassuming Aelemians to stumble onto their path, but they are the minority, not the standard. You will be a spectacle," he smiled, "but you will also be safe."

"Well then I am in!" Cal said, cheerfully. "No offense to you lot, but I need to be around other people for once. I can't wait to actually be part of a crowd again."

Rasha was quite certain he had never experienced the longing that Cal spoke of, and from the eye rolls exchanged between Mauria and Garreck, neither had they. However, as there were no true objections to the dalliance in Gaian, they readied their horses and filled several water pouches in preparation for the trip. The road to the capital was not a long one, but Rasha and the others had learned to prepare for even the most unexpected of happenings.

Cal

Cal had expected the people of Devoran to be as eclectic as the landscape. Instead, once they reached Gaian, Cal found himself slightly underwhelmed by how very ordinary the Devora were. The foreign men and women meandered about at no particular pace, pointing at goods and chatting with friends. None of them seemed as wild as Damean, and Cal wondered if their sorcerer was an outlier rather than the norm in this place.

Cal was also a bit surprised by the absence of coin purses, but Damean explained that Devoran's commerce subsisted solely on barter and negotiation, much like the Aeslish. Because of this, booths and stands were in deep competition to win the attention of passersby, and their decor was ostentatious to say the least. Some stood out for their painted signs and free samples, while others were more drastic in their attempts. Cal was startled to see one stand crackling and popping, smoking slightly as stars erupted from the top and sides of the structure.

"It's not sorcerer owned," Damean said, as he saw Cal's expression. "It comes from a powder we develop here. Pretty, isn't it?"

Cal nodded, and moved cautiously towards the booth. "It's spectacular." *This* was the flash and pop he'd been hoping for.

"I have to head toward the livestock," Damean said, breaking away from the group as he did so. "I'll leave you to your own devices." He shook his head a bit as he turned, clearly bemused by Cal's excitement.

Rasha followed Damean as he headed toward a fenced-in flock of large, tawny birds. Cal and the others split off, and eventually Cal was on his own, winding through a sea of busy shoppers.

After stopping to watch a young woman as she juggled viper-sharp swords, Cal decided to rest. He found a beverage kiosk, traded a joke for a steaming mug of lacquer liquid, and sat down at a wooden table already occupied by several strangers. As he took a large, searing sip of the bitter drink, Cal felt satisfied.

Settling into a comfortable position, Cal looked around at his table companions. Across from him was a woman with wild curls, people-watching from her small place in the world. Next to her was a young girl huddled with a faded book clasped tightly to her knees. A few chairs down sat a middle-aged man in hushed but animated conversation with a handsome gentleman with a salt-and-pepper beard.

Cal was drawn to this last pair. While he could not make out much of what he said, he heard bits and pieces that were not only audible, but familiar to him as well. He turned his body casually in their direction, propping his feet up on the seat beside him so that a lean in their direction was almost natural.

"Then it *is* Rien," whispered the bearded man. "We always assumed."

"We did," the other said, "but that means it will be quick. The others might have stood a chance, but the Rie do not believe in weapons. They will fold easily."

"I wonder if the others will try to stop them."

"Not likely. They have grown polarized and cautious, they will watch, writing policy and singing songs and hoping they are not next."

Suddenly, their conversation stopped. Cal turned to see the handsome one jerk his head in Cal's direction. They got up, walking away just as a hundred questions sprinted into existence in Cal's brain.

They had to be talking about the weapon. Between the lazy days of the light toil and relaxation, Cal had almost forgotten the reason for Damean's appearance in their lives. He got up quickly, running to catch up with them.

"Excuse me!" Cal yelled, pulling on the sleeve of the salt and pepper man. "How do you know?"

Affronted, the man acted as though he did not understand Cal's question.

"You said Rien was the target," Cal clarified quickly. "I know what the Cantics are up to, but how do *you* know they are targeting Rien?" Cal dropped his voice as he clarified, noticing that his aggression had drawn the eyes of a few passing shoppers.

The man glanced to his friend for a moment before looking back at Cal. "Word travels quickly here. I heard it from a friend that was recently drinking with a few of the Cantic workers. Apparently they are not as secretive as their employers."

Unwilling to let them leave until he learned as much as possible, Cal nodded, "Thanks. There isn't anything else you can tell me, is there?"

To his disappointment, both men shook their heads. As they walked away, Cal sat back down and attempted to process what he'd just been told.

For some reason, knowing that Rien would bear the might of that powerful force made the threat real in Cal's mind. He pictured Rasha, so small and wholesome, facing the heat and hate of fire, and his hands curled until his fingernails dug into his palms.

They would have to do something, and that meant they would have to leave soon.

Rasha

While the others branched off to make their own way through the crowds of Gaian, Rasha stayed close with Damean; he had no desire to lose himself in the tangle of trade.

Damean went first to a collection of squawking beasts that he called torkes. They glabbered on, bumping into each other in their enclosed space. However, their disordered floundering quickly settled as Damean approached.

This was not the first time Rasha had seen Damean's effect on animals. He had stilled one of the sows back on his land after it had been shaken by a wild dog and had even coaxed a chicken off of her precious eggs. Rasha chalked this ability up to Damean's identity as a sorcerer. Though he had yet to see anything truly spectacular, there was no denying that Damean was able to shape this world to his own wants and needs.

After the torkes, they traded milk for a few yards of strong burlap and folded it into their sacks. As they did, Damean explained that the material was extremely useful and that it yielded rope of incredible strength when woven correctly. As the hours passed, their purposeful ventures turned to irresolute browsing, and Damean declared that it was time for a snack. After spotting the desired cart, Damean tossed a few shining river stones to an attendant in exchange for two sticks laden with meat and roasted vegetables.

Together, they leaned against the corner of a small kiosk. Damean and Rasha ate their meal and took in the scene around them. The sounds coming from eager salesmen and impatient children were enough to keep them entertained, and they enjoyed a few quiet moments of companionable silence.

Their leisure was broken by a ruckus on the far side of the busy road. A horse reared, bucking and pawing. Dust clouds rose up in all directions and the wagon attached to the beast wobbled threateningly. One of the children looked up as the cart towered over her, alarmingly close to her frozen figure. Damean dropped his meal and pushed down, his arms making a controlled movement toward the ground. As he did, the horse steadied, but the damage to the dray had been done. It snapped off its supports and fell toward the child. Damean flicked his hands up, and a sudden wind brought the wagon back. It settled, broken but immobile in the dusty haze of the event.

Rasha looked up at Damean, mouth and eyes both wide. He had not been surprised to see Damean tame the horse, but the vision of him summoning and controlling the wind was another thing entirely.

Damean's face remained placid, his breathing steady; he seemed wholly unaffected after just saving a human life.

Rasha continued to gawk, but with a tentative voice managed to ask, "What exactly can sorcerers do, Damean?"

Damean paused for one beat, and replied, "We can speak the language of everything."

The phrase meant nothing to Rasha, but still he stared as Damean returned to his snack. He picked up the kabob from the ground, dusted it off with a casual air, and continued eating as if nothing at all out of the ordinary had happened.

And perhaps, Rasha thought, it was because nothing extraordinary *had* happened. Events like this could very well be daily occurrences for someone as magical as Damean.

For the first time since his pilgrimage, Rasha felt a longing for knowledge so deep within him that he was surprised by its intensity. He didn't understand Damean's magic, that much was clear. Still, his mind itched to uncover the mystery, wanting desperately to understand it.

Garreck

It was a quiet trip back to Damean's home after their time in town. Garreck wasn't quite sure *why* the mood had changed so drastically; he'd had a surprisingly nice time wandering around. He and Mauria had ended up together for the last half of their visit and had spent a good hour or so away from the chaos. They'd ventured over to an adjacent field, and Mauria had agreed to teach Garreck some of her combat techniques. He would never be a star pupil—he was clunky and out of practice—but it was fun to try and match her graceful movements.

When they met up with the others, however, Rasha and Cal seemed off. They walked deep in thought, each lost in a world known only to them. Damean was unchanged, but Garreck doubted there was much that could phase that man. Even his plea for them to help deter a violent attack in the west had been given with a level, dispassionate air.

It was not until they had reached the cottage and returned to their attic room that Garreck discovered what was on Cal's mind. Cal had asked Mauria to join them as well, and when they were assembled, he looked solemn.

"I think we need to do as Damean asked."

It took all of Garreck's flimsy self control not to laugh. He let Cal continue, but could feel a fresh smirk creeping through his features.

"I heard some men talking in town today. They seemed to think that Rien would be the Cantic target. We can't let that happen."

The smirk disappeared from Garreck's mouth, not because he was surprised, but because he had feared this from the beginning. The confirmation made him nauseous.

Cal continued, "I think we need to go home. We need to tell people what is happening. Maybe if the secret comes out, Cantor will simply stop. It is easier to act when the eyes of other lands are distracted. Maybe the attention will be enough to keep Cantor at bay."

"And what if it isn't?" This came from Mauria, who had gone pale.

"Then we ask them to stand against Cantor. I know my people will do the right thing. Mauria, do you think your people would be willing to fight? I know they've never really had the need, but Marcan West is the most extreme in their pacificity. Would the other sections lend their help?"

"I'm not sure. Marcan West is our governing faction. The others would most likely follow whatever path they set. We might help, but that aid would come in the form of support, not soldiers. They might provide supplies?" Her voice sounded unsure, and Garreck understood. The Aelish were not warriors of any kind. Helping Rien, if it came to it, would mean putting themselves at risk, and they would not be able to defend themselves if their turn came to fight.

"Well, hopefully it won't come to that," Cal said. Garreck wasn't looking at him, but he could feel Cal's gaze shift and settle in his direction. "Garreck, I know this is a lot to ask, but I need you to talk to your father."

It *was* a lot to ask. But it was also a futile assignment. Marten was not interested in him or what he had to say. The idea of Garreck persuading him to halt an imminent invasion was one of fantasy. "He won't listen, Cal."

"You have to try. At least tell him that you know—that *we* know. Tell him about Rasha and his people and make him see the pain he will cause. You yourself said that Cantor has no reason to attack Rien. They don't need anything from them, so maybe you will be enough to see what little value there is in this."

Cal's pleading hit Garreck at the core of his being. The urge to concede fought madly with the knowledge that he *wasn't* enough, and having to face that truth over and over in the span of a minute was crushing. He wanted to help Cal. He wanted to show him that, somehow, miraculously, he had changed since they first met. He found that, in that moment, this desire overcame that crippling pain of Marten's eternal rejection.

"I'll try."

Through his angst, Garreck realized that one in their gathering had remained silent during this crucial discussion. "What about you, Rasha? How do you think Rien will react?"

Rasha looked at him and said very calmly, "I don't know if I can go back yet."

Cal must have seen the shade of eggplant that Garreck's face quickly turned. Before Garreck could explode, Cal asked "What do you mean, Rasha?"

"I still have things I need to work through, and I think this place is where I am meant to do that searching. It will not make a difference if I leave now or in a few weeks. My people have only one course of action—they will await whatever Taklam has in store for them."

Garreck didn't realize he had been holding his breath until a rush of air came cascading out of him.

"You are going to let us do your work for you then, are you? You'll let us go back and face this whole damn mess while you 'find yourself'?" Garreck's anger flared, and he tried not to yell when he spoke. Still, the words came out like a strikes of a whip, every consonant lashing dangerously toward Rasha. "If you haven't noticed, Rasha, my people hate your people. We all know it was Cantics who attacked your pilgrimage that night you found us. We all know it was for nothing other than blind, poisonous resentment for you and your religion. You would let that type of danger threaten your people?" Garreck's eyes were steel, and they bore into Rasha.

Rasha looked stricken and began to cry. Mauria put a hand to his shoulder, but did not coddle the boy. She seemed as angry as Garreck was. "I'm telling you, the Rie will not do anything to help themselves. It would be pointless for me to try." When the others said nothing, he added, "I'll come back soon, I promise." Rasha's last words faded, as if he knew they wouldn't help his cause.

There was silence, apart from Garreck's loud breathing as he tried to calm himself down. Cal, always the reasonable one, replied, "Do what you need to do, Rasha, but the rest of us need to act quickly." Turning to Garreck and Mauria he added, "We'll leave tomorrow, if you can be ready."

Cal

Cal did not sleep well that night. Try as he might, he could not stop his mind from running through every possible scenario that might play out in the months to come. In the most terrifying visions, Marten moved unimpeded to Rien and engulfed the country in plumes of green fire. In the best situations, Garreck was able to move his father to cancel the mission, and all was well. It was not encouraging that Garreck seemed to believe the second scario to be less likely, but Cal appreciated him trying. There was clearly a lot of trauma associated with Garreck's childhood, and facing it showed true courage.

Eventually, the sun came up, and with it some of Cal's anxiety ebbed away. Instead of the normal grumbles and stretches from the other beds in the room, Garreck and Rasha rose quickly. Maybe Cal hadn't been the only one awake all through the night.

Cal and Garreck packed silently while Rasha shuffled about getting dressed. The boy did not deserve the level of derision he had received the evening before. Still, it was smart of Rasha to leave quickly, restricting the opportunity for a new round of Landsing anger.

When it was just the two of them in the attic room, Cal looked at Garreck. "Thank you," he said. "I know what it will cost you to talk to Marten."

Garreck sighed, but simply shrugged and said, "You're welcome."

"I wouldn't ask you if I didn't think it was necessary. You're our best shot at stopping this thing before it goes too far." Cal believed it, even if Garreck did not.

"I promise you, it won't do any good." Garreck said in a strained voice, "but I'll give it a go. You're right, we need to try."

Garreck's face was one of sadness and uncertainty. He looked more conflicted than Cal had ever seen him. Whether it was to ease some of Garreck's suffering or because he had wanted to do it for some time now, Cal leaned in and kissed Garreck softly on the lips.

Cal expected Garreck to react angrily and violently. Instead, Garreck raised his eyebrows and leaned into the kiss before pulling away and looking Cal squarely in the eye. He said nothing, and Cal wished he knew what was going on inside that Cantic brain.

Cal waited for Garreck to speak. Just when the silence was beginning to feel unbearable, Garreck said, "And I thought this trip couldn't get any more complicated."

Rasha

Rasha watched his friends depart, feeling an overwhelming combination of regret, guilt, and anticipation as they made their way out of Damean's clearing. He had expected Garreck to yell at him once more before they left, but instead Garreck had ignored him. Rasha even thought he had seen Garreck smiling. The absence of yelling was almost worse, for Rasha was left to cope with his own, self-inflicted shame.

He knew he should be leaving with them, that his own country was at risk and he was choosing to delay all thought of aid. There was something pulling at him, however, that he needed to resolve before he left Devoran.

Turning back through the cottage door, Rasha sat down quietly at the kitchen table. Damean had not questioned his choice to stay, but Rasha knew he would need to provide an explanation.

Sitting up straight and feigning confidence with each syllable, Rasha said, "I'd like to learn how to be a sorcerer. I'd like to learn to speak the language of everything."

Damean did not laugh, which had been Rasha's deepest concern. He was not joking, nor was he lightly asking for this favor.

"Tell me why," Damean replied.

It came spilling out of Rasha before he could properly articulate his thoughts.

"I can't remember a time when I wasn't searching for something. I have been disappointed my entire life, and the last few weeks I thought I would have to give up on ever feeling any kind of passion or connection. I didn't know what I wanted and I didn't know what to do if there wasn't something to search for—if there wasn't something to live for." He paused a moment, looking at Damean with an intensity that would have been uncomfortable for any normal person.

"But then I found this place, and I saw what you are capable of. You have a connection with the world that is profound and meaningful and rich and mysterious and I think … I think it's what I've been waiting for. What if the thing I'm meant to dedicate myself to is your 'everything,' *our* 'everything'?" I thought about it all night. The others have their gifts. They can persuade and heal and influence. What if I can believe? What if faith is *my* gift, and I just never knew what I was supposed to devote myself to?"

Damean waited as Rasha caught up with himself. Rasha looked down, afraid to hear Damean's rejection should it come, and equally afraid to give away the unadulterated joy that would accompany his acceptance.

"We will try," said Damean. "You do not have much time before you have to go back to your country. And though there is magic that runs through your veins, it may not be enough to yield the power of my people. That said, I will try to teach you what I know while you are here, and we will see if you are capable of learning."

"Thank you," said Rasha. He got up slowly and held out his hand to Damean. The act was too mature for him, and Rasha felt foolish the moment his arm jutted out. Damean smiled and took it, shaking it firmly with his own.

"You're welcome."

PART THREE

Find courage in the failing.
Find solace in the sin.
When once a path has come to term,
Then others must begin.

And if those roads should call for valor,
Do not hesitate. Attend!
Cast off thoughts of wickedness.
Resist! Rebuke! Condemn!

Inhale—and look to victories,
Let goodness set one's worth.
Take up true bravery and
Set all fears upon the hearth.

Mauria

Mauria's plan of attack was to approach her country's delegates at the next Gathering. During each Gathering, all four divisions of Aelemia were represented by invited attendants as well as any other concerned citizens. She could only hope that the unity felt during the Gathering would be enough to spur her pacifist country to action. Each assembly took place in Marcan West which was, coincidentally, physically and politically closest to Cantor. It would take a compelling argument to sway them to sever that union.

Traveling all the way to the Gathering House made Mauria's trip longer than it would have been otherwise, but she didn't mind. The thought of parting with her friends chipped away at her heart, and she welcomed the extra time.

Mauria's separation from Rasha sliced through her with each step, but it helped that none of the others wanted to discuss their friend's betrayal. And it was a betrayal … to Mauria at least. They were all going out of their way to return to their homes and fight for Rien, and Rasha was staying for his own selfish reasons. A fraction of her brain understood why Rasha had chosen to remain in Devoran, but a larger part could not fully forgive him for it.

Fortunately, the days spent travelling with Garreck and Cal were merrier than ever, and she was able to forget her bitterness toward Rasha more often than not. The reason for their cheer was obvious; the relationship between the boys had changed noticeably, though Mauria could not for her own life determine the catalyst. She'd always suspected the two boys might have feelings for each other, but something must have happened in Devoran to make them aware of it, too.

In similar situations, Mauria would have felt extra and out of place. Instead, the three became closer during that final leg of their journey. Cal had always been comfortable and charming, but it seemed that she and Garreck both smiled and laughed more than ever as they twisted their way back from Devoran—true testaments to the power of self-comfort and confidence.

Their merriment had to end at some point, however. The night before they separated, Cal ran through the plan once more. Wind flicked shadows wildly about his face, but Cal acted as though he did not notice, intent on reviewing their strategy.

"Mauria and I," he said, "will try to convince our countries to act on the threat. Pressure from Cantor's political allies will go a long way." Turning to Garreck, Cal added, "Garreck, you will speak directly to Marten. If you can get Marten to stop, then there won't even be a need for our interventions."

"And if he doesn't listen? What do I do after that?" Garreck asked. Mauria thought he looked very skeptical, despite Cal's confidence.

Cal shrugged, "You can come meet me in Cratos. It won't be prudent to hang around if the conversation with your dad goes poorly."

"We all need to agree to keep each other updated," Mauria said, shuffling closer to the fire as a particularly strong wind whipped through them. "No matter what, it's important that we know what we're up against."

The others agreed, and soon they had put all matters of Cantor aside. There would be time to worry about all that in the days to come, and they spent the rest of the night discussing topics that were not about the pending struggle. The echoes of their laughter rang through the night—testaments of their need to be children, if only for a few more hours.

Too soon, the moon faded into morning light, and the group said their goodbyes. Garreck continued West, Cal went North, and Mauria finished the last day traveling to a community close to the Gathering House. Once she was there, Mauria bunked with a kind Aelemian family for that final night, and forced herself to repay their generosity with friendship and attentiveness, though it was difficult to focus on anything but the task that lay ahead.

Mauria

When it was finally time to appeal to her country, Mauria mustered all of her newly gained self-worth and walked boldly through the doors of the Gathering House. Aelemia would not be the only country to sit back and watch others suffer. She would make sure of it.

The Gathering House was perhaps the only thing grand in all of Aelemia. Marble walls, raw but stunning, made up the base of a large, circular building. Inside were ornate wooden benches, carved with details specific to each division of the country and polished to perfection. Though beautiful, they were not comfortable—such a thing might promote dawdling. Always considerate, they discussed, decided, and dismissed within a single day in order to avoid wasting time and resources. A sturdy bench and sore bottom expedited even the most complex issues.

Mauria spotted and went to sit with the West faction. She walked swiftly over to them, greeted a few familiar faces and settled onto one of their benches. In the center of the circular room stood a man at a podium, shuffling papers and looking about at the crowd. When the seats were full and side discussions began to die, he welcomed them.

"Thank you for coming to this season's Marcan Gathering. As most of you know, my name is Wilson, and I will be helping to guide today's discussion."

Wilson's voice prattled on, and Mauria found it hard to listen closely. The proceedings were dull recounts of the different progresses and shortcomings of the season. She knew from her parents that there was an open forum at the end of each Gathering as they had come several times to request volunteers and to plot out new areas of farmland. Mauria waited impatiently for this segment to come. Eventually, after each division had been given the chance to share, discuss, and appeal, the floor was offered to anyone with a cause. Mauria nearly ran from her seat to the center of the room and was the first to reach the forum line.

The crowd laughed indulgently at Mauria's eagerness, and Wilson smiled as he gestured for her to take his place. "Please state your name, division, and position, please," he said before moving aside.

"My name is Mauria Hoan. I am from Marcan West, and I am a healer." She saw a few nods of appreciation run through the audience. For all their talk of equality, it was certainly an advantage to be one of the gifted fifty percent.

"I am here today because Rien is in danger." Mauria felt her audience's discomfort, but pushed forward, knowing the true difficulty was still to come. "A few weeks into the summer season, my friends and I traveled to Devoran, and we happened upon a Cantic mine. A local man told us that Cantor has been excavating an element called moridium for many years, and that they plan to weaponize it. We have specific reason to believe their target is Rien, and I came home to ask for your help." Her report was practiced and concise, but still she breathed a sigh of relief, glad that the bulk of it was over.

Silence and starring greeted the end of her speech. For good measure, Mauria added, "Aelemia is built on the belief that we must help, protect, and provide for each other. We must extend this to our peaceful brothers and sisters to the South."

Wilson looked awkward and moved forward, responding to her but looking out toward the rest of their countrymen as he did so. "Mauria, there is much about your story that is troubling, and I hope you can understand how unlikely it sounds." His voice was light and airy, almost patronizing. "This alleged threat chimes tones of fantasy, rather than reality."

"I understand," Mauria told him. And she did. She knew for a fact that she would have been one of the sceptics if the situation were reversed. As such, she was ready with a reply. "What if I asked you to speak to Cantor? To confront them with this allegation and gauge their reaction? It can't hurt, even if you believe it is for nothing."

A woman in the benches rose and looked at Mauria. Her face was steady, but subtle lines near her eyes hinted at an underlying anxiety. "Such an accusation, however politely delivered, would be seen as an offense. The Cantics are not known for their patience when threatened." There was a tittering of uncomfortable laughter at this, but the woman continued. "If it came to a fight, Aelemia would not survive."

Mauria's mouth almost fell open, but she caught herself and replied in as even a tone as possible. "There are three other divisions of Aelemia. Surely we could support each other if it came to that. What I am telling you is true, and if the Cantics attack Rien, they can just as easily turn their wrath towards us. How can we wait, watching our neighbors burn and hoping we will be spared?"

The woman was already shaking her head. "What you're saying cannot be true. But even if it were, doing nothing keeps us safe for the immediate future, interceding welcomes the risk of conflict."

The sea of faces in front of Mauria began to shift, murmuring their agreement in a low rumble that grew, rippling out from epicenters of fear.

"I'm sorry Mauria," Wilson had shifted her out of the way, and was now gesturing for her to return the stands. "It seems the Gathering has not accepted your notion. Thank you for sharing your story."

Her audience clapped politely as she walked away, but Mauria did not go back to her seat. Instead, she stormed out of the Gathering House and leaned against the cool perimeter.

"Aargh!" Mauria yelled so loud a few nearby pigeons jumped and tweeped away. She felt like kicking one but held back the impulse, knowing she'd just feel guilty once she'd done it. As a substitute, she brought her fist back, ready to drive it into that gorgeous marble wall.

"You're about to break your entire hand, idiot." The voice behind Mauria came just as someone grabbed her fist, stopping it before she could release her pent up fury. Turning around, Mauria found a powerful looking woman raising an eyebrow at her. The woman was slightly below average height, but her thick arms and legs told stories of strength.

"My name is Jay Cardit," she said, still giving Mauria a look of mingled amusement and disdain. "And as long as you're done acting like a child, Hoan, I've decided to take you seriously."

Mauria bit back the snarky rely that played on her lips and glared at Cardit. "You heard them, there is nothing they will do."

"I know," Cardit said, her voice impatient. "Which is why we will not be asking them again. Come, let's talk." Cardit sat down against the wall and Mauria sank beside her.

"What are you proposing?" Mauria asked, her temper still pricked and sizzled, but she could feel her pulse settling.

"There happens to be a community in Marcan South that would be very interested in helping with this cause," Cardit told her, "but I'm going to need a few answers before we go any further."

Mauria nodded her head, "Of course, what do you need to know?"

Cardit was direct in her questioning. How certain was Mauria of this threat? *Absolutely.* How many soldiers would she need? *All of them.* How much time did they have? *Not much.*

"Most importantly," Cardit asked, the last in her line of questioning, "Who else will stand with us? You say you need everyone I can provide, but will there be others fighting at our side?"

Mauria nodded enthuiastically. "Yes. I have a Craitan friend who is positive that Cratos will come to our aid as well. And I'm asking Rien, even though I've been told it's no use."

Cardit did not seem heartened by news of either of these allies, but she simply nodded, filing the information away for later.

"How long have you all been together?" Mauria asked, as it appeared Cardit was done speaking.

"We've been a community for about five years now. People come and go as they wish, so our numbers are always changing. Some have been with us for a while, and they help me to train the new recruits."

"Why have I never heard about you before?" Mauria asked, amazed that there had been such a community in Aelemia all this time.

"We don't like to draw too much attention to ourselves. You saw how the group in there reacted when they were forced to *discuss* conflict, never mind actively prepare for one."

Mauria nodded in agreement, trying not to get worked up again. "Well, I'm glad you exist. Thanks for believing me."

They chatted briefly after that, but Mauria could tell Cardit was a woman of action, with little patience for small talk. When she had all the information she needed, Cardit left for Marcan South; Mauria was to join her there when she was ready.

Part of Mauria wanted to follow Cardit that very moment—to feed off her strength and assurance in a time of so much uncertainty—but there was one place she needed to go first.

For whatever reason, Rasha was still in Devoran. And without knowing when he would make his way back, Mauria felt that someone needed to warn the Rie what was coming.

Because of this, Mauria did not leave with Cardit. Instead, she found herself in a cramped Rie Caravan, hitching a ride back with a returning pilgrimage. In exchange for safe passage with them, Mauria allowed the group to use her horse to carry supplies. She would have rathered the fresh air of horseback, however, and secretly hoped that she could survive the wagon's confines long enough to make it to Rien.

Garreck

When Garreck finally made it back to Cantor, his father was not home. It was a small blessing, for he didn't think he was quite ready to talk to Marten, never mind confront him about his plot with the moridium. Garreck still held out hope that this was not his father's plan, and that they had somehow gotten it wrong. Maybe the attack was a fabrication—suspicions manifested by Devora who still had chips on their shoulders.

He would have to wait to find out. For now, he focused on dealing with his mother. She had burst into tears when Garreck walked through the door. Eyes brimming, she sobbed into his shoulder for a full five minutes before pushing against him, those safe eyes turning to flame.

"How could you leave like that? I thought you were dead! We were so worried, Garreck."

Garreck raised an eyebrow. "*We* were worried? Are you sure it wasn't just *you* who was nervous? I don't see dear old dad here to welcome me home." He regretted the words immediately, for his mother stomped away, too mad to speak.

She still wasn't talking to him, but Garreck couldn't help but be touched by the initial emotion she'd displayed. His mother had never been one to show her affection, save a proud smile or thin-lipped disappointment. Knowing that she cared in that way meant more than he liked to admit, even to himself.

As the days went by, Garreck waited for Marten to arrive, but he also made productive use of his free time. Rather than falling into his old patterns of solitude and angst, he set to work breaking the palpable tension that pulsed through the Landsing home. He bought a plant for their living room, introducing life to the home and hoping that the metaphor wouldn't be lost on the others. He even went 'round to an old bookshop—one of the only ones left in Cantor—and bought colorful novels filled with fantasy with which to stack the shelves at home.

He also reached out to his brothers, attempting to make peace. About a week after he arrived, he knocked on Ronan and Benji's door to see if they wanted to spend some time with him.

Benji answered his second knock. "What do you want?" he asked lazily.

"Are you guys up for some fishing? I was thinking of going down to Bush Lake."

Benji eyed him suspiciously, but then called to Ronan, "Ronan! Do you want to go fishing?"

Garreck heard the creak and thump of limbs swinging to the floor, and then his other sibling appeared.

"You want to go fishing with us?"

"Why not? We've got some catching up to do, and I'm bored as hell." Garreck cringed internally at the last addition. One of the things he had learned during his small hiatus was that admitting he had a soul wasn't just okay, but actually felt quite nice. He wished he didn't have the urge to appear emotionless in front of his brothers, but it was long-engrained, and would be a tough habit to shake.

The twins looked at each other, shrugged, and nodded. Without saying anything, they slammed the door in Garreck's face. He heard objects shifting and footsteps padding before they opened it again, changed and ready. Garreck smiled. He couldn't remember the last time they had spent the day together just as brothers.

At the lake, they didn't speak much, but the twins did catch him up on bits and pieces of life after his departure.

"Dad was really mad when you left, but he was angrier when he heard you got arrested." Beji admitted.

"Yeah, it's probably good that it took you a couple months to come home because he would have killed you," laughed Ronan.

They all went silent after that last comment. Though Marten wouldn't have *killed* him, necessarily, Garreck was sure they were all picturing that scene that would have occurred, and the vision was only slightly more pleasant that death.

Garreck told them about Aelemia and Devoran, omitting the major events and focusing more on the locals and scenery. When he first mentioned the Aelemians, his brothers chuckled, ready for Garreck to rip into those "tree tugging, grass grubbers" as Ronan so affectionately referred to them. Garreck just shook his head, and talked about their gifts instead. His brothers were impressed by this and asked if he had seen any in action.

"They healed me," he replied, and showed them his fully healed ankle. "You should have seen it before. It looked like when Ronan snapped one of my arrows in half that time I outshot him." He nudged Ronan fondly as he said it, while Benji laughed at his side.

"The only time," Ronan grumbled. "How were the people you traveled with? Mauria and Cal and Rasha? They sound really weird."

"They *were* really weird," Garreck said, chuckling, "but they were my friends. Better friends than most I have here, actually."

He turned back to his rod at that point and let the conversation blend with the silence of the sport. He had not told his brothers about the extent of some of those friendships, and he did not plan to. They were having a more pleasant interaction than they had had in many years, and he would not ruin it with the truth—that he was a cank.

In truth, Garreck hadn't spoken about his kiss with Cal since it had happened. That kiss had not been their last, though. They had been close on their way back from Devoran, holding hands when the way was calm, and enduring Mauria's knowing smile every time her eyes fell on them touching. But they had talked of other things, and Cal had not pushed him. Cal knew that Garreck's ability to cope with their new levels of friendship was limited by both real and imagined borders.

Maybe someday he would be brave enough to tell his family, but for the moment Garreck was simply happy to be on speaking terms with most of them. Even as they packed up to go home, Garreck felt the privilege that their small moment had been. He had stolen this time with them, and he relished how uncomplicated it was to sit and fish with Ronan and Benji. The second Marten got home, his life would become complicated and cold once more. As they made their way back, he made sure to turn his face up so he could feel the warmth of the sun.

Cal

Cal's thoughts were with the others as he tried to decide on the most effective way to approach Rien's situation with the Cratian government. Cal believed that Cratos was Rien's best chance at survival, and he eventually decided to tell his mothers first so that they could help him navigate the intricate workings of the political bodies in Cratos. While he was sure that Cratos would feel obligated to use their power to come to Rien's aid, he also knew how long it could take to pass any kind of legislation in his country. Because of this, he wasted no time catching Cora and Caroline up on the existence of moridium when he arrived home.

It took them a while to grasp the situation as fully as he hoped they would, but once both women understood the violence that Cantor intended, they did not disappoint. Caroline acted quickly, much to Cal's relief and wonder. She wrote out an appeal while he talked and had it ready to send off within minutes of his tale's conclusion.

When the dust settled, however, it was Cal's job to wait and to answer for some of the smaller matters that had been only briefly touched upon in his haste to save Rien.

Getting arrested, for instance, was high on Caroline's priority list.

Cal endured questioning about his brush with Cantic law, but when his parents realized the details of the crime, both Cora and Caroline immediately put the matter to bed. They'd both warned him of the dangers that Cantor promised, and after a moment of smugness, they saw no need to further the lesson. Cal was grateful.

He was eager to tell them every detail of the trip, however, and set about to recounting everything that he had encountered while away. Each night, he enjoyed breaking into a bit of his journey, sharing a sampling of his travels like one of the beloved fireside stories he had started on the road.

He kept it simple at first. He tried to bring the quiet passion of Aelemia to life, as well as the roguish spirit of Cantor. Nothing was akin to the wonder of Devoran, however, and most nights were spent answering countless questions about this one elusive realm.

"Tell us more about Damean," Cora asked one night. "We haven't learned much about him, other from his part in the moridium business."

Cal had purposefully brushed over much of Damean's past. He'd told them about the existence of a dangerous element and about Cantor's scheme to exploit it. Those were facts that they could examine, analyze, and digest easily. The rest of Devoran would be more difficult for them to understand.

"Well," Cal began, carefully looking anywhere but their eyes.

"Damean lives in a house that looks as natural as any tree; it's as if it grew right out of the ground." Cal pictured the structure and could almost see it clinging to the mountainside like a thick, unyielding vine.

"What kind of person was he? You were all so lucky that he was friendly. To think what could have happened if he had been dangerous."

"He was wonderful to us," Cal said, thinking back to Damean's gruff, yet accommodating ways. "He is a sorcerer," he added, hoping to add this most important matter unnoticed at the end of his thought.

Cora laughed uncomfortably, but Caroline snorted, eyes rolling grandly, her mouth taking on an almost pitying smirk.

"Please, Cal, be serious."

"I am," Cal shot back, defensive now. "We saw him do some magic while we were there; he tamed animals right in front of us. It's the reason we have gifts—I mean, knacks." When his parents continued to look doubtful, he launched into an explanation of the past according to Damean. He told them of the feuds, the divisions, and the consequent loss of history. He recalled the factions and what they became, and tried to impress upon them how much sense it made, looking at what Colliptia had become.

"But, Cal, if this were true, we would know of it. There would be texts with this knowledge; it would be documented, preserved." Apparently even if Caroline could accept the idea of real magic, it was nothing without organized files to prove its existence.

"The other countries were afraid, Mom. They didn't want curious children running off to get a look at magic first hand. They cut ties. Eventually fact becomes rumor, and middle-aged women laugh at it without giving it a chance."

Cal was very annoyed now, and angry tears threatened to spill out over his reddening cheeks. Cora got up and put her hand on his shoulder, looking at Caroline for support. Caroline paused only a beat before joining her.

"I promise to try to believe you," Caroline said. "But you need to be ready for the very real possibility that the rest of Cratos won't. They might attend to the threat you've reported, but do not think for a second they'll give merit to stories of magic and ancient wars. It is not our way, and you know that."

Cal nodded. He hoped the moridium would be enough to move the Cratians to act. If it wasn't, they were in for a much larger, much more complicated fight than he had expected.

Garreck

Marten arrived home just as Garreck was beginning to feel comfortable. He had settled into a new pattern of familiarity with the other members of his family that was both foreign and welcome. They laughed at dinner time, and joked with each other indulgently, rather than aggressively. It hadn't been until his time with Cal, Mauria, and Rasha that Garreck had learned there was even such a thing as "poking fun" at someone. In the Landsing household, there had always simply been scorn and degradation. It felt wonderful to be happy in his own house.

But Marten, of course, changed all that. Garreck's father strolled through the front door early one evening and went straight to his office without so much as a hello.

"Asshole," Garreck muttered under his breath, accompanied by a deep sigh. Garreck would have indulged this bit of angst more, had he not noticed his mother out of the corner of his eye. She was staring at the wall, face pale and crumpled. She did not cry, but somehow Garreck knew that meant nothing; perhaps she had run out of tears long ago.

He walked over to her, catching her in an inescapable hug. "It'll be okay, Mom," he told her. "I'm sure he's just tired. He had a long trip home."

Neither Garreck nor his mother believed the words, but she nodded all the same, somehow managing a small smile. She said nothing, just touched her hand carefully to his face before turning to seek solace in some mundane task.

Garreck could not believe he had ever hated his mother. She was just as damaged as he was by the cold apathy of his father. Marten left people broken and in need of repair.

The emotion brought on by this small but endless moment of realization breathed new life into Garreck, and he marched toward his father's study.

His courage lasted mere seconds. By the time that Garreck had burst through the ornate wooden doors of Marten's office, he had lost his voice and was unable to shout and rage as he had intended. Garreck found himself staring, mouth open soundlessly, with his father barely looking up from his work. The effect was less than ideal.

"What on earth can you possibly want?" Marten asked, dismissively.

To shout at you. To throw you into those stupid books I know you've never read. To make you play with Benji and Ronan. For you to you look me in the eyes. For you to love me. "I just want to talk."

"Fine then." Marten shuffled through papers for another few seconds before looking up halfheartedly at his eldest son. "Let's hear it."

Garreck didn't know where to begin. "I know I have been gone a long time. But it has been good for me. I've changed since I left."

Marten interrupted him. "My sources told me you were last seen leaving a jail with a cank. Is that true?"

Garreck had been gone for *months.* He had gotten arrested and then freaking disappeared, and his father asked him about *that?* Garreck willed himself to ignore it.

"I went for a bit of a vacation. I made my way through Aelemia and even made a couple of friends. We were all up for a bit of adventure, so," Garreck pushed through his anxiety, "we decided to go to Devoran."

Marten shifted. It was infinitesimal, but Garreck was used to his father's ablity to sit, resolute and unmoving for hours on end, and it had become easy to notice slight alterations. "And what did you find there?"

"Well, many things, really, but seeing you was a bit of a shock." Garreck kept his voice casual, but his face hardened, his forehead coming together at the center.

Marten was quiet for an uncomfortable amount of time; he just sat there, gazing at Garreck with an impassive expression on his face. It got to the point where Garreck began to worry that there was an explosion coming. Eventually, however, his father looked him right in the eyes and did the most terrifying thing he could have in this scenario. He smiled.

"Amazing, isn't it?"

"Excuse me?" Garreck didn't understand how they had gotten here. There was pride in his father's voice where he had expected terror or anger or shame.

"We've been working on it for years, but the project is just about finished. I'm so glad you got a chance to see it in its glory. When we started it was nothing but a tall, vast tableland." Marten's eyes glinted at the memory. "And look at it now—its potential is finally unlocked."

"Dad, I know what you're mining there." Garreck did not try to hide his confusion. His father's reaction was so unexpected that he felt thrown even more off his guard than he had been.

Marten frowned. "How do you know?"

"A local told us," Garreck said, not wanting to reveal too much information about Damean on the off chance that it might get him into trouble. "He said you were planning to use the moridium against Rien. Is that true?"

A vein in Marten's temple popped as his jaw clenched. "Well, Garreck, you have to understand. There have been reports of some very serious activity on the borders of Rien for years now. They've even been creeping up into Cantor." The words sounded worn down and practiced, as if this was not the first time Marten had said them. "It has become a matter of security, and we must respond."

"How do you know the incendiaries were Rie?" Rasha's face flashed through Garreck's mind, and his hands balled themselves into hard fists. It was preposterous to think of a country full of people like Rasha containing even a fragment of the evil that Marten accused them of.

"I told you—I have my sources," said Marten, casually and with an idle wave of his hand.

"Then your sources are wrong!" Garreck made two large steps and his hands came slamming down on Marten's desk. The bitter, resentful, wrathful side of him that had all but disappeared came bubbling to the surface now. "The Rie have done no such thing. Either your sources are idiots, or they are liars."

Marten remained exasperatingly calm. He got up and walked toward one of the orderly bookshelves, only turning to Garreck after a few moments of tense stillness.

"We can't take any chances." There was something behind Marten's words that Garreck only now recognized—an awareness that transformed uninformed violence to calculated crimes of hate. He knew that the Rie were not dangerous.

As Garreck processed this, Marten continued. "I was hoping you would want to join and help with this cause, now that you are aware of the situation. We are set to move very soon." He raised an eyebrow, "It would appear, though, that you will not be accompanying us."

Garreck shook his head once, firmly.

"Very well. I wonder, though, what caused this sudden defensiveness for a country full of *violent* heretics?" That panther smile played across Marten's face once more, making Garreck feel more like prey than progeny.

"One of the friends I traveled with was Rie. He was sweet, peaceful even. When we found him, his pilgrimage had just been attacked by a group of Cantic monsters." His father raised an apathetic eyebrow at this news, but said nothing. Disgusted, Garreck spat out his next words. "I won't destroy a group of people who are nothing but good, and I'll do everything in my power to keep you away from them."

Marten walked across the room with that same tempered nature and slapped Garreck firmly across the face. "You have always been the weakest, most disappointing of all my sons."

And then, just like that, he went to sit back at his desk. "If that is all, you may go. You've wasted my time, just as you always have."

Garreck would not let his father see him break, and so he turned to go. Before reaching the door he turned. "You're wrong," he said as evenly as possible before walking away from the cruelest man that he had ever known.

Months ago, Garreck would have believed his father's claims. He would have yelled, commiserated, and drank away the words he both hated and took as dogma. But he had grown; he had found his strength and his voice, and he would not let the scum he called a father define him once again.

He left a note for his mother and brothers letting them know where he would be, sent another off to Cal, and then left. He hoped that news of this setback would reach Cal before he did; it would save him having to relive it.

He found a wagon heading to Cratos, and he did not look back.

Cal

The council's rejection came the same day as Garreck's letter. Together, they were a crushing blow, and Cal's joy at the prospect of seeing Garreck was not enough to outweigh his chagrin. The return response from leading Cratian politicians made Cal's blood curdle. He had always thought of himself as mild-tempered, maybe even a bit too passive? But violence coursed through his veins as he read their cowardly reply.

Dear Mrs. Hanson,

After careful consideration of your appeal, We the Council cannot find just cause to intervene in this global matter. Should the events you so fear someday come to pass, Cratos will welcome all Rie citizens in search of refuge, and will initiate funds to their benefit.

Yours in Reason,

Gillian Hough
Council Secretary

The statement was too short, too dismissive. He struggled to understand what had gone wrong and wondered if he or his mother had left any crucial information out that had jeopardized his goals.

He found Caroline in the living room, quietly pouring over an old legal manuscript. It was one of the ancient texts that she enjoyed so much—remnants of archaic trials, the subjects of which seem so obviously correct in hindsight.

Without bothering to apologize for his interruption, Cal flung the letter on top of the pages his mother was reading.

Caroline raised an eyebrow but read the page, her expression changing from annoyance to acceptance in one fluid shift. When she was finished she looked up, her eyes searching his, "What about it, Cal?"

"What about it?" he asked her, his anger at the council seeping out and latching onto her instead. "What happened? How can they refuse to do something, *anything*, to help Rien? We tell them that Rien is going to be destroyed and they tell us there is nothing they can do?"

Caroline looked at him calmly. Cal noticed that although she appeared sad, she did not seem surprised.

"What?" he demanded, when she still did not speak.

"You must have known this was a possibility, Cal," Caroline said to him, slowly. "The council has other responsibilities to attend to, and some of them involve close political dealings with Cantor. *I* believe you, and Cora believes you, but put yourself in the council's shoes; would you be willing to alienate an ally on the word of a teenager?"

"But you submitted the appeal! You vouched for me. That has to mean *something*." Cal struggled desperately to find a way to undo their decision.

"My name might go a long way in some matters," Caroline said, "but it has its limits. I'm sorry, Cal."

Cal was irate. He was sure that he had never known this level of resentment before and had no idea how to cope with it. "I need to take a walk."

He stormed out, and Caroline did not try to stop him. She must have seen the emotions raging across his face and known it was better to let the storm pass.

But Cal doubted his anger would ever subside. The council was supposed to be the voice of Cratos, and though he'd questioned some of their rulings before, he had never suspected them of ill intent. Now, however, his rulers had blurred the lines between what was right and what was easy, and he would not stand idly by as they waited to clean up the carnage of Rien. His country had chosen cowardice, but he would not.

Cal

It had never occurred to Cal that the Cratian Council would deny his request for aid. Without their support, Rien's protection would be limited to the army of Aelish recruits that Maura had found. When she'd first written about Cardit and her community, Cal had pictured them as support—a welcome but unnecessary supplement to the justice of Cratos. Now, those volunteer fighters were all that they had. The idea of the Aelish alone standing up to Marten was unnerving, and Cal knew that he had to do something. He refused to admit defeat so easily. If the Council would not provide the bodies needed to make a stand, Cal would find them on his own.

Well, not entirely on his own. Cal knew that if he was to succeed, he would need the help of his friend Jane.

Jane was not a hard person to find in Cratos, but she was one of the more difficult to keep engaged. She was energy materialized, and she flitted between causes the way that others did their hobbies. Ever the advocate, Jane loved to saturate her audience with persuasive rhetoric and impassioned tones, sparking flames and leaving them for someone else to tend. Because of this, Cal knew that he could get Jane's attention when he told her of the threat to Rien, but he was not sure she would carry through with the level of commitment he needed.

Cal eventually found Jane on one of Cratos' busy streets in the center of the city. She was nailing protest papers to every storefront that would let her and calling to people as they walked by.

"Only two nights away! Educational inequity impacts everyone!" Jane's voice boomed towards passersby. Most people politely took a flyer, but it was likely only to keep from being screamed at any more than they had to be.

"Oy!" Cal yelled towards her, and she spun, her face poised for a public argument about Cratian learning.

When she saw that it was just Cal, her face relaxed and she bounded towards him. "Where have you been!" she asked, giving him a hug and hitting him playfully upside the head. "Your break from lessons is almost over and we've hardly spent any time together." She gave him an exaggerated facial expression that did nothing but make him laugh.

"I'm sure you've kept yourself busy," he told her. "Actually, Jane, I've got something that might pique your interest."

"Do you now?" she asked, eyebrows raised and mouth flashing an excited grin.

"Yes, but can we talk somewhere else?" If Cal was going to go through his story again, he wanted a seat and a cup of tea.

They ducked into a busy tavern, two drinks—non-alcoholic, of course—and found somewhere quiet to sit. As Cal had assumed, Jane's eyes lit up as he relayed the details of Cantor's plot for what seemed like the hundredth time. Her blond hair buzzed wildly about her round features as he spoke, and when Cal was done he could almost feel the connections as they zipped about Jane's mind.

To Cal's surprise, Jane was calm when she finally emerged from her thinking. Where normally Jane was scattered and focused intensely on the big picture, the seriousness of the situation seemed to have tamed her. It was actually quite jarring. If Cal had not already understood the seriousness of the situation, this would have tipped him quite over the edge.

"I can get you a crowd," Jane told him, "and I can get them going, but it's going to take much more than a pretty speech to collect the numbers you need to make a difference down south."

"That," Cal said slowly, "might not be as hard as you think."

"You have something up your sleeve?"

Cal smiled a bit, "Not me, per say, but I know someone who might be able to convince the masses."

Garreck

Garreck arrived in a cloud of frustration and profanity. Although much of his pent up angst seemed to have flooded out of him after confronting his father, the bit that lingered had emerged in full force during his travels. Just before he'd reached the Cratian border, Garreck's horse threw a shoe, and he was forced to leave her with a local farrier. After paying the man and promising to return, Garreck unhappily took a wagon for the rest of his trip northward. The ride had been just long enough for the Cratian passengers to start getting on his nerves, and he was not proud of his parting words to one particularly frustrating rider.

Dusting himself off from the journey, Garreck paused momentarily to examine Cratos, home of Cal. The city sang with consideration and cleanliness—both quintessential pieces of who Cal was. People mingled quietly, politely accounting for the feelings of those around them. Garreck could have laughed at how many "beg pardons" and "my pleasures" he heard as he strolled toward the shop where Cal had instructed him to meet.

Cal was there—early, of course—leaning effortlessly against the storefront and talking to a blond woman he had never met. When Cal saw Garreck, his eyes lit up, and Garreck felt himself smiling in response. His friend seemed unsurprised by their small exchange, which meant that Cal must have filled her in on the nature of their relationship.

If he hadn't, she certainly would have known from the lingering kiss that Cal gave him once he got to them. Garreck burned and looked around, embarrassed and afraid of such a public display of affection.

"I'm sorry," Cal told him, squeezing his hand in an attempt to comfort. "Things are different here, I promise. It's normal."

Garreck gave him a nervous laugh and fought the urge to yank his hand from Cal's. Instead, he took a deep breath and squeezed back.

"I'm Jane," the girl interrupted, shaking his other hand hand and making some of the most direct eye contact he had ever experienced. "I hear that you have some very impressive talents."

Garreck was confused until he saw Cal pointedly tap on his temple. He couldn't help but roll his eyes.

Garreck's skepticism must have been noticeable, for Cal hastedly added, "And I also told her that you were a bit out of practice. But I think we can use it tonight to help us get some support."

Garreck opened his mouth to argue, but instead he found himself saying, "I'll do it." The answer came quickly and unexpectedly, but for all his surprise Garreck also felt conviction solidifying deep in his bones.

"Oh. Well, perfect! I was prepared to put up quite the fight to get you to agree." Cal seemed confused, but pleased.

"I am nothing like my father," Garreck said, and the courage that truth brought him was beyond description. "Maybe using my gift will undo what that bastard has done."

"Wonderful!" Jane said as she ushered them away from the building and onto the busy street. "Then come on, we've got some work to do."

"Oh! There is one more thing," Garreck had almost forgotten this most crucial piece of information. "Marten confirmed that they will be moving against Rein very soon. So whatever we do, we will have to do it quickly."

Cal's face darkened but Jane, whose energetic disposition seemed impervious to all negativity, just shrugged. "Then that's what we'll do."

Garreck

Jane led them all to her own small apartment so that Garreck could practice his gift in peace. The home was clean but cozy, and it was easy to see Jane's personal style mixed with her Cratian need for order. Her book collection was comprised almost exclusively of nonfiction accounts concerning the state of Cratian affairs. Yellowing flyers from past political events hung on many of the walls. As Jane went to find them chairs, Garreck's eyes strayed to the glass casings surrounding Jane's candles. Each was tinted a different color, and Garreck was sure that the effect when lit was marvelous.

They spent little time relaxing, to Garreck's displeasure, and most of their day was devoted to helping him hone his skills. It was exhausting—like using a muscle he had not exercised in a very long time. Eventually though, he found his rhythm.

After going at it all day, Jane finally declared herself satisfied with Garreck's progress. Relieved, Garreck followed Cal and Jane out of the apartment and into a dingy hangout that was more like something he would have found in Cantor. It was small and cramped, but warm; the atmosphere was festive and prints and flyers hung all about in disarray.

"We're still in Cratos, right?" Garreck joked.

"Of course! Cortez Tavern simply honors clientele that are a bit more colorful than most." Cal was smiling broadly, feeding off the energy in the room.

As they meandered through the clusters of bar goers, Jane returned with three glasses of water and a conspiratorial look. "We're going to wait until the open performances start," she told them, guiding them towards a few vacant barstools. "Let a couple sops do their thing and then introduce Garreck."

Garreck took a long gulp of his water. He would have much preferred an ale, but apparently it was forbidden in Cratos—along with everything else fun. The thought of going up in front of everyone without a bit of liquid courage was daunting, but in the end it was probably for the best; he needed his wits about him tonight. Like he'd told Cal so many weeks before, drink gets in the way of the Cantic gifts, dulls the senses, and he didn't want to take any chances.

"Now Cal," Jane continued, "You know how much I love to stir the pot, but I need to ask one more time; do you have any moral reservations with what we're about to do?"

"Of course not!" Cal swatted his hand dismissively. "You felt for yourself that Garreck doesn't *make* anyone do anything. He just manipulates the emotions in the room—makes people more willing to do what they already would. We've got a house full of rebels and revolutionaries at our feet; they'll want to help. We just need to get them past the initial skepticism surrounding the situation."

"As you wish," Jane said with a wink at Garreck. He smiled back. Jane was one of the strangest people he had ever met. She treated everyone she encountered as though she had known them for ages. And while Garreck had never known anyone quite like her, he was happy to have her there with them.

The next hour or so passed quite pleasantly. They laughed together, lightly heckling the performers and fully enjoying each other's company. Garreck particularly enjoyed listening as Jane told story after story of young Cal.

"He was such a little rake when he was younger," she laughed, rolling her eyes as Cal feigned an innocent look. "Caroline and Cora must have gone out of their minds trying to keep track of all the names."

"Ha! But you admit I brought each and every one home to meet them!" Cal countered. "I took my relationships *very* seriously."

"If you count a lakeside encounter when you should have been at lessons *a relationship*," Jane muttered, but she smiled at him affectionately nonetheless.

Garreck was already so blown away by Cal's confidence, that it was hard for him to imagine the hormone-raging, less-restrained version. He was also once again glad that Cal grew up here and not in Cantor; they would have eaten him alive.

"I know everyone is having a great time at my expense," Cal cut in, "but I believe it is showtime."

Cal

Cal watched Garreck fidgeting nervously before it was his time to go up. He would be incredible, Cal was sure of it, but he could do little to calm his friend's nerves. Instead he simply gripped Garreck's hand and smiled. "You can do this," he told him just before Jane whisked Garreck away to stand by the stage.

Once the lutist had finished her tune, Jane strutted out to introduce Garreck. She was expressive, impassioned, and if it weren't for the gravity of the task at hand, Cal was sure she alone could have convinced the crowd of anything.

Polite applause followed Jane offstage, and Cal saw her whisper something to Garreck just before she pushed him out to replace her. Garreck's steps were slow but sure, and Cal took an involuntary breath, praying to every god he didn't believe in that this would work.

His prayers proved unnecessary; Garreck was dazzling. From his opening words Cal felt at ease, and as he began his explanation that ease shifted to interest. Interest became deep concern when Garreck described the project they had found in Devoran, and concern became eagerness when he appealed for the audience's help.

It was difficult but not impossible to identify Garreck's knack working away in his mind. It was as if his brain all of a sudden had a temperature, and that temperature fluctuated in effective ways whenever Garreck moved to a different position. Concern, for instance, was cooler, while eagerness warmed. It was subtle and strange, but most likely unnoticeable for someone who didn't know what was happening.

Cal thought back to the squirrely man who had tried to sell him rucksacks at the beginning of the summer. He realized now that the nasty little man had been using *his* knack to swindle unsuspecting shoppers.

That scoundrel, Cal thought, he temper flaring.

Momentarily irked, it took a conscious effort for Cal to pull himself out of this digression, but he forced himself to focus on Garreck's last point—his call to action. The audience's response would determine whether or not they brought anyone back when they inevitably joined Mauria down south.

"I walk around this country and I feel like I am home," Cal listened as Garreck brought his voice lower, more intimate. "I see peace and acceptance and security. There is probably no one in this room that has ever feared for their family, who has ever been threatened with hunger or war or pain. If you have, you knew that those crimes would be met with justice. Right now, there *are* people living in the shadow of such a threat—of a boundless hate that knows no law or order." Garreck's voice shifted now, filling their somber hearts with hope.

"I do not ask you to fight. I simply ask you to stand with us. Meet us in one month on the border of Rien and Cantor, and show the Cantics that Cratos will not allow such intolerance. It is not happening here—yet. Do not give them a chance to spread northward. Protect your foreign neighbors. Protect yourselves."

The tavern was silent. Cal, who had been near tears, spun about, trying to read the sea of silent onlookers. However, when he looked toward Garreck he was met with a wink and a triumphant expression.

Unsure of where Garreck was getting this confidence, but relieved by it, Cal turned towards Jane, who was now addressing the room.

"Please see me or Cal," Cal waved as she said his name, "for specific information about the rally. We need you."

She added the last part desperately, but it wasn't necessary. Every chair had scraped at her words, and soon Cal was flooded with patrons asking him for details. They spent two hours answering whatever questions came their way, and when all was said and done, they had ruined the open performance section of the evening, but had gathered upwards of 300 volunteers.

Mauria

Against all odds, Mauira *did* survive the trip from Marcan West to Rien, and as she got out of the wagon she took in a breath of clean, hot air.

Mauria realized suddenly how low her expectations had been for this country. If she was being honest with herself, her perception of Rien had been something akin to desert huts and somber streets. Instead, she was met with gorgeous, textured buildings the color of sandstone and raw beeswax. The people around her were not rowdy, but there was a sense of happiness and purpose as they mingled and laughed and socialized through the streets. Strong scents of cooking caught on warm winds, and if she squinted she could see small spires glinting off of a few magnificent domed structures.

She'd had to ask someone from the pilgrimage who she should see when she arrived, for she knew only that Rien was based in religion. Mauria was surprised to learn that the country actually had an elected official who was separate from their faith. His name was Binda Botros, and with the help of a few friendly strangers, Mauria found him with little trouble.

His office was housed in a modest building in the center of the main city. The decor, while simple, was lovely, and Mauria's fingers danced slowly along the carved walls as she waited for an audience with Botros. Lulled into a reverie as she traced the delicate stonework, she almost didn't hear the assistant call to her.

"He can see you now." She said it softly, but Mauria jumped all the same. She scrambled up, composing herself quickly before walking into Botros' office.

Botros was a slight man with piercing blue eyes and coffee skin. He smiled at Mauria as she entered, and gestured a long arm warmly for her to take a seat across from him. She couldn't be certain, but she guessed that if he stood, he would have been at least a foot taller than she was.

"I'm sorry that you had to wait," Botros told her, "but this is certainly an unexpected request. You've come a long way from Aelemia." His gaze was quizzical, as if he was trying to read the truth in her eyes before she told it to him.

"It was certainly last minute, and I'm sorry if it was an imposition," she said quickly, trying to get formalities out of the way, "but there is something fairly pressing that I was hoping to discuss with you."

His eyebrows pinched together, "Forgive me, and I do not mean to offend, but if this news is so important, why are you the one delivering it?"

It was a fair question, but that didn't keep a small sigh from escaping before Mauria could control it. "Well *I* don't mean to offend, but it's because I'm the only one who cares, sir."

Botros gave a small laugh and, shaking his head slightly, said, "Well then, what do you need to tell me?" Mauria was not sure if his tone was one of condescension or amusement, but she decided it did not matter.

She gave the same speech she had prepared for the Gathering, but left out the appeal for aid. This was *his* country, after all. She didn't need to ask for his help, she just needed him to *know*. She needed an adult other than Cardit to give a shit about the looming catastrophe.

He was patient, and did not interrupt; Botros even nodded a few times as she spoke. When she was finished, he paused for a full minute, choosing his words carefully.

"We are aware of the threat from Cantor." He said it simply and pretended to ignore Mauria as her jaw dropped. "We did not know the extent of the weapon they have acquired, but it also does not change our course of action."

"What action?" Mauria's shock turned to anger faster than even she had expected. "What are you doing to protect yourselves?"

"I assume Rasha told you of our way of life while you traveled together." It wasn't a question. "You are aware, then, that we rely on and believe in the protection that our faith provides us. We nourish our minds and bodies through prayer, and our beliefs keep us whole. We can't sacrifice that essential fact by taking up arms as you might have us do."

"So you will do nothing?" The derision was sharp in her voice, but Mauria didn't care.

"You might see it as nothing," Botros allowed, "but we do not. We see it as our only option."

"But you'll let others protect you? You'll let others put themselves in danger?"

"You sought me out, Mauria, not the other way around. I have not asked you to help us, nor will I ever."

Mauria felt stricken. She looked Botros in the eyes, searching for fear or madness, and found only a tinge of sadness in that penetrating blue. "Okay," she finally said. "I guess I'll show myself out then."

She turned to go, but then whirled around. "Why not leave? At the very least evacuate the city until it is safe again?"

Botros sighed. "And to where would we flee, Mauria? You just admitted to being the only person who cares enough to warn us about Cantor."

And with that, he walked Mauria to the door. She followed, shame and anger warring within her.

It was raining when Mauria stepped outside, but she did not avoid the warm drops falling freely around her. Instead, she sat on the ground and looked up, meeting them head on, and let herself feel. She felt the pain of Rasha's small betrayal, felt her own frustration with the world's apathy, and felt the creeping suspicion that she simply wasn't enough to save this place. She felt it all, and for the first time since Kent had fallen out of their Yew tree so many years ago, she wept.

Cal

High with the buzz of success, Cal and his friends left Cortez's and settled at another tavern to relive their victory. They sifted through hundreds of names, rejoicing at the numbers and imagining the Cantic faces once they eventually met the hoards that they'd amassed. Their celebration lasted hours, and it wasn't until the curfew warning had rung out that Jane finally left their small celebration, yawning deeply as she said she goodbyes. Now just the two of them, Cal and Garreck moved from the bar to the street. They ambled slowly back to the Hanson house, taking their time. Where the inside of the tavern had been boisterous and loud, the street was peaceful, and Cal revelled in the ability to speak at a normal volume.

Garreck walked next to him, his soldier-straight posture clashing with his mood which was utterly relaxed. Now that it was just them, though, Cal posed the question that had been nagging at him all night. "All right, you have to tell me how you knew."

"Knew what?" Garreck chuckled.

"When you finished your speech back at Cortez's you were smiling, like you *knew* your audience had bought it. I thought we were done for, but you seemed so sure that they'd been convinced."

"Well, for one," Garreck put a hand up to his chest in mock offense. "I take issue with your use of the phrase "bought it." You make it sound like we were trying to dupe them, which we were not." Cal laughed, but continued to look curiously at him.

"Fine," Garreck said. "To answer your question—I knew that they believed us because I *felt* it. That's the way the gift works. Tell me," he smirked slightly and Cal's insides turned to mash, "what did you feel when I was done talking?"

"I felt warm, almost hot," Cal tried to remember. "Like someone had turned up the temperature in the room to the point where I was aware of the heat, but not uncomfortable."

Garreck nodded. "It was the same for most of the people in front of me. Some people who weren't convinced had different energies, but for the most part I could feel a crowd full of ready people, even if they weren't saying it out loud."

"That makes sense," Cal said. "I guess it would be hard to influence someone's emotion if you couldn't identify what you were starting with."

"Exactly," Garreck said, smiling at Cal and then turning his grin upward towards the stars, totally at peace. Cal could not believe how different Garreck was now that he was honest with and confident in himself; he had never seen him this utterly satisfied. There was something, though, that kept Cal from joining him in his contentment.

"So, are you always aware of other people's energies?" Cal said it casually, but there was a weight to the question that he couldn't escape. He cursed his fair skin as he felt a blush spread rapidly over his cheeks. Cal hoped it was dark enough that Garreck would not notice.

"Up until today I wasn't using my gift, so I wasn't aware, no. But ever since I decided to tap into it again, I guess I do."

"Is it distracting?"

"Well, that depends." Garreck reached for Cal's hand and squeezed it, and Cal was once again thrown by his increased self-possession and assurance. "Right now for instance," Garreck said, "I am very aware of it."

Cal leaned in and kissed him, and then sighed and pulled away.

"That is wholly unfair. I'm going to have to be on high alert from now on."

Garreck laughed and shrugged, "A small price to pay, I hope."

"Entirely worth it," Cal said, putting his hand out to Garreck. "But are you ready to go head to head with someone who can resist your manipulations?"

"Who did you have in mind?"

"Well, we're almost home, and I know that Caroline and Cora are just *dying* to meet you."

Garreck

The Hanson sisters were asleep when the boys arrived home, but Cal's mothers had waited up for them. Garreck was pleased to discover that Cal's ominous warning about his parents had been unfounded, and that upon the boy's arrival Cora and Caroline both gave Garreck enormous hugs that would melt even the coldest person. When everyone had said their hellos, the four of them sat drinking mugs of melted chocolate while Garreck was lightly interrogated. They did not ask about his family; Garreck guessed that Cal had warned them it was a touchy subject. Instead, they asked about his goals and ambitions, and for the first time ever, Garreck allowed himself to consider the answers.

"I honestly never really thought about it. My father liked to tell me what to do, and I liked to disappoint him, but I think deep down I believed I'd eventually end up doing what he wanted." Speaking this truth out loud was terrifying, never mind doing it in front of Cal's parents, but they didn't seem thrown by the answer. In fact, Caroline was nodding to herself.

"Did you enjoy speaking tonight?" she asked him.

"I did. It felt great, actually." Garreck's mind flitted back to the scene at Cortez Tavern. He could still feel the rush of pride and ability that had accompanied the use of his gift.

"While it shouldn't be the only answer, you might want to think about taking your knack into consideration while you explore what makes you feel truly fulfilled. That's how I came to be a lawyer, actually."

Cora gave a bark that startled the rest of them. "Remember what you were doing before the firm?" She was shaking with restrained laughter as Caroline pushed her away teasingly.

"I was molding young minds," she said, face turned away from Cora to hide her grin.

"You were screaming at children for being children, and I was worried that either you or a student would eventually end up physically injured."

Caroline looked ruefully at Garreck. "It turns out I have a sense of justice that doesn't translate well into the world of tattling and cheating at lessons. Eventually, though, I found a place where all the pieces fit together. I've got a second home standing in front of a jury of adults who can appreciate reason."

Cora settled down and smiled at her. In that instant Garreck could see how unconditionally they valued one another, and the tenderness of the moment hit him in an aggressive way that he was not prepared for.

"I'll definitely think about that, Caroline," Garreck said, getting up a bit too quickly. "I'm actually a little tired, do you mind if I head to bed?"

"Not at all!" Caroline told him, and once again there was too much sincerity—too much love. "We're up far later than we should be anyway; we just couldn't wait until tomorrow to meet you."

After brief "goodnights" between them all, Garreck let Cal lead the way to his childhood bedroom. Trying to focus on something other than his own self-pity, Garreck peered intently around at the small space. There were books everywhere. All of them were on shelves of some sort, but the titles had been placed haphazardly so that some spines were facing away from the reader. There was an enormous map nailed squarely to one wall and a mural drawn delicately on the other.

"Cora drew that," Cal said, noticing Garreck's eyes scanning the creation. "She would have put it on the ceiling, but I hate sleeping on my back."

Garreck moved closer to the scene: a beautiful starscape so detailed Garreck had to squint to catch the more minute details.

"She said it's the same stars that they could see on the day I was born, but I'd wager that some of the smaller ones are made up."

Garreck stared at the constellations, at the love that had gone into each delicate drop of paint. To his utter horror, he felt himself beginning to tear up. His mind searched desperately for images that would stop the coming emotion in its tracks, but as he scrambled, Marten's face flitted quickly to the surface. It only served to exacerbate the situation. Soon Garreck's silent tears threatened to progress to more dangerous territory. He wiped quickly at his face, but as he did so, he felt Cal's hand reach inexplicably up to stop him. Cal neither laughed nor mocked this moment of weakness; he just stood in front of Garreck, attempting to decipher his sopping face.

"What's the matter?" Cal asked. "I promise, you can trust me." It was a request, not a demand, and Garreck fought against the instinct to reply with a typical "It's nothing," or "Everything's fine."

Keep it together idiot, he told himself sternly before responding, "I just can't help but compare your family to mine."

He was embarrassed by his jealousy, but it burned through him now even harder than it had back in the living room with Cora and Caroline.

Cal seemed at a loss for words, and Garreck didn't blame him. Cal knew how distant he and his brothers had been; he knew that Garreck's mom had failed to defend him against an abusive, selfish father.

"I can't even imagine what it was like for you," Cal finally said, "but it seems to me that you did the only thing you could do. You survived. And you know, you'll never be able to control what they do and how they are, but you do have ownership over your own decisions. Since I've known you, Garreck, you've made choices that allowed you to become an incredible, developed, empathetic person."

As an afterthought he added, "You were such an asshole the first time we met." That got Garreck to laugh, and he turned to see Cal beaming at him.

"And somehow you are still as *annoying* as when we first met," Garreck jabbed, grinning back.

Cal laughed with him before sitting on the bed and gesturing for him to sit down.

"Seriously though," Cal said, "you care about people now. You told me you took your brothers fishing because you knew they'd like it. You did things just to make your mother smile. You changed yourself and in turn the Landsings were able to grow a bit as well." He paused for a moment before adding, "Maybe someday Marten will, too."

Garreck threw himself back onto the bed, hands resting behind his head, "Oh, definitely not! But I can be satisfied being loved by most of my family."

Cal lay down beside him, curling so that his head was on Garreck's shoulder. "And you've got a backup family here," he said quietly, "for when you need it."

Mauria

Mauria almost didn't make it to her last stop in Rien.

Once the storm passed she thought briefly of getting up on her horse and finding her way back to Cardit in Marcan South. In the end, however, she swallowed her pride and made her way to Rasha's house.

It took a while to get there for as she moved away from the center of the city, the streets grew smaller and more twisting. Fortunately, most of the Rie people were friendly, and after asking around, she found herself knocking on a sturdy wooden door, silently hoping that no one was home.

To her disappointment, Mauria heard footsteps approaching, and when the occupant opened the door, she found herself face to face with a beautiful woman who could have been Rasha's twin. The woman was petite, and had it not been for the creases below her eyes, it would have been impossible to determine her age. She had Rasha's face exactly, except that it lacked the light freckles with which his was spotted.

"Can I help you?" she asked, curiosity slowly etching her features.

"Yes," Mauria said quickly, reaching out to shake her hand. "I'm Mauria. Are you Lira?"

"I am," Lira said, a bit taken aback.

"I'm a friend of Rasha's," Mauria explained, and as she did relief flooded Lira's face so profoundly that Mauria silently scolded herself for even considering not coming.

"So, you have seen him then! And he is all right?" Lira's joy was palpable.

Mauria put out a comforting hand, much like she would have done for Rasha. "Yes, he is. I came here to tell you that he is okay and that he hopes to come home soon."

"Come in," Lira said, guiding Mauria into a warm kitchen. She sat her down at the table, and brought over cookies and tea, even when Mauria insisted she couldn't stay long.

"Please, tell me everything. I had heard his pilgrimage did not make it to Torp, and when he was not one of the survivors who returned, I assumed the worst."

Mauria felt an instant pang of guilt for not writing to her parents at all during her trip to Devoran, but also knew that her situation was not quite the same. They had no reason to think she'd been slaughtered as Lira believed of Rasha.

"We met just after the attack. He was fine physically, but mentally the ambush really affected him. He needed some time to think, so he joined my friends and me on a trip. He was like a little brother, right from the start," Mauria was surprised and happy to find that even with her anger towards Rasha, her affection for the boy was still strong. "We had a lot of fun together," she added, her words enriched by her fondness.

"Where is he now? Did he not return with you?" Lira pressed.

"No, he stayed behind to learn a bit about other parts of the world." It was less than half of the truth, but Mauria didn't think Lira needed to know more. Mauria herself hardly understood why Rasha had stayed in Devoran, and she didn't want Lira to worry about her only son lost in a foreign country: particularly one that most believed to be dangerous and wild.

"Is he safe? Lira's eyes were pleading.

Mauria nodded. "Yes, he's safe."

"And happy?"

"Very," Mauria told her. *Right until he totally lost his mind.* Again she was only giving Lira a partial truth, but she decided it was probably kinder not to speak the second part out loud.

"Can I write to him?" Lira's voice was quiet and earnest. "If you had an address I could reach out to him … let him know I love him."

Mauria silently scolded Rasha for worrying this wonderful person, but simply said, "I don't have an address, but I would be happy to give him a letter if I see him before you do."

Lira smiled and went to get a scrap of paper and something to write with. She wrote quickly, but paused at the end before added one last line. Folding it carefully, she handed Mauria the letter. "I was also hoping you could get this to him?" She held out a piece of finely woven cloth the color of burnt topaz. "It's a scarf. I finished it after Rasha left. It would mean so much for him to have it."

Mauria nodded, and Lira's answering smile was breathtaking.

"Thank you. I am so lucky that Rasha found such friends."

"I was the lucky one," Mauria said, with complete sincerity, taking the scarf and the letter and stashing both items in her bag.

Lira walked her out and pointed her in the direction of the road that would take her to Marcan South. Mauria turned back to see her waving, and she imagined the same scene but with Rasha leaving for his pilgrimage.

Mauria waved back, smiled, and hoped Rasha had waved, too.

Cal

Even though they shouldn't have, Cal and Garreck spent a few extra days with his family. It felt like stolen time, but it was necessary. Neither one had truly rested since they'd left Devoran, and the hope that their volunteers had brought provided momentary respite and an excuse to breathe freely again.

Eleanor and Emilee took to Garreck right away, and he was surprisingly gentle with them. He played their nonsense games and listened to their wild stories; he even helped them set a trap for Fendrel. It was hilarious to watch the three of them crouched behind the sofa, watching intently as the cat walked cautiously toward a tantalizing pile of treats.

"Now!" Eleanor would shout as the other two threw a blanket over Fendrel, rushing over to grab him up.

"Enough!" Cal finally called, once again acting as the cat's savior.

"Fendrel is fifteen years old, and I'll be damned if you three will give him a heart attack before he makes it to sixteen."

Garrack sighed and leaned over to Eleanor and Emilee. "I guess he's probably right. Besides, I think we should set our sights on larger prey." He wiggled his eyebrows conspiratorial at the girls and then flung the blanket up at Cal.

The girl's exploded in giggles, springing up on Cal as the cat sprang from his arms to safety. They were all about him, but Cal fell backward trying to catch his breath as he laughed and struggled for freedom.

"All right! I surrender!" he called, heaving himself into a sitting position and catching each of his sisters in a one-armed hug. "You two are far too clever for me."

"We know!" They trilled together, laughing and dashing away.

Garreck, who'd had a chance to stand during the assault, offered Cal a hand. He took it, pulling himself to his feet and giving Garreck a grin.

"You're wonderful with them," Cal told him.

"They are demons," Garreck laughed, "but they are cute demons."

Cal nudged him, "Your brothers are lucky to have you."

"I've still got some damage control to do with that relationship once I finally make my way back home," Garreck shrugged, "but it's nice to know I've got it in me."

For the rest of the day they lounged, thinking about as little as possible. Eventually, though, Cal and Garreck sought out Cora and Caroline. Cal knew his mothers would not be thrilled with the news that he wasn't returning to lessons once the season began, but he hoped they'd understand.

They did him one better and expected the news.

"We figured as much," Cora said after Cal told them their plans. "Just promise us that you'll study on your own. We've gotten used to having a bright son, and it would be a shame if you lapsed into a dullard."

Cal rolled his eyes while Caroline pulled him into a hug. "And *please* write this time, for reason's sake. Let us know how everything goes. I'm sorry we can't come with you, but with our jobs and the girls it's just not in the cards."

"It's all right," Cal told her, giving her one final hug. "We've got numbers now. I feel really good about our chances."

His next words were directed at Garreck. "Are you ready?"

With a sigh Garreck said, "Sure. Thank you, Mrs. and Mrs. Hanson. This has been really nice."

They beamed at him. "You're welcome back anytime, Garreck" Caroline said. "I'd love to test our knacks against each other at some point—experiment to see which is stronger."

"It's a deal."

Rasha

Rasha breathed heavily from exertion and dropped to rest on one knee. He'd spent the last twenty minutes snapping apples from trees and whizzing them about. It was difficult, combining several elemental connections in quick succession, and though rewarding he was completely drained.

He sighed deeply, lying back and allowing himself to sink into the tall brush. When they first started together, Damean had warned Rasha that not everyone possessed enough magic to practice sorcery. Well, over the last two months he had listened closely to everything Damean told him about magic, and though he was nowhere near as powerful as his mentor, Rasha couldn't help but be pleased at how quickly he'd picked up on all Damean's teachings.

Even now, face tilted towards the sun and arms crossed comfortably behind his head, he felt thousands of connections to the warm rays that hit him. He knew that he could tame that heat with a soft wind or amplify it, igniting a flame that would act according to his will.

The sun had slowly begun to set while he practiced, and rather than continue training, he heaved himself to his feet and made his way back to Damean's house. Afternoons were typically reserved for verbal lessons and discussion, and while he looked forward to these talks, today he was also conscious of the slow, churning dance of his empty stomach.

Damean was still out when he arrived at the cottage, so Rasha started a fire and began chopping root vegetables and grinding spices that he would eventually stew. He'd always enjoyed eating meat, but ever since he began his training he's eaten less and less of it. Damean didn't seem to mind, but there was something about connecting with animals that then made eating them seem very wrong to Rasha.

Dinner was almost ready when Damean came through the door. He looked concerned as he kicked off his boots and sat down at the table. Rasha brought over two bowls of stew, and waited for Damean to tell him what was on his mind. It took him a while to talk, and nearly an hour had gone by before he looked to Rasha and said, "You have to leave tomorrow."

Rasha dripped stew down his front and was thankful that enough time had passed that it was no longer scalding. "Why on earth do I need to leave tomorrow?"

Damean raised an eyebrow. "Why do you think? The Cantics are ready, and are moving on Rien very soon. You have to go back."

Rasha let that news sink in. Of course he had not *forgotten* about the moridium, but he'd also let it fall back into one of the many crannies of his mind. How could he focus on anything when there was so much more to learn from and ask of Damean? He thought he would have more time. There was one question in particular that Rasha had wanted to ask since he'd begun working with Damean, but he had, thus far, feared the answer too much to approach his mentor.

"I'm not finished here." Rasha looked away, his voice quavering from equal parts indignance and worry.

"You have to be. But let us take tonight to review all that you've learned. You will want to do all that you are willing to when the time comes to stand against Cantor."

Rasha's head snapped to Damean. His use of the word *willing* was not an accident, and Rasha knew this was the conversation he had both feared and craved.

Damean saw that Rasha was about to speak and stopped him. "One step at a time. I want to review before we add another piece tonight. Tell me why we are able to harness magic."

Rasha nodded. "Because we speak the language of everything. We recognize the connections—not just between living things—but between elements. If the world is a drum, we know its many beats and rhythms."

"Well said," Damean told him. "And what of our responsibility to that magic?"

"We must honor our connections and use them for need rather than want. We crave vibrancy, and life is the only thing we should want in excess."

"Good," nodded Damean, but his already serious face darkened. "Now, I have only ever shown you how to manipulate connections: how to push and pull, expand and tighten. However, as I know you have guessed, connections can be broken." He closed his fist as he said it, and a flower that had been blooming in the kitchen window burst. Where the plant had once stood healthy and green there was nothing save for a few bits of glinting mass, and even those were quickly disappearing.

Rasha gawked. "What happens to those connections? Once they're broken, I mean."

"The fragments go into everything."

Rasha looked at Damean, his face pale. "I don't know if I understand, Damean." He carefully asked, "Is this what happened all those years ago? Did Devoran split because the sorcerer's used their magic to break *people's* connections?"

Damean grimaced, "They did what they thought they had to do. I cannot imagine the choices they had to make. But ever since, it has been an unspoken rule among those of us who still practice magic to harness connections—never to break them."

"Manipulating connections drains me," Rasha told him. "What kind of toll does this take on you?"

"Physically? It is the same. But as you have learned by manipulating connections, we are all a part of everything. And so each time you destroy a connection, you become aware of it, and you feel its absence. Just breaking the connections in that small flower was like puncturing my lung or some vital organ. It stays with you. You feel it with every breath."

"Damean, I don't know if I'm prepared to do that when I leave. I don't know if I can."

Damean gave him a small, sad smile. "I wouldn't let you go if you thought you *could*. I only wanted you to know so that you had the option, should things become that utterly desperate.

"But what if things do get that bad and I still can't? Then I watch my people die and know I could have stopped it."

Damean shrugged. "Let's hope it doesn't come to that."

PART FOUR

Though blazing are the embers
which survive long through the night.
The cyclic sun must surely rise
and threaten firelight.
Burn on!
As hotly as the night of cinder's first rebirth,
Fight wildly for space to flare
and smolder on this earth.

Mauria

*W*hen Mauria finally arrived in Marcan South to meet Cardit, she had a hard time believing that she was actually in Aelemia. The camp was small, housing only fifty soldiers. Tiny tents were pitched in precise rows; there appeared to be room inside each for only a person and perhaps a few possessions. Searching about, Mauria spotted the occupants of those tents off in a field a few hundred yards away, practicing drills in perfect unison.

In some ways, Mauria thought, the Aelish were the perfect soldiers. They were raised to believe in helping others, sacrificing for a community, and selfless acts of service. It was only the potential for violence that clashed with their way of life.

She made her way to a larger tent that had been pitched on the far side of the space. Cardit was inside, rifling through papers and furrowing her brow.

"Laz, our ration count is off; I'm going to need you to go through it again before we send them out on another hunt."

"Numbers were never a strength of mine," Mauria teased, coming to sit in front of Cardit. "But I'll do my best."

Cardit rolled her eyes but came to hug Mauria all the same.

"Glad you made it, Hoan. How did the meeting in Rien go?"

"Not well. I talked Basta. He knows and is still unwilling to act."

Cardit's face fell as Mauria skimmed through the important details of the meeting. She also gave her the most recent word from Cal, which was that Cratos would not be sending aid.

"So it is just us?" Her voice was calculating, trying to figure out how they could succeed against these new and worsened odds.

"For now," Mauria told her, "but I've heard nothing from Cal and Garreck yet. When he last wrote, Cal was going to try to recruit protestors to help pause the Cantic advances. If they succeeded, maybe it doesn't have to come to a fight."

Cardit raised an eyebrow. "You think that a Cantic army is going to stop because some bleeding-heart reformists yell at them? If Marten Landsing is really bringing a weapon powerful enough to destroy all of Rien, he won't be keen to just turn around and go home."

Mauria, who had just felt invigorated at the sight of their army faltered slightly at this but pushed through, desperate for positivity. "But look at what we have here! If it comes to a fight we will be ready."

"You are right about that. But do we have a chance of winning? I think you overestimate our abilities. You've only just arrived, and although we have a solid group of soldiers here, many are new like yourself." Cardit paced a bit and then looked back up at Mauria. "You say this is a weapon that will do all the dirty work for Marten. That means he won't need invasion numbers, that's good for us. But he will most likely bring anywhere between twenty and fifty armed guards to travel with him and the moridium." She sighed but continued. "I *am* good with numbers, and that puts us at a 2-1 advantage at best, and 1-1 at worst."

Mauria was at a loss for words. She had been at the camp less than an hour and Cardit was already crying defeat. Flustered, but also frustrated at Cardit's pessimism, Mauria threw her hands up in the air. It was a childish gesture, but she didn't care. "Then what do you propose we do? Shall we just pack up and watch Rien explode in a cloud of fire? We can find a cozy spot to watch it all happen. I'll bring snacks."

Laz, or so Mauria assumed, chose this particular moment to walk in, head buried in a few pieces of paper. At the sight of Mauria's emerging panic attack, he turned wordlessly and walked out of the tent.

Smart boy, Mauria thought wryly.

"Look, now you've scared away Laz." Cardit said it lightly, trying to bring Mauria's energy back to a healthy place. "He's going to be useless when the battle finally rolls around."

Mauria looked up. "You still want to fight? After all you just said…"

"I said things were bad. I didn't say we wouldn't try." Cardit took Mauria by the shoulders and stared intently at her. "We need to be honest with our own people though. We'll wait for word from Cal and then let them know what we know. They need the opportunity to leave should they fear the risk."

Mauria nodded, anxiety leveling back to the normal it had established when Damean first told them about moridium. She hoped that the rest of the army was as brave as Cardit.

"Let's get you set up," Cardit told her briskly, followed by a sharp, "All right, Laz, get in here."

Laz, who must have been waiting just outside the door, shuffled in and gave Cardit a firm salute. "Ma'am?"

"Can you find Hoan a tent? But hustle back, I really do need you to go through the ration count again." Cardit spoke with an authority that Mauria coveted. Her face must have betrayed her because Cardit turned to her and whispered, "I promise I'm not as formidable as I sound."

Mauria smiled but shook her head. "On the contrary, I feel like I'm only getting a taste right now." Cardit gave a snort of humor, but said nothing in reply. She turned away, leaving Mauria to follow Laz out of the tent, intrigued and excited for her time with this crew.

Mauria

Mauria was in Marcan South for a few days before Cal's letter came. While she waited, she joined the daily drills and strategy sessions, immersing herself in the life of an Aelish soldier. The phrase *Aelish soldier* was so contradictory that every once in a while Mauria checked to make sure it wasn't all some elaborate, wicked dream.

But it was real, and although she had been surrounded by family and community her entire life, it took only those few days for the camp to feel like home.

Cardit was right when she said there were many beginners in their ranks. Mauria herself was behind in most areas, but her passion and previous study helped her advance quickly as she shadowed the more advanced fighters. Others did not have the blessing of prior experience, and Mauria took it upon herself to target and help these individuals. She admired their willingness to break away and try something so alien to their way of life. It had taken two lost boys and an opening to pry her away from the comfort of her community; these men and women did it simply because they wanted to.

Despite their varying levels of aptitude, a current ran throughout the camp, and it kept them alive; it kept them strong.

That is, of course, until Cal's letter came.

It arrived while Mauria was in the middle of a sparring drill. She'd been paired with a more experienced fighter. They'd found that integrating ability levels led to better and more advanced learning for everyone.

Her partner was a man named Chasten Marks, only a few inches taller than she, but with sinewy muscles that he used skillfully. He'd just set up his next offensive move when Mauria heard Cardit call her name. She looked up at the wrong moment and was caught below the chin with a hard swipe. She turned to glare at Marks who looked appropriately apologetic, but also pleased with his placement and form.

"Sorry about that, I didn't see you look away," Marks said, reaching his hand out to check the damage.

"Whatever," Mauria grumbled, swatting his hand away. But she shot him a grin all the same. "It was a good punch."

They both tilted their heads to acknowledge the end to the spar, and then Mauria jogged away to see what Cardit wanted.

Cardit was holding Cal's letter open in one hand, and a hard, yeasty roll in the other. Mauria could tell something was off by the number of times Cardit brought the roll absentmindedly up to her mouth, only to bring it down unbitten a few seconds later. After a long minute, Cardit passed the letter to Mauria, saying nothing.

Mauria glanced down, hoping that Cardit was having a go at her, and that the letter was not the death sentence it appeared to be.

Mauria,

With any luck this letter is only a few days ahead of us. We had great success in Cratos, and got nearly 300 volunteer signatures. Garreck was incredible—you should have seen him! They will meet us on the Rien border with Jane. She plans on travelling soon so that there is a core group ready to welcome the others as they arrive. We promised they would be protestors and nothing more, but I think that with Cardit's army it might be enough to stop Marten, even if—as you wrote before—Rien will not fight for themselves. I don't know what your numbers are, but if the soldiers are anything like this Cardit that you described, we've got a chance at actually making a difference here.

I haven't heard anything from Rasha. I know he'll come—he promised he would. I just don't know if he'll be able to find us when he comes to meet us. I know everyone is still raging at him, but I miss that kid.

See you soon,

Cal

It was as if she'd received a few more hits from Marks.

Thud, "*Protestors, nothing more.*"

Thud, "*Don't know what your numbers are.*"

Thud, "*Rasha.*"

Cardit came and laid a hand on Mauria's shoulder. It was as simple gesture, companionable. She seemed to understand that Mauria needed to be reminded that she was still among friends—that she wasn't alone.

"I didn't pay attention to anything other than the part that implies you think I'm something special," Cardit joked, taking a bite of her roll and grinning at Mauria. "Don't worry, I let it go to my head."

Mauria tried to laugh, but nothing came out. She felt so empty that although she felt like throwing herself on the ground and weeping, she knew no tears would come.

"What do we do now?" she asked.

"We tell the others," Cardit said, simply. "They need to know the gravity of what they've signed up for."

Mauria nodded, following Cardit out and back to their drills and daily chores. It was nerve wracking to picture their group any smaller than it already was, but Cardit was right. They could not assume that their soldiers' allegiance would extend to an undertaking as risky as theirs had quickly become.

And so they told them. After dinner, during a time that was normally reserved for jokes and jests, Cardit explained the situation.

Yes, they would have 300 others there to support them. No, those supporters couldn't fight, and most likely would refuse to do so. Yes, the

Cantics had a weapon that could destroy all of them. No, they probably wouldn't waste it before getting to Rien. Yes, their stand would almost certainly end in a fight. Yes, their stand would almost certainly end in Aelish casualties.

When she was done, and a noiseless pall had settled among them, Cardit took a deep breath, and said, "If you want to leave, I would not fault you for it. Some of you have been here for a long time, training and waiting for a moment to test your skills. Some of you, however, are young and new—more interested in the community aspect of this army than the act of protecting others. Neither is better or worse, but we don't need those who fall into the second category. We need people who are willing to sacrifice. I do not mean crops or skills or time, but *lives*."

And some did leave. Mauria counted fourteen members who got up, apologizing quietly to those around them as they left. Some of the deserters were new members, but there were a few experienced fighters in the mix. She noticed that those veteran soldiers said nothing, their shame palpable as they made their way to their tents.

When they had gone, Mauria looked to Cardit, whose face remained impassive throughout the small exodus.

"For those of you who are left," Cardit said the words loudly and clearly, offering power to powerless troops, "nothing has changed. As far as we know the Cantics have not yet moved, and until we hear otherwise drills will continue as planned. We start at dawn. If your normal partner has left, find another. I am proud to be among you, and I will be honored to fight with you."

As Mauria turned to leave, Cardit stopped her. "At the Gathering, you said you were a healer." The statement caught Mauria off guard; she was surprised Cardit had remembered.

"Yes, but it is only a part of who I am." Mauria said. She was a *fighter*, that was why she was here.

"I am going to need you to be both," Cardit told her, and upon seeing the look of rebellion in Mauria's eyes added, "Any other healers among us will be asked to do the same. Surely you would not deny our community the small gift of safety, or at least the semblance of it."

Mauria sighed but nodded.

"Good, then I'll say goodnight." Cardit turned, and Mauria knew that just like everyone else in their camp, Cardit would not sleep soundly tonight. Their dreams would be filled with horrors that only the unconscious mind can concoct. There was a grim humor to it—the Aelish even shared their trauma.

Garreck

Garreck and Cal probably should have journeyed with a bit more haste on their way to meet Mauria, but it was hard to quicken their pace knowing how drastically their lives would change once they reached their friend.

There was joy in traveling together. Autumn had reached every corner of the thick trees of Marcan West, and he and Cal crunched through the woods, hand in hand. Cal's prattling, which Garreck had once found insufferable, was now endearing; although, he would be lying if he said he took in every word. He found a way of politely tuning Cal out when he really got going.

The nights were cold enough now that they slept close to the fire, curling their blankets close when the flames had burned down and the chill air was finally able to sweep over them. On clear days they'd lie on the forest floor, looking at the stars and talking until they slowly slipped asleep.

Their conversations frequently revolved around *after*, for Cal had been jubilantly optimistic ever since their success in gathering protestors.

"I can't imagine much will change, honestly," Garreck told Cal one night.

"Why not? I mean, for reason's sake, *we've* changed. Why wouldn't our countries follow suit?"

"Because if we stop Marten, then things stay the same. Part of me thinks that for things to change, we'd have to lose." Garreck said, turning to face Cal. "Say we aren't able to stop Marten, and he manages to annihilate the Rie. That's when people would react. That's when Cratos would come to their aid, angry about the injustice of it. That's when Aelemia would come with supplies and welcome survivors to live in their communities. I know it sounds dark, but maybe violence is the only way things *ever* change."

Cal frowned at these last words. "I disagree. I think there are peaceful solutions to every problem." He paused and then asked, "Are you rethinking our stand against your dad?"

Garreck shook his head quickly. "Not at all, I just wouldn't expect things to change if this all works out. People tend to stagnate when they're comfortable."

He saw Cal running this through his brain, eyes fixed on the stars above. Garreck could tell Cal was not convinced, so he added, "We all changed because we were unhappy with our lives when you think about it. I was a complete disaster, Mauria's community was driving her crazy, and poor Rasha had a crisis of identity and faith and *then* watched a wagon full of people die in front of him." Garreck sighed, hoping Cal wouldn't take offense as he said, "You have this unquenchable thirst for adventure. Sometimes I wonder if you'll ever feel complete."

Cal smiled, "I feel pretty whole right now."

Selfishly, Garreck wanted to believe him, but he knew that Cal was wrong. Cal's eyes sparked with the same electric excitement as they had when they first met at the beginning of the summer. Still, Garreck quietly hoped he had been able to fill a small section of whatever was missing.

Garreck

When they finally arrived at their destination in Marcan South, Garreck and Cal were met with an intensity which was all encompassing. For Garreck, this was an unwanted energy, for it solidified his reality in an unwanted way. Despite Damean's descriptions of the power of moridium and his own knowledge of Marten's capacity for evil, part of Garreck had always felt as though they were simply playing hero, inflating something that would find a way of working itself out in the end. As he and Cal had discussed, they were all the perfect recipe for a serious savior complex. But when confronted with the drive and focus of the Aeilsh army, this tiny hope was dashed.

Cal, of course, had the opposite reaction, and barrelled ahead in a blaze of excitement. This was something new, and Cal couldn't help but be taken in. Garreck was quite sure that if Cal held his hand out it would be shaking with the buzz of a new experience.

"Excuse me," he heard Cal asking a passing soldier. "We're here to see Mauria and Cardit. Could you point me in their direction?"

The soldier looked confused. "Mauria?" She asked, but then something seemed to click. "Oh, you mean Hoan." She smiled but shook her head, "They're both out training, but I can walk you to the main tent. Wait around and they'll show up eventually."

Garreck followed behind them as Cal asked endless questions. The soldier, whose name turned out to be Anderson, took Cal in stride and did not seem perturbed by his pestering. She explained the daily patterns and procedures as they made their way through lines of greying tents and tried her best to explain their recruitment process to a skeptical Cal.

"It's true; we've never approached people about joining our group. We just wait for them to come, and they always do." She shrugged as if this was obvious.

"But this is so different from how most Aelish live. How do you *know* you'll attract others?" Cal seemed unconvinced.

"We don't, I guess," Anderson told him. "But when someone grows up surrounded by people that they don't connect with, you can be certain they'll eventually find someplace they belong."

Those words triggered something in Garreck, and he found himself listening less to what they were saying, lost in his own thoughts. Until very recently he'd never had something that felt like a home. But now? Did Cratos provide him with just that?

"Here we are!" Anderson's voice jogged Garreck out of this reverie. "I'll leave you here. Hoan should be back in a bit. It was nice to meet you," she added, shaking Cal's hand, then Garreck's.

It ended up being almost an hour before Mauria was done with her drills. When they finally spotted her walking in their direction, she was rolling her shoulders gingerly and looked exhausted.

Her entire disposition changed when she saw them. She rocketed forward, grinning broadly and crashing into them with her arms flung wide. Garreck hadn't realized how much he'd missed her until this moment, and he hugged back, inadvertently crushing his two best friends.

After they broke away, Mauria's eyes went back and forth between them, her expression slowly shifting from joy back to exhaustion.

"We've got a lot to talk about," she said. "Let me show you where you're sleeping, and then we can find Cardit."

Cal

Ever since the night at Cortez's, Cal had been operating under the assumption that they would win their struggle against Marten. The second those volunteers signed their names to protest the Cantic plans, a weight had been lifted that allowed him to enjoy his time with his parents, his trip with Garreck, and those first moments of wonder as they entered the Aelish camp.

Because of this, he did not take it well when Cardit gave her forecast for the battle. The idea that the Aelish troops were planning to fight and die to stop Cantor stunned him, and while somewhere in the room Cardit gave facts and strategies, his brain worked to keep his lungs breathing and his body functioning.

"Cal, snap out of it." Cal looked up to see Garreck staring intently at him, an expression of concern shadowing his features. Mauria and Cardit seemed taken aback by Garreck's words. Clearly they hadn't noticed Cal's burgeoning panic attack.

"I'm fine," Cal told Garreck before turning towards the others. "This is just a lot of news that I wasn't expecting. We are bringing so many supporters from Cratos—won't that count for anything?"

"It would if they were going to be armed," Cardit told him. "But you were specific in your description of them as peaceful protestors. Has that changed?"

Cal sighed. "No. And at their core most Cratians are opposed to violence. Even if they were given weapons, I doubt they would agree to use them. Or know how to use them, for that matter"

Cardit nodded. "Garreck, what do you think Marten will do when he sees three hundred protestors?"

"He won't even flinch." Garrecks voice was flat, but there was an underlying anger that steamed through.

"If our own numbers were larger, maybe things would be different, but there are only about thirty left in our army." Cardit's voice was still conversational, even calm.

Cal just gaped. "Well then, for reason's sake what do you suppose we do?"

Mauria closed her eyes and put her middle and pointer fingers to both temples, as though she were attempting to subdue some growing frustration. "She was trying to tell you earlier, but you were apparently too bothered to listen."

"But I will happily continue, now that we've all caught up," Cardit said briskly. "We think the only plan worth merit at this point would be to catch Marten's troops by surprise. As Garreck confirmed, the Cantics will most likely not take the Cratian opposition seriously. We'd like you to try to reason with your father, Garreck, just one last time so that we know there is no choice but Aelish intervention." Cal thought Garreck looked uncomfortable at this suggestion, but he stayed quiet and did not interrupt. "If Marten attempts to move on Rien despite your objections, our army will converge from the sides and attack. The goal will be to eliminate Marten and hope that his troops surrender once he has fallen."

She shot Garreck an apologetic look as she delivered this last piece. Cal looked to see Garreck nod once, though his face remained impassive. At the beginning of the summer, Cal would have believed this to be a true absence of emotion; now he understood that it was simply a practiced, perfected facade.

Mauria put her hand on Garreck's shoulder and said, "We can talk more about it tomorrow. Until we hear that the Cantics have moved, we have time to process and flesh this all out. But from what we've been able to come up with, this is the best course of action that we have."

They all said goodnight to Cardit, and Mauria walked them to a tent pitched close to hers on the outside edges of the camp. "I'd like to say it will be okay," she told them. She sighed and shook her head and hugged them once more. "I'm so glad we're all together."

Garreck didn't want to talk once they had settled in for the night. He wasn't asleep, but his eyes were shut and Cal tried to respect his privacy. After all, Garreck had just been told that he would be the last line of defense, and if he failed the Aelish would assassinate his father.

So, Cal was left to his own thoughts. For the most part, Cal dwelled on two questions that he had wanted to ask Cardit, but which he had refrained from asking. What would happen if the Cantics did not stop once Marten had died? Even more troubling—what if the army was unable to get to Marten in the first place?

The answer to both was the same, and it was simple—they would lose.

Garreck

It probably should have taken longer for the darkness of that first visit to be replaced with the exhilaration of training, but it didn't. Garreck threw himself into the Aelish sessions to keep his mind off his father and because it was a physical outlet for the rage and anxiety that had once again taken up residence within him.

Cal, on the other hand, had begun training simply for the joy of discovery. Garreck was certain of it. Cal glowed at the opportunity to explore untapped knowledge. Though they had discussed Cal's aversion to violence before, Garreck knew that the drills and practices were all merely fun for his friend. They were something to do while they waited for Cardit's scouts to send word of Marten's activity.

And so they practiced. For Garreck, the trainings were nothing new. He had gone through the seemingly endless recruitment camps that Marten sent him to as a child, and because of his experience, Garreck even found himself helping to teach the newer members of their small army. There was a biting resentment each time he gave a tip to or fixed the stance of one of their members, but he knew that ignoring the stores of unwanted knowledge would only be doing himself and the others a disservice.

Garreck had one additional, private reason to hone his skills— something that pushed him to practice harder and exercise discipline more than he ever had before. Ever since their first night at camp, Garreck had been unable to clear his mind of the ominous truth—someone would have to kill his father. He didn't believe that anyone actually expected him to have an effect on Marten, and if they did, they were foolish and naive. If anything, Garreck would be able to stall his father a few moments longer, giving the Aelish more time to press their attack. But there would be an attack—that much was clear to him. And when it came, he wanted to be the one to finish off his father.

There was certainly a part of Garreck that wished his father was dead. However, there was a part of him—larger than Garreck cared to admit—that screamed for Marten's survival. His father was a wicked, callous, selfish worm of a man, but he was also his father. Garreck thought of a life without him, and instead of the relief he expected, there was a deep fear of that unknown. Garreck knew he could not let his own cowardice be the ruin of Rien, and the idea of taking ownership over the situation brought him some small comfort. Attempting to normalize the imminent patricide, each time he shot an arrow, threw a dagger, or charged an opponent, he pictured Marten.

Cal

Cal had taken a break from training when he saw Mauria walking towards him.

"Oy! Slacker!" she yelled across the space between them, smiling and holding her arms out in a very *"What the hell?"* gesture.

Cal grinned and shouted back, "I'm keeping watch!" But at that point she was only ten feet away. She shook her head, laughing, and plopped down next to him. She was sweaty and breathing heavily, clearly having just finished some kind of drill. She sighed deeply and reached into the back pocket, passing him a letter.

"It's from your mom," she said. She let herself fall backwards, closing her eyes and smiling as a cool breeze swept over them.

Cal had expected a letter from either Cora or Caroline. They didn't know exactly how dangerous his plans had become, but that didn't mean they weren't worried. Opening the letter, Cal found two pieces of paper. One was a short note written in Cora's handwriting. She had a lovely, clean hand that was easily deciphered; Caroline's was more of a scrawl, and typically took some guesswork. The other note was folded into a perfect square, with a Cantic address given in the corner.

Cal decided to read Cora's first. He opened it up, scanning its contents quickly. Rather than asking how he and Garreck were it simply said:

> *Cal,*
>
> *I hope that you are well and happy. A letter for Garreck came a few days after you left for Marcan South. It looks like it might be from his family, so we wanted to make sure it got to him. I know you said things could be contentious in their household; I hope everything is okay!*
>
> *Love you bunches,*
>
> *Mom*

Cal's eyes flashed quickly to the second letter. His immediate instinct was to rip it open, but knew he would have to wait until Garreck was given a chance. If Garreck's family was sending him something, it was almost certainly related to the moridium. There was a small chance, however, that his brothers or mother were just trying to connect, and he didn't want to intrude.

"News from Cantor," Cal told Mauria.

She sat straight up at his words. "What did they say?" Her voice was casual, but Cal could detect an underlying urgency that mirrored his own.

"I'm not sure, I don't want to read it without Garreck."

Mauria gave him a skeptical look, but did not argue. Instead she got to her feet and grabbed both of Cal's hands, pulling him up with her. "Then we need to find him. It's too important to wait."

They hurried back to the camp and walked hastily between trainings. They finally found Garreck in the fencing arena, helping a few soldiers with their stances.

Cal caught Garreck's eyes and gestured for him to join them. Much to his annoyance, Garreck rolled his eyes and held up a hand, indicating that they could wait. He turned away from them, resuming his lesson. Cal was about to call out to him when Mauria snapped.

"Hey! Practice is over. Clearly we have something important to talk about, so get your ass moving before I lose my goddamn mind!" Her face was red, and Cal could tell that the composure she'd been able to manage before was slipping fast.

Even from a distance, Cal could see Garreck's puzzled expression, clearly taken aback by the outburst. He nodded once, recognizing Mauria's shout, and said a few words to his students before making his way over. Cal saw Garreck's face flicker through several stages of emotion. His initial anger became confusion, and by the time he was standing in front of them apprehension was etched in his features.

"What is it?"

Cal held out the letter. "We haven't read it yet, but it was sent to Cora from Cantor. She thinks it might be from one of the Landsings."

Garreck took the letter and read. Cal tried to read his expression but found it guarded. Garreck revealed nothing as he digested the mysterious message. After a moment, and without looking up from the page, Garreck said, "Marten will be in Rien within the next few days."

"What?" Mauria snatched the letter from him and read it herself. "This says they plan on leaving in two weeks."

"Yes, and the letter traveled between three countries before it got to us. For all we know Marten could already be there. We could be too late."

Mauria stood, stunned by her mistake. Cal could hardly wrap his head around the horror that it would be if they did not make it to Rien in time. He needed to get word to Jane. Fortunately she was already there with many of their supporters, but it would be devastating if Marten arrived before they had backup.

Mauria finally shook her head, snapping back into action. "Garreck, spread the word that our soldiers need to be packed and ready to leave within the hour. We'll be traveling in darkness, which will make the going slower, but a little extra cover could end up being to our advantage." She took a breath and focused; Cal understood that she was

140

working her way through a mental checklist. "I have to go tell Cardit," she said, finally.

She spun on the spot, looking over shoulder to give Cal one final order. "I need you and Garreck to ride ahead and join Jane," she told him. "Our goal is to remain unseen by Cantor, and so we'll take our troops an alternate way; we can't risk exposing ourselves if we don't know Marten's location."

Cal nodded. Garreck was already gone, off to alert the men and women who had probably been looking forward to some dinner and a moment's rest. Cal tried to keep himself from shaking as he walked toward the stables, but his legs vibrated against his will, and his hands trembled as he saddled their geldings.

Rasha

It hadn't taken Rasha long to find his friends. Not knowing exactly where to begin his search, he had gone first to Mauria's community in Marcan West. Even if the group wasn't there, he'd hoped the Aelish would at least be able to point him in the right direction.

They had done him one better. News of Mauria's stand at the Gathering had reached her old community, and her parents told him that Mauria had gone to a military community in Marcan South. Both seemed to disapprove of their daughter's choice of location. Still, they wished Rasha good luck and gave him directions and a few supplies for the trip. He'd borrowed a horse from Damean, so his only needs were food and drink which they gladly provided. Though uncomfortable with their level of generosity, he was grateful nonetheless and in return promised to say hello to Mauria for them when he finally reached her.

Stocked and ready, Rasha made good time on his journey south. In fact, Rasha spent almost two days observing the day-to-day routines of the Aelish forces after he arrived, willing himself to join them. He found a small hill about a half mile away from the site on which to sit and think, and had planned to wait another day before approaching the camp. However, the sudden action below surely meant that they were preparing to move. Knowing that his deadline had moved up and understanding that the time to join his friends had arrived, Rasha still found himself hesitating.

He had no reservations about seeing them. On the contrary, he wanted nothing more than to be with Cal and Mauria again. Even Garreck would be a welcome presence, though Rasha was not sure Garreck had yet forgiven him for remaining in Devoran. No, what kept Rasha from rushing to the familiar faces below was the truth that he was so unwilling to share with them.

If he told them the kind of magic that he was capable of, they would expect it from him. They would ignore whatever strategies and plans they'd previously prepared and put him at the center. But he would not let himself be pressured into breaking the Cantic connections. His resolve to avoid this path was as strong as it was when he had last spoken to Damean.

The selfishness of this choice weighed heavy on him, but he knew the consequences of any other decision would outweigh his current burden tenfold.

The sudden movement of the Aelish forces worked to inspire a third option in Rasha's brain, and as it formulated he clung desperately to it. What if he could be their *hope*? What if he could reveal only a small portion of his abilities? After all, they had seen Damean work small bits of magic back in Devoran. If they accepted that there was a finite limit to what he was capable of, he'd be able to march with them, to help them, without the burden of having to choose between his people and the Cantics. With just a bit of Rasha's magic, they stood a chance of winning on their own, emboldened by the idea sorcery on their side.

Motivated by this revelation, Rasha packed the few possessions he had brought for the trip. As he fastened the last strap on his bag he paused, feeling the singularity of this moment—this last bit of *before*. The connections in this part of Colliptia were duller than those in Devoran, but they hummed with life nonetheless. Even given the state of melancholia in which he seemed permanently trapped, Rasha smiled.

Then, with renewed strength and sense of purpose, he made his way down to the camp.

Mauria

The sun had nearly set when Mauria saw him. In the absence of light, she noticed Rasha's silhouette long before she could make out his features, but she didn't need those details to recognize him.

Moments before she had been dodging between tents, communicating with any troops that Garreck had failed to reach. But now she froze, staring as the outline of her friend grew larger as he drew closer. She thought she would be angry. She *had* been angry. There had been pain and betrayal and fear and confusion when he'd left them. But instead she felt only relief. *He was safe. He was here.*

Mauria ran straight at him, stopping just a few feet away. Rasha was startled, but composed himself quickly, looking at her questioningly. She smiled, and closed the space between them, enveloping him in the widest hug she could manage.

"I am still mad at you," she said, but even she didn't believe the words as she said them.

"I told you I'd come back," he said, smiling back at her.

Now that Mauria was really looking at him, she saw that he was not the same boy they had left. He had the same dark, wavy hair and the same olive skin, but his eyes looked older, creased at the corners in a way they never used to be.

Rasha noticed her silent evaluation and raised an eyebrow, but she just shook her head. "Come on, let's find Cal and Garreck. They'll want to see you," she told him, beaming. Rasha raised both eyebrows at the second name. "Yes! Even Garreck. You're not the only one who's changed." She saw Rasha smile a little at that. Had he thought she wouldn't be able to see those changes? He was a noticeably different person than the lost boy they'd picked up so long ago.

She steered him toward the center of the camp, and together they made their way to the others, walking swiftly but carefully so as not to collide with the soldiers as they prepared to leave.

"We just found out Marten left earlier than we anticipated," Mauria explained as they went. "The Cratian protestors are there already, but they've agreed only to a non-violent stand. Without us they're vulnerable."

Mauria saw Rasha's look of concern at this. "You are the only ones who will be fighting?" he asked her.

"Yes. We're planning to take them by surprise—ambush Marten and his men from the sides if Garreck and the Cratians aren't enough to stop them."

Rasha nodded slightly, and Mauria could tell he was thinking deeply. She left him to it. She herself knew that their plan was risky at best and foolish at worst. She couldn't allow herself to doubt the only course of action that they had.

"I might be able to help before you and your troops make your stand." Rasha voice was steady, revealing nothing, but Mauria's head whipped towards him at the words all the same.

"What do you—," she started to question him, but was interrupted by Garreck's booming voice.

"You've got to be freaking kidding me!" Garreck, apparently, was not ready to shed his anger as quickly as Mauria had. He bounded toward them, walking with large steps that hit heavy on the earth with each stomp. When he reached them he paused, glaring at Rasha with utter contempt. Before Mauria could stop him, he punched Rasha in the face.

Rasha didn't move. It was as though he wanted Garreck's punch to land. He didn't put his hands up, or turn, or do anything other than close his eyes before the fist collided hard with his cheekbone. Rasha spun on impact, his hand going up to his eye and a grimace on his face, but he seemed otherwise unfazed.

Mauria watched as Rasha turned back to Garreck. "I deserved that," he said.

Garreck looked stunned, but mustered a rather lame "Yes, you did," before Cal came up behind him.

"Garreck! What the hell?" Mauria couldn't be sure, but there seemed to be a bit of amusement deep within Cal's reprimand. She remembered how disappointed Cal had been when Rasha stayed behind in Devoran. Cal might have missed him, but maybe he thought Rasha deserved a good smack in the face.

If he did, Cal hid it well. Mauria smiled as Cal shook Rasha's hand and said, "Welcome back."

Rasha smiled back and nodded. "I'm sorry it took me so long, but I came to help … if you'll let me."

"Yes!" Mauria had just remembered what they'd been talking about before the interruption. "What can you do to help, Rasha?"

Rasha flicked his finger and a rock flipped up from the ground, changing direction once it was eye level with Garreck. It bounced off Garreck's head and Rasha grinned. Mauria held in a snicker as Garreck's face turned purple.

Mauria could tell Garreck was not to be pushed right now. "I hope you can manipulate something a bit larger than a pebble," Mauria told Rasha.

Rasha nodded. "I've got it covered. I think I can do enough to frighten them or to even cause the damage necessary to make them turn around. I'll let Cal and Garreck stand first, but I'll be there to back them up."

Mauria nodded enthusiastically. For the first time in a long while she felt hopeful.

"As long as you're not planning on ditching us again, that sounds like a plan." The comment came from Garreck, but a small part of Mauria had been thinking the same thing.

"I'm here to stay," Rasha told them. "I promise."

"Hear! Hear!" Cal clapped Rasha on the back. "Garreck," he said, turning toward him, "We've got to go. The horses are ready and Jane is still waiting with no support. I'd hope that if anything had already happened, we'd have heard, but I'll feel better once we're on the road." Cal then faced Rasha and Mauria. "We'll see you both soon."

Mauria watched him go. She guided Rasha off towards Cardit's tent so that they could fill her in. Things were still not resolved, but they were certainly looking up.

Rasha

Later that night, Mauria came dashing up to Rasha, her arms laden with objects.

"Just a few provisions," she explained, "things I'm sure you forgot

145

to pack and may need." She gave him a very sisterly nudge and pushed what looked like an entire queen-sized bed's worth of blankets and sheets into his hands.

"You're more like your family than you think, Maur," he told her with a grin, gesturing to the provisions her parents had given him.

She blushed and shot him a look of mock annoyance. "How dare you," she chimed, digging into her bag and presenting him with a package wrapped in heavy brown paper. "A thoughtful, caring Aelemian wouldn't have forgotten to give you this. I'm terrible, but it completely slipped my mind in all the craziness earlier."

He took the package and tore it open. Inside was a letter and a silky ball of fabric, its color falling somewhere between roasted yams and rust. Rasha looked up to see Mauria smiling at him. "I went to see your mom while I was in Rien, and she sent these along."

Rasha was momentarily confused, but when he realized what the material was he broke out into a dazzling grin that only his mother could inspire from him.

"She's wonderful, isn't she?" It was all he could say. He dared not read the letter for fear of breaking down in front of Mauria, but he could hardly wait to see Lira's familiar handwriting, to feel her presence in his life again.

Mauria bobbed her head in agreement and seemed to know that Rasha needed some privacy. She patted him on the shoulder, and then scurried off, back to making sure the camp packed up as quickly as possible.

Once he was alone, Rasha opened the letter carefully. He savored the familiar scents of caraway and clove that rose faintly from the paper, and he could almost picture Lira sitting at their kitchen table while she scrawled her message. His eyes drifted to the words, and though she had not written much, their impact left Rasha in quite the daze.

Rasha,

I can't describe how relieved I was to hear that you are alive and well. Only a few people made it back from the attack on your pilgrimage, and when Abi told us that you had been separated, I feared the worst.

But you lived, and it seems you found your adventure,
even if it was not the one you had planned. I know I don't
often speak of your father, but he would have been proud
to see you off and exploring the world. He was a traveller
himself; sometimes I think that is why he left. He had a thirst
that Rien could not quench, and I loved him for that.

Though I know you cannot stay, please come back, if only
to visit. I love you so much, and want nothing but the world
for you, sweet boy.

Be well,
Your Loving Mother

Rasha read and reread the message to the point where he could have recited it from memory. There was a bittersweet tone to his mother's words that lingered with him, a joy and a sorrow that conflicted on the page. She seemed to know, before Rasha understood himself, that he would not be returning permanently to Rien.

Even more jarring were the lines about Rasha's father. Lira had *never* spoken of his father before. Never in his entire life had they talked about that missing entity, to the point where a large part of Rasha had believed his father to be dead. This was not the case, though. Apparently the man had chosen to leave them. He was out there, somewhere, and Lira did not seem angry. On the contrary, what little she'd written was tinged with awe and admiration. How could she not begrudge him? Even now, it must surely sting to know that she finished second place all those years ago.

And here was Rasha, fourteen years later, ready to make the same choice. His face burned with self-loathing, and he promised himself that he would see his mother as soon as it was possible. The second that this whole ordeal was over he would set off for their small home in Rien and prove to Lira that he would always come home, even if the visits were brief.

A sudden crashing sound from somewhere in the Aelish camp brought Rasha back to the crisis at hand. Knowing that he would soon have to rejoin the fray, Rasha took a few moments to collect himself. In that time, he thought vaguely of what Damean had first told him about sorcery. Back then, Damean had warned Rasha that he might not have enough magic in his veins to manipulate connections. Rasha had taken to his studies, though, and not just adequately; he had been an exceptional student.

What if his talent was not the product of luck or chance? What if his father had been magical—maybe even a sorcerer? He would probably never know. But the possibility that he had yet another connection to Devoran coursed through him, giving him strength and confidence that he knew he would soon need.

Cal

Other than Devoran, Aelemia was the largest country in Colliptia. As such, it took almost a full day of riding across Marcan South for Cal and Garreck to reach Jane and her volunteers. It was clear as they approached that Marten had not yet made it to the border, and Cal breathed easier as they neared the group. Cal was also relieved that the numbers they'd been promised back in Cratos appeared to have showed. However, he was concerned by the general lightheartedness of the gathering.

An enormous collection of Cratians had congregated, and their positive energy could not be contained. There were groups making wooden signs with phrases like "Don't Ruin Rien!" and "Cantor Can't DO This!" and Cal was more than mildly appalled by the playfulness of the words. Other groups worked on chants to shout against Marten, and others simply sat, enjoying the company of other charitable souls.

"Excuse me, sir," Cal used the hand that was not guiding his horse to tap one volunteer on the shoulder. "Remind me again. Why are you here?"

The man's face went momentarily blank, but he was saved by the woman next to him, who shouted, "Never Again, Marten!"

A chorus of "Never Again, Marten!" rang out around her. Cal paused for a moment, then turned and walked away. He shouldn't have been surprised. He had seen this happen with other movements in Cratos, but had hoped the severity of this cause would push their message into the minds of the volunteers.

Ah well, he thought. *At least they are here.*

He and Garreck became separated in the hoard, but Cal knew they'd find each other eventually. He continued to weave through the crowds, guiding his horse and looking for Jane. When he finally found her, she was chatting animatedly with a few friends.

"No, what you're saying is that you'd rather be *comfortable* than free!" Cal could almost hear the implied *moron* attached to the end of Jane's words. The man she was talking to threw his hands into the air, and Cal decided to interject before things got too heated and he lost any chance of getting Jane's attention.

"I'd say it's poor practice to shout at our volunteers, wouldn't you?" Jane whirled at Cal's words and grimaced at him.

"This one can go. We don't need him" she said, but Cal could tell she was already coming down from her zeal. "Where have you been, Cal? I thought we were going to have to end bigotry all on our own."

They hugged hello and Cal caught her up on all that had happened since they'd left each other in Cratos. Cal was thankful for Rasha's return the previous day; it saved Cal from the dire conversation he'd been planning to deliver to the Cratians. Now, his news didn't have to be quite as bleak.

He reassured her that the Cratians would only be asked to protest. He told her of Garreck's plea that would hopefully dissuade Marten from his move against Rien, and without going into too much detail, he mentioned Rasha's contributions should they be necessary. Finally, Cal described the Aelish ambush that would be their final option if all else failed.

Jane took everything in with an attentive expression, never interrupting or asking for more information. When he was done, she simply asked, "Do you think Rasha will succeed?"

She must have believed, like Mauria and Cardit, that the protestors would not be enough to stop Marten. Cal considered this and said, "Yes, I do. I haven't seen much of what Rasha is capable of, but anyone who has met Damean knows the potential for power that he holds. If Rasha's skills are anything close, we'll be fine."

After a beat, Cal realized her other implication. Frowning slightly, he asked, "Do you not think Garreck will be able to end it?"

Jane shook her head sadly. "I think any father who has treated a son as cruelly as Marten has treated Garreck has been confronted with his own evil many times before. Who knows, maybe Garreck's words will strike some unknown chord, but I wouldn't put my faith in it." Noticing that she had worried him, Jane touched Cal's arm and added, "But if you are confident in Rasha, then I am confident in our cause. Our people will be safe, and a great movement will have succeeded."

Cal gave her a small smile and hoped that she was right. Maybe in the next few hours he would venture into Rien to find one of the religious meeting houses. If there was ever a time to take up prayer, Cal was sure it had come. For now, he would go and try to find Garreck.

Garreck

Garreck had broken off from Cal in the chaos of the Cratian mob and had been resting by the horses ever since. He didn't love socializing much anyway, never mind doing it on his own with a bunch of overenthusiastic strangers. He might be evolving as a person, but time and time again he was reminded that some things were simply a part of who he was at his core.

That punch at Rasha, for one. Garreck did not regret his emotional response to Rasha's homecoming. He'd been furious with that spineless numpty back in Devoran, and time apart had left the wound raw. A small part of Garreck also knew that the only reason he had been so hurt was because of how fond he'd grown of Rasha up until that last day in Devoran. He had evolved to consider Rasha a friend and then Rasha had ruined it. Garreck was sure that the boy had his reasons, and that eventually they'd come to understand what had made him abandon his friends. For now, though, Garreck was happy to lie stagnant in his resentment.

Garreck's rancor melted a little when he saw the smile on Cal's approaching face. There was nothing behind that smile other than affection, and although the foreign nature of unconditional love still made him slightly uncomfortable, it was a welcome kind of discomfort.

Cal plopped down next to him. "Could you have picked somewhere that smelled worse?" Cal joked.

"The smell keeps the rest of them away," Garreck told him, gesturing to the group of protestors. "I know how you Cratians value personal care. I'm honored you decided I was worth the trip over."

"There isn't a stench around that could keep me away," Cal laughed, putting his head on Garreck's shoulder.

It was moments like this that caught Garreck off guard. Even when Garreck was being sarcastic and glib, Cal found it in him to forgive such roughness. Garreck leaned his head on Cal's, hoping the return gesture said all that Garreck was unable to articulate.

"I was actually going to ask you for a favor," Cal said, twisting to look up at Garreck.

So much for unconditional *love.* "What do you need?"

"I was hoping you could give one final speech to the group tomorrow—a pep talk to kick off their efforts." Cal's voice was innocent and unassuming. *Sneaky*, Garreck decided, *might be a more appropriate word for it.*

"Did we just walk through the same assembly? Those people don't need confidence. They need a slap in the face and some sense in their heads," Garreck said with a snort.

"Oh, come on," Cal's tone was playful but had an undercurrent of defensiveness. "They're here and they want to help. I think we owe it to them to prove that we're as committed as they are."

Garreck didn't answer at first. He was pretty sure the Cratians were excited enough without any additional support. In fact, he was quite sure; he could feel it. Ever since they'd made it to the border, he had felt how heightened their energy was. Their attitude consisted of an intense combination of hope, rebelliousness, anticipation, and naivety—not a great blend in Garreck's opinion. More than anything, though, there was a blind confidence emanating from the group that made him extremely nervous.

Given that assessment, there was no way they needed a pep talk. However, maybe they *could* benefit from a few words of wisdom. It might not be the call to action Cal was asking for, but if the mob was to be of any use in the days to come, they would need a reminder of why they were all there.

"All right," he said after a few beats. "I'll get started on it now." He stood, grabbing Cal's arm and pulling him up. Garreck leaned in and kissed him quickly, smirking. "But no distractions. You go back to your crazy countrymen, and I'll stay out here and write where it's quiet."

He watched Cal go, grabbed some scraps of paper that had been shoved into his travel bag, and began to write. He wrote and rewrote until the first stars began to come out and Cal had been back twice to visit and bring him a warm drink. As Cal approached for a third time, Garreck had just about finished.

"You promised to stay away, I'm nearly done here!" All jokes aside, Cal actually did interfere with Garreck's process, even if it was otherwise nice to have him there. Cal asked questions and tried to peer at the words Garreck was squeezing into the unused corners of his pages, and there were a couple times Garreck had suppressed the urge to swat Cal away.

"Don't worry, it's just another delivery. I went with something a bit stronger this time." Cal handed Garreck a mug of amber liquid that smelled like oak trees.

"Look here!" Garreck put a hand up in mock rejection. "Isn't alcohol forbidden in Cratos? What rapscallion in that bunch decided I was above the rules?"

"Ha, ha. Very funny. Yes, it appears that many of them have taken liberal advantage of the flexible laws in Cantor and Rien." Cal swirled the drink in his hand thoughtfully, and then with a casual gesture tipped the glass so that the contents were millimeters away from spilling onto the ground below.

"I'll forgive them this time. They're only human." Garreck reached out and took the cup as Cal laughed. "Actually," Garreck said as Cal began to walk away, "I'm nearly finished. I can call it a night."

"Wonderful!" Cal turned back and sat down in the nest of blankets that Garreck had fashioned into a passable workspace. He'd lit a fire as well, for his task had become difficult once the sunlight started to filter away.

They sat together, listening rather than speaking. They could make out the faint sounds of their rowdy volunteers in the near distance, but they were far enough removed that nature made its presence known as well. Crickets and katydids buzzed about them while larger wildlife softly stepped through fallen leaves, unseen by either man.

"You know what, Garreck?" Cal said, breaking their trance. He was still looking away, through the fire and off toward some unknown point.

"Hm?"

"I know that the rest of you are supposed to be the ones that believe in magic and religion and all that, but I think I'm starting to come around."

Garreck had not expected this. Cal was so practical, so sure of his rules and his way of being. "What do you mean?"

Cal turned to look at him. "I mean, I've always believed in chance. I thought that if I tried my best and helped others I'd feel fulfilled, but I also knew that at any moment something out of my control could happen. I didn't believe in fate or destiny or anything like that. And I definitely never believed in magic."

Garreck took Cal's hand. Cal squeezed back, but continued. "Then we both got thrown in jail, and all of a sudden it was like something or someone had been waiting to take the reins. We met Mauria and Rasha and we found magic and danger and purpose. Now we're about to try and stop a horrible attack that we never would have even known about if it hadn't been for that one catalytic moment."

Cal paused, but Garreck could tell he wasn't finished. He waited for Cal to find his words.

Finally Cal said, "Does it terrify you to think there's something bigger than us out there? Does it make you feel small?"

Garreck had to think about that before he could answer. "Honestly? Knowing that I'm part of some grand design makes me feel safe. I don't want everything to be an unpredictable act of chance. With fate, everything evil serves a purpose, even if we're not able to see the reason."

Cal nodded at this. Garreck could still feel his concern, but it was quieter now—a pale orange flicker as opposed to the sun-burned feel of true anxiety.

Garreck wanted to make him smile. "All this seriousness. Tell me, Cal, what happened to the debonair charmer that Jane talked so much about? *He's* not implying that he's found someone he's *destined* to be with?"

But Cal didn't smile. Instead he looked very seriously at Garreck and said, "Of course. Don't you feel it?"

Cal

Cal was not able to sleep at all that night. He and Garreck stayed awake together, watching the darkness deepen until eventually soft colors broke through black emptiness. It was the most intimate night of his life, and yet all he had shared was his soul.

Unfortunately, the emotional impact of restructuring his system of beliefs, coupled with the physical toll of sleeplessness, left him spent. Hopefully, whatever speech Garreck had concocted would be impactful enough to whip him into shape because he could hardly drag himself back to camp to meet Jane at their agreed-upon time. Garreck stayed behind to pack up his things, but promised to meet him when he was done.

When Cal arrived, Jane was pacing back and forth, looking frazzled. "Where have you been?" she demanded, striding toward Cal.

"I kept Garreck company when he was done writing."

Jane rolled her eyes and mimed vomiting. "Today is too important for you to waste an entire night on anything but preparation. While you were frolicking, I divided our people into quadrants so that each group has an equal mixture of signs and cheers. Everyone knows to meet us in twenty minutes to hear Garreck talk. Does he even have something prepared?"

Instead of addressing her many incorrect assumptions, Cal simply said, "He's ready, don't worry."

Fighting to keep his eyes open, Cal let Jane guide him toward an opening in the mess of tents and people. Immediately, Cal noticed Rasha's robes clashing brilliantly with the Cratians' neutral clothing. He waved his hands, attempting to get Rasha's attention, but eventually was forced to shout, "Oy! Rasha!" over the noise of the gathering.

Rasha looked up, gave a slight nod, and began working his way over towards them. Once there, he shook both Cal and Jane's hands before asking, "What's this all about?"

"Garreck is going to address the group," Jane said authoritatively. "Give them something to hold onto today."

Rasha looked skeptical, his eyes tracing over the obviously upbeat bodies around him, but said nothing.

Others had started to congregate around a wooden table which would presumably serve as Garreck's stage. When most of their group had assembled, Cal scanned the crowd, hoping to find Garreck. At first he didn't see him, but then suddenly a portion of the group began to quiet. He turned toward the lull and saw Garreck nudging his way through to the table. In his wake people instantly calmed, and Cal was sure it was due to Garreck's influence.

Garreck climbed onto the makeshift stage in a less-than-graceful manner, and as he did, Jane groaned at Cal's side.

"Give him a chance," Cal told her in a tone of light admonishment. "I would think that you have nothing to fear. You've seen what he can do."

The woman in front of Cal and Jane turned to shush them, and something about the assuredness of the gesture reminded him inexplicably of Mauria. If Rasha had arrived, then she and the troops would have made it to their position. At that very moment, they were most likely waiting out of sight, poised for what was to come.

Cal wondered if they would be able to hear Garreck's speech, too.

Mauria

As a matter of fact, Mauria *could* hear Garreck. After a smooth trip, the small army had eventually settled on a wide, wooded hill about a quarter mile east of the volunteers. Scouts had identified it as an ideal location to launch a potential ambush. They were not particularly high, but the breadth of their station was such that they were able to spread out just below the ridge, able to hear and see what was happening below through gaps at the forest's edge.

Mauria wouldn't have known to listen if it hadn't been for the sudden silence that permeated the space beneath them. It was a good thing that the protestors were not relying on stealth, for their liveliness had not ceased since she and the others arrived. Honestly, they were so loud that when the volunteers finally shut up it was more conspicuous than their clamor.

As Garreck began, Mauria couldn't help but question his choice of message. She had expected an inspirational, uplifting speech with which to rally their troops and prepare them for whatever was to come. Instead, his words were severe—biting. He cut through pretense with phrases sharper than any blade and did nothing to coddle or to appease his audience. As his talk neared its close, however, Mauria understood the significance of the choice he had made. Even among her own troops, there had been a sense of intense joy and positivity ever since they had left their camp. With the arrival of Rasha and his news, there was very little chance they would be needed. Consequently, many had been treating the move as an excursion or exercise, a work outing that they would enjoy and return from in a few days' time.

Garreck's words chipped efficiently away at that feeling of security. He knew, and Mauria recognized, the danger of complacency, and his speech had clearly been designed to remind everyone of the reality of their situation. It might have been too bleak had it not been for his final words. Right at the end, he gave them something to hold on to.

Remember that you are surrounded by allies—by friends and neighbors and strangers who share your ideals and fight your battles. We will stand together when the Cantics arrive, and we will remind them that where there is wickedness, justice will also be found. You have built your lives around rule and law. Implement those values now. Be prepared to face the dangers that today may bring, unflinching and united. We do not stand because it is easy, we stand because it is right.

Mauria had grown cold. It was not a normal chill of fear or terror; rather, it had a delicate, tenuous quality. Never experiencing his gift before, Mauria could not be sure if Garreck was behind this shift inside her, but she suspected that he was—his words matched her emotions too perfectly. She felt the cold of a frost before it is scattered by daylight—the chill of winter fighting against the push of spring. She felt guarded, defensive, resilient, and if the others were experiencing the same, Marten would not be ready for the crowd he was about to face.

Cal

Garreck's speech was not what Cal expected, but it was exactly what the volunteers needed. They walked away from the rally highly affected, and more serious than Cal had yet seen them. Unfortunately, the haunting success of the address was somewhat wasted, for Marten and his troops did not arrive that day.

You've got to be joking, Cal thought dolefully. Hopefully their lot could hold themselves together until their foe arrived. He never thought he'd be rooting for Marten to hurry up.

Garreck

Without realizing it, Garreck's father had played a power move that would rival that of the best negotiator. Marten's delayed arrival put everyone on edge, and they spent an entire day of nervous waiting and subdued fellowship before the Cantic army finally came.

Garreck first received word by way of an Aelish scout whom Mauria had sent to relay the news of Marten's appearance. An hour later, three small figures could be seen approaching the protestors' camp. Without delay, Garreck, Cal, and Jane rode out to meet the unknown visitors, not wanting them to get too close. It wasn't that Garreck believed his father would send these three to attack the protestors. In truth, he was more afraid that one of the Cratian's would throw something to provoke their opponents before they were done trying to negotiate.

His father's last words to Garreck played over and over in his head: *You've wasted my time, just as you always have.* With bitterness, Garreck realized that this statement most likely still held true. Although Cal believed in the value of the upcoming plea, Garreck knew that it was only going to gain them some time. He was, as usual, just getting in Marten's way. Well, his father might find him as irksome as an insect, but he would continue to be that gnat, flying time and time again into Marten's emotionless eyes until it had the necessary effect.

Too soon, the parties had reached each other. Marten was not one of the three who had come to meet them, and though Garreck was disappointed, he should have realized that his father would not lower himself with an attempt to parlay in person. Although it made the dealings a bit less daunting, there was still much to be cautious of. Garreck noticed grimly how reinforced the Cantics were. He, Jane, and Cal wore only their normal clothing. Garreck had his bow, but it felt woefully insignificant compared to the fully armed soldiers they now faced. If he stretched, one of the enemy's longswords could have cut fully through him.

Garreck knew that he could whisper and any of the five others would hear his words. But he did not whisper. Instead, he raised his chin, and spoke loudly and clearly in an attempt to appear as brave as he wished he felt.

"You took longer than we expected, Price." Garreck had recognized her and Bernhardt once they were close enough for him to see their features. They were two of Marten's most trusted advisors. Both had occasionally been over for dinner at the Landsing house while he was growing up. He did not know the third man; he was young and dodgey, obviously uncomfortable with the situation. Perhaps a protege or officer in training?

Price didn't react to Garreck's words. If it hadn't been for their close proximity, he might have thought she hadn't heard him.

"We're glad you came to talk with us," she said as though *she* had begun the negotiations. "We hope that you will consider letting us by without escalating the situation."

She glanced over Garreck's shoulder, and he felt her eyes resting on the vast mass of people and tents behind him. The Cratians might be worthless in a fight, but their presence and scope were undeniably useful.

From out of the corner of his eye, Garreck saw Cal lean forward on his horse, head tilted toward Price conversationally. "I'm sorry, but we can't let you do that," Cal said. "We have it on good authority that you're business in Rien is less than whatever trading excursion you've made it out to be." His voice was light, harboring no signs of aggression or apprehension.

The man whose name Garreck did not know shifted on his horse as Cal spoke. "We come under no false pretenses, you stupid Cratian cank. We are here to stop those dangerous Rie radicals once and for all."

"Sasse!" Price said the name in a loud, clipped voice, but remained otherwise unaffected. The Cantic soldier stopped speaking immediately, but continued to glare at Cal.

Addressing Garreck as if they had not been interrupted, Price said, "Your father is worried about you. Your mother has cried ever since you left. Your brothers need a role model. Why do you choose to abandon them when you could be back, protecting them from all of this hurt?"

If Price had expected to move him with her words, she was sorely mistaken. Garreck laughed in her face. The sound was cold and humorless; of course his father would resort to manipulation as his first tactic, even if it was through a proxy.

"We've known each other for so long, Price. Even you can't believe that my father cares what happens to me."

Her eyes widened, affronted. Perhaps she actually believed that Marten was a noble, loving man, but Garreck doubted it. More likely she was just a very good actress.

"You're right, Garreck. We do have a history. Tell me: what happened to the upstanding young man I used to know? What happened that set you on such a ridiculous path?" Price's eyes were searching, as if she could find the remnants of that long-lost child and summon them forward.

Garreck shrugged. "That 'upstanding' person was also depressed, bitterly angry, and blind to the evil lurking all about him. Tell me…if my father is so worried for my well being, will he turn back in order to keep me safe?"

Price had no response. How could she? Or course Marten had no notion of returning to Cantor without completing his mission.

"I thought so," Garreck nodded. "Well, please tell Marten that we will leave when he does. And if he chooses to move through us, he will have to do so while risking the lives of hundreds of Cratian innocents." For good measure Garreck added, "I know he doesn't care about the death toll, but think of the publicity nightmare."

Bernhardt shook his head. "Is there nothing else you'd like us to say to your father when we return? Nothing else a son might wish to convey to the man who raised him?"

Garreck paused. He tapped his finger pensively on the side of his face, pretending to be lost in thought. "You know what," he said, pointing at Bernhardt, "You can tell him to piss off and go to hell. Why don't you tack that on to the end of our message?"

The man named Sasse snorted in disgust at Garreck's words, and Garreck rounded on him. "You laugh now. But if this is how that monster treats his son, how much do you think Marten really cares about *you*? It can't be much, can it?"

Sasse said nothing. He simply have his horse a rough kick and turned, Price and Bernhardt falling in line behind him.

Thus ended the negotiations. Jane and Cal would surely scold him for not even pretending to come to a peaceful agreement, but Garreck didn't care. There had never been a reality where his father cared about him enough to alter his plans, and anyone who thought otherwise had been deluded. At least this way, Garreck got a few good jabs in before his father took the knockout punch to his heart.

Cal

After the negotiations, they rode back to camp silently. Cal could tell that Garreck was avoiding his eyes, and he wished he wouldn't. He wanted to connect with him, to share a bit of what had just happened. But Garreck gave nothing away in the short stretch between no man's land and their waiting volunteers.

Those volunteers, who had been chatting at a normal volume, hushed when the three of them approached. Cal was grateful for Jane in that moment. She simply swung herself around so that she was sitting sidesaddle, faced the crowd, and said, "What? They're still coming. It was always a possibility and nothing has changed. Grab your signs, summon your chants, and let's get ready." The words weren't harsh, but they were resolved.

Jane seemed calm as she joined the masses, barking the occasional order, and Cal found that he did as well. Their failure to find a compromise with the Cantics was of little importance now that Rasha had promised to help them. Without Rasha, Cal was certain that his mind would have been in a much darker, graver state.

As everyone around him took Jane's directions, Cal swung down and went to Garreck, who seemed frozen on his horse. Cal put his hand lightly on Garreck's arm, looking into his stony face. "Come on, let's go get them something to drink before we head to the front of the group." Cal knew Garreck needed a moment to deal with his own demons before any other conflict began.

Garreck nodded. The two led their horses to a roughly made trough, and for several moments there was just the slurping of their animals drinking and the general bustle of the activity behind them.

"All right, go ahead," Garreck's words came suddenly, and Cal was taken aback by their rigidness.

"What do you mean?" Cal asked, perplexed.

"I just ruined things back there. I didn't even try to cooperate, and now they're coming and it's all my fault." Garreck's voice was defensive, but his face looked stricken.

Cal was shaking his head before Garreck was even finished. "You think I want to shout at you? Are you kidding?"

Garreck's armor cracked a bit. "Don't you?"

"No!" Cal's anger was unexpected, but he couldn't believe what he was hearing. "What just happened was terrible for you. You were brave and strong and stood up for yourself. Those were people you've known since childhood and they acted like you were scum." His voice got gentler as he added, "I want to hold you, not yell at you. I want to let you cry and rage and feel whatever you what ... because you deserve that. You don't have to pretend that all of that was fine—it wasn't."

Maybe it was because of the betrayals of Price, Bernhard, and Marten, or because of Cal's emotional response to their cruelty. Maybe it was simply eighteen years of steely grit and forced emotional suppression. Whatever the reason, Cal saw it eat away at Garreck's carefully controlled mask, and without warning, Garreck began to cry. Cal reached out instinctively, and Garreck allowed it. They sat, arms around one another, while the tears came quickly and forcefully.

After a few minutes that felt like months, Garreck looked up. His face was splotched and his breath came in quiet shudders, but he was steady enough to look at Cal. He smiled the kind of grin that is burdened by pain and said, "You need to get yourself together, Hanson, there's a battle about to begin."

Cal didn't grin back. Instead, he reached in to kiss Garreck softy. His friend's face was damp with tears but he did not care. After he looked Garreck in the eyes. "You don't need to joke about it. I don't want you to joke about it. Bits like this are normal and natural, and they help. How do you think I'm so happy all the time? If I didn't let myself cry there would be no room for all my pep."

Garreck rolled his eyes, but Cal remained serious. "I'm not kidding. You have to let yourself do that sometimes." And then with his hand on Garreck's cheek, he added, "But thank you for letting me be a part of it. Thank you for trusting me."

After a few more moments to compose themselves, they packed up their things, gathered their horses and made their way back to the others. As they approached, Jane came hurtling toward them, seemingly out of nowhere.

"Where have you been?" she demanded.

"It's all good, Jane. Our horses needed some water," Cal explained, hoping she would pick up on his tone.

She did not.

"Well, if you hadn't noticed, Garreck here pissed off the Cantics even more than they already were, so we've got some things to do."

Cal saw Garreck's expression fall and attempted to defend him before all of his progress was undone by Jane's tactlessness. "The Cantics were never going to turn around and leave, Jane," Cal told her. "I was the only one dumb enough to believe otherwise. But now we know, and we can start working towards our next steps. Have you seen Rasha?"

Jane jerked her head to her left. Following her motion, Cal saw Rasha sitting quietly, eyes shut and apparently deep in concentration.

"I'm told he's been like that since the beginning of negotiations. If one of you could talk to him that would be helpful because he's starting to make our people nervous." As she turned to leave, Jane shot Cal a look that was clearly a *he's your problem, figure it out.*

Cal could understand why it would make people uncomfortable to see Rasha—their last chance before combat—kneeling silently by himself on the ground. He checked with Garreck to make sure he was all right and then made his way over to Rasha.

Cal noticed as he drew closer that Rasha's mouth was moving. The boy said nothing, but his lips worked quickly, forming unheard words.

"What are you up to? Are you praying?" Cal knelt down next to his friend, touching his shoulder with an imploring hand.

Rasha looked up and smiled a bit. "I am. For the first time since the accident, actually. Plus, my beliefs shifted entirely the moment I started training. Nothing has changed since then, but it seems there's something about mortal peril that makes prayer a comfort."

These were not the words of a confident man. Cal fidgeted uncomfortably, and in a rare moment devoid of delicacy or charm, Cal asked, "Rasha, do you really think you can stop Marten before this goes too far?"

Rasha's response came quickly, but in a steady, resolved voice. "I have to. For my own sake as much as everyone else's."

Cal didn't fully understand what Rasha meant, but as long as he was sure of his plan, Cal did not object to being left in the dark. He simply nodded, "All right then. Well, you're almost up, so let's make it count." Then he turned to go find Garreck.

Marten

Marten smiled to himself as Price, Bernhardt, and Sasse returned from the parlay. They looked deflated, which meant that they had failed to convince the Cratians to disperse.

"We're sorry, sir," Price said, regret slipping through her otherwise formal tone. "But Garreck refused to see reason. I'm afraid he and the others are set in their stand against us." Bernhardt and Sasse both nodded quickly behind her, confirming this report.

"Well then," Marten said coldly, the grin vanishing from his face, "you know what to do. Ready our troops. We move on my order."

They scurried away, and when he was sure they were gone, Marten allowed the smile to creep back over his features. It was true—the presence of Cratian protestors made their going more difficult than he'd originally planned. However, a small part of Marten was thrilled to have met some resistance. He was begrudgingly proud that Garreck—spineless and disappointing as he was—had not folded so easily after their argument back in Cantor. His eldest son was soft and full of weakness, but at least there was still some fight left in him.

And as luck would have it, Marten was ready to give him that fight. He turned and made his way among the troops. There was no notion of failure as he rallied his men and prepared them to move. The Cratian resistance would be as distressing as a passing snowdrift on their way to using the moridium. Those foolish protestors could bluster all they wanted, but it would not slow the inevitable.

If it *did* come to a fight, he would try to contain the damage done. Not that the world couldn't benefit from fewer emotional activists, but the political fallout of such a slaughter would be nightmarish. It would be hard, though, to temper their destruction when the fight was so clearly unbalanced. He had brought just short of one hundred eager and capable men to accompany him south. He doubted anyone from Cratos even knew how to hold a sword. His army had crossbows, swords, and infantry armed with caltrops, and they were trained to wield those weapons at his command without question.

No, it would not be pretty if the Cratians refused to get out of his way, but Marten was ready to do what was necessary; he would deal with the repercussions after he'd accomplished his mission. The efforts expended over the last nine years were now building to a triumphant crescendo, and he would not be stopped.

As he signaled a forward march, Marten was surprised to realize that a small part of him feared for his son. He was taken aback by the sudden burst of anxiety, but was quick to douse that nagging, paternal flame. If Garreck *did* die during this fight, at least it would be a death worthy of the Landsing name—a death Marten could respect.

Mauria

When Mauria sent word of the Cantic approach, she chose not to tell Cal how many soldiers had come with Marten. The troops were far enough away that it would be impossible for the Cratians to know the scope of their foe, and informing them would serve no purpose but to instill fear and unease. It was probable that Cal, Garreck, and Jane were not even able to tell how many Cantic soldiers there were when they met halfway between parties.

Mauria barely watched *that* interaction, knowing it was unlikely to be of much consequence. Before Rasha joined them, she had allowed herself to be coddled by the idea of a son's emotional plea to his father, but their new situation gave her proper perspective. The parley was a stall and nothing more.

This was confirmed when Mauria watched the parties separate, neither looking too pleased. From her post, Mauria saw the Cantic army ready for battle, while the Cratian mob organized itself into protest groups. The contrast was stark, but despite the pitiable appearance of Cal's people, Mauria could think only of her own soldiers.

They were *all* she thought about in the short time between the failed negotiations and the onset of the battle. There had to be one hundred Cantic soldiers poised and ready to attack. Even in Cardit's worst-case scenario, they had had better odds than this. If Rasha failed, those Aelish men and women were doomed to lay down their lives in a fruitless attempt to stop Marten. She'd told them very little about Rasha's abilities and had kept her description of their plan short and sweet when talking to her troops. They would wait, they would watch, and—if all else failed—they would fight.

A part of her believed so fully in Rasha that she allowed herself to think *if*, rather than *when*. She resented that hope, almost as much as she resented the parts of her that anticipated Rasha's display of power with excitement. This was not a spectacle to enjoy, and yet she yearned to see the extent of his abilities.

Whatever the urge was, she needed to assume a position that would allow her to observe both the melee and her own waiting troops. Mauria rested, back-straight against a tree at the ridge of their perch. Cardit was at the opposite end, closest to the Cantic forces. If they were needed, Cardit would lead half of the Aelish to circle around behind Marten while Mauria and her group charged the front. For now, they would sit, poised and ready. As her thoughts drifted to the many possible outcomes still waiting to materialize, Mauria pressed her back as far as it could go into the ragged bark, caring more for its cover than comfort. If they were seen before it was necessary, they would be faced with an entirely new set of problems.

She settled in, and the Cratians began to chant.

"What the hell is that?" exclaimed Arla, one of the older recruits who had settled close to her. "What are they chanting?"

Mauria listened closely, trying to make out the garbled words shouted by the mob below. Instantly, she wished she had not. From what she could piece together, they were shouting, "Banish the Cantics" and "Can't-issues be resolved?"

It was all she could do not to sink directly into the tree. How embarrassing this was for them. They were utterly worthless as nonviolent observers, and yet their enthusiasm knew no bounds. They were passionate in their cries. She was happy to have their support, but more than ever she was critically aware of how insignificant their words were. Words, she'd come to believe garnered support before and renown after. But those moments of change demanded action that the Cratians simply weren't willing to provide.

Trying to ignore Cal's volunteers, Mauria watched Marten's troops draw closer and closer until finally they were only fifty yards from Garreck, Cal, and the rest of the protestors. All was still, and in this moment of calm, Mauria's eyes raked across the crowd, searching for Rasha. He had not drifted toward the front of the groups as she had expected. But he still wore his long green cloak and eventually Mauria saw that he was stationed off to the side, on the very edge of the congregation closest to where she hid. It was a smart place to position himself. From there, Rasha would be able to maintain a clear view of the Cantics without becoming an immediate target. Apart from his clothing, no one would be able to single him out from the hundreds of other witnesses. Even his actions were subtle. The effects of those actions, however, left Mauria speechless.

Rasha

The Cantic army approached, and connections buzzed through Rasha as he contemplated his first move. He felt the human lives about him as distinctly as he felt the trees lining the forest to his left and the moridium contained just beyond the Cantic line.

It was because of the moridium that he couldn't use fire. Yes, it would have been the most effective method of keeping Cantor at bay, but it could also have disastrous consequences. He shuddered to imagine what would happen if moridium and fire met.

Instead of fire, he decided on elements that might be less intimidating, but would hopefully be just as impactful. He turned towards the heavens and felt above him, connecting with the water that saturated Collipia's endless sky and pulled the wetness closer to him. As he drew upon it, darkness rolled across their company as clouds gathered overhead. It began to rain.

All about him people shivered and looked up, confused by the sudden change in atmosphere and light, but Rasha continued. He sent a huge wind crashing over them, whipping the Cantics and carrying leaves and other debris with along it. Refuse swirled in a beautiful, mangled mess before knocking into the opposition, blocking their view and obstructing their path.

Rasha connected with the energy that buzzed among his summoned clouds. Independent from the traditional rumble of thunder that warns of its arrival, a bolt of lightning shot out, quick and powerful, striking just in front of Garreck's father. Marten's horse reared, but its rider did not budge. Rasha noticed with satisfaction, however, that the man looked shaken.

Growing more confident in the effects of his magic, Rasha turned his attention below, and the ground beneath Marten's troops began to rumble. Land split, breaking off in places and shifting so that the humans above were forced to fall out of formation. Behind him the Cratians cheered, and their chants grew louder.

Rasha allowed himself a smile. He looked over and saw Cal's beaming face mirroring his own satisfaction, and for a moment he knew that they had done it—they had saven Rien.

But, even as he watched the celebration around him, he saw Cal's face shift from joy to fear. Marten had cried out, and although Rasha could not make out the words through the chaos he himself had created, he saw the result.

Cantor was still moving.

Slowly Marten's soldiers were pushing forward, fighting against the forces that Rasha had set against them. Rasha acted in turn, pressing the wind harder and faster towards them, sending bolts of lighting streaking down, carefully avoiding the center of their party where the carriage of moridium could be seen.

Not a single Cantic man or woman retreated. It was a testament to either Marten's leadership or tyranny—and Rasha suspected the latter—that they persevered despite odds that would strike fear in the hearts of the bravest individuals. They pushed forward, and Rasha knew that within minutes they would begin slicing through the volunteers.

From the other side of the observers, Rasha heard Garreck yell "Fall back!" Heavily muffled by distance, weather, and the shouts of frightened people, still his voice rang out. No sooner had Garreck's words reached his ears than Rasha saw their saving grace.

Cal

The sight of the Aelish rushing towards the fray was welcome, but did not automatically assure the safety of his people. The Cratians were flailing about, tripping over dropped protest signs as they raced to put distance between themselves and the approaching Cantic soldiers.

A group of observers no older than Cal had fallen on the ground, crying rather than moving with the rest. Cal went up to one and yanked him to his feet.

"Go, now!" he shouted, but the man was stunned by fear. Cal slapped him.

"I said move!" Cal yelled again, this time pointing at one of the others as he added, "Take him and get out. You're going to kill yourself and others by staying here. You're in the way! Do not go straight back into Rien. Hide in the woods. Marten won't follow you there!

That was, unfortunately, the only way to keep some of them alive. They would have to clear the path to Rien to save themselves, and if the Aelish failed, Marten would all but stroll over the border before destroying the small, unguarded country.

His orders seemed to rouse the fallen activists and they got up and shuffled quickly away. Beyond their moving bodies, Cal could make out Garreck leading a small group of Cratians, each carrying a weapon and heading towards the danger, not away from it.

Cal sprinted after them. He forgot about all other obligations and ran toward Garreck. His pace, coupled with poor visibility sent him hurtling into Garreck's back, knocking him down onto the now-muddied ground.

"What the—," Garreck cursed angrily and spun around, softening only slightly when he saw that it was Cal. "What the hell are you doing?" he demanded.

Cal stood up, gasping for breath. "You can't go out there. It's too dangerous," he managed to get out.

Garreck nodded his head, "Yeah, it is too dangerous. But my father is the maniac responsible for all this. I'm not just going to watch it happen."

Cal could see from Garreck's hardened expression that he was not going to budge. By keeping Garreck from the fight, Cal was only prolonging the inevitable. "All right then, but please for the love of reason, be careful."

Something in Garreck's face shifted, and for a moment Cal thought he might stay behind with him. Instead, Garreck gave him a swift kiss, murmuring, "I'll be back," and then he was gone.

Garreck

When Garreck turned away from Cal, he scanned the battle for his father. It was not difficult to spot Marten. He was fending off three Aelish soldiers with relative ease on the far side of the field. With mortal resolve, he worked his way determinedly across to where Marten was fighting. All about him were screams and roars as individuals dueled and raged, but Garreck focused only on what was ahead of him. The training that he'd been subjected to as a child paid off, and he bowled his way through each foe who approached him. In those moments, Garreck realized with grim satisfaction that he was finally using Marten's cruelty against him.

If he could just make it to his father, and if he could manage to get a clear shot, he would have a chance of destroying Marten. He knew he could do it, too. He knew with every fiber of his being that he could release his bowstring and let fly a lethal arrow. Whatever familial blood flowed in their veins had long ago been poisoned by unhealthy doses of contempt and derision.

As he fought his way closer to Marten, the density of soldiers, both Aelish and Cantic, began to thin. Wreckage from upturned supply wagons was strewn about the field. Garreck took advantage of the destruction and hoisted himself up so that he was standing tenuously on the side edge of one of the carts. He crouched low, attempting to keep himself steady as he prepared his bow.

Finding his target, Garreck pointed his weapon at his father and called out, "Oy, Marten!"

Marten looked up, neck twisting to scan the chaos, his eyes landed upon his son. They were close enough that Garreck could see the cruel smile as it spread across his father's lips. Garreck's insides boiled at the sight, but to his horror, he found his hand frozen, unable to release the arrow. He had been so certain in his resolve to be the one to end Marten's life. Yet, now that it was upon him, the weight of patricide hung heavy, staying his shot.

From Marten's expression, Garreck could tell that his father understood the turmoil raging within his son, and from where he stood he mouthed one word, slowly and deliberately, "*Weak*."

Garreck had one fleeting second of surprise, heard a warning shriek from close behind, and then everything went black.

Cal

Cal had witnessed the standoff between Garreck and his father. However, unlike Garreck he was unable to focus on Marten. His attention was fixed on the Cantic soldier who had silently crept up behind Garreck. Without thinking, Cal raced to tackle the assailant. He pushed and prodded his way through the crowd, but was unable to reach him in time. In one terrible, wrenching moment Cal felt all the air rush out of his body. He gasped, staring at Garreck with fear and confusion in his eyes. All at once, Cal's world ended.

Rasha

Even in the presence of so much physical pain, nothing compared to the agony of watching Garreck fall. The emotional ache of the scene ripped through him. Rasha was only a few yards away when it happened, and once again he was too cowardly to do anything other than cry out. It was the pilgrimage all over again. Rasha felt the heavy weight of shame immobilizing him even as the battle continued around him. He watched, afraid to make his move, afraid to suffer for the sake of a friend who now lay crumpled on the ground, bleeding from a wound that Rasha could have prevented.

And Garreck *was* a friend. Despite Garreck's initial hatred of Rasha, each had grown to respect the other. Rasha had watched Garreck transform into someone who empathized with people he had once despised, had seen him grow into a man who was good and brave and loving. The heartbreak of his loss tore through Rasha. He already felt *everything*, but this was unlike anything he had ever experienced. In one moment, he thought of what would happen if Marten continued on, if he carried the moridium all the way to Rien and destroyed all that Rasha had ever held dear.

The thought of it was too much to handle. Within seconds of watching Garreck tumble from his perch on the wagon, Rasha decided he could not live with the pain of any other casualties.

And so, he reached out, tightening his hold on every Cantic connection, but one. He felt the evil souls mixed with the sheeplike followers of Marten, but did not discriminate in his purge. He brought his hands up, holding invisible lines of life above his head. He pictured the dead bodies of the pilgrimage members, Garreck's motionless form on the ground before him, and the countless casualties of their ruthless Cantic hate. Grief flooded through him, and then Rasha screamed, slashing his arms down through the air, destroying each connection in one swift, fluid motion.

The effect was instantaneous. Rasha doubled over as he felt the absence of each broken connection. They rushed from him, puncturing him again and again, leaving him shredded and weak. He cried for the family he had saved and for the lives he had taken. He cried for dead friends, the wickedness of the world, and the humanity he had lost trying to defeat it. Anyone walking past him would have thought Rasha dying, a casualty of the battle. But he was very much alive, and the implications of that survival would stay with him long after other wounds had healed.

Mauria

Mauria was fighting furiously one moment, and then the next she was not. In an instant her sword came down heavy on empty air where there had once been a person. Panting and confused, she looked around to see that the rest of her soldiers were experiencing similar phenomena. The air glinted with a slight haze, as it does when hot earth creates a shimmer in the space above. But the enemy was nowhere to be seen. The Cantics had gone. They had *won*.

Cheers rang out among the Aelish and few Cratians who had stayed to fight. She was sure that the others who had hidden would soon begin filtering back, drawn by the sounds of victory.

Her eyes were alight with the glory and relief of their win, but only until they found Rasha. He was slowly sitting up. His face was pale, his eyes vacant. She ran to him, but was confused when she saw that he had not been harmed.

"Rasha?" she asked, not understanding the reason for his exhausted, confused state.

He stared at her, not really seeing her, and then he turned, and her eyes followed him to Garreck, who lay still on the ground.

"No," she breathed, throwing herself from one friend to the other.

Unlike Rasha, Garreck was neither conscious nor unharmed. A deep sword blow to his back had bled profusely, but was slow when Mauria checked, and she knew it was because the blood supply had all but drained from its host.

He did not have much blood, but he did have breath. Mauria felt it against her hand as she tilted Garreck's head up. It was so faint that it would have been missed without such close proximity.

With a flutter of hope, Mauria threw off her armour and reached for her medicine bag, silently thanking Cardit for pushing her to embrace both the healer and the fighter. She dug out a thick balm, globbing in onto each index finger before slathering it directly onto Garreck's mangled back.

Nothing happened. There was not a flinch or stir as she worked to mend her broken friend.

"Come on you brute! You moron!" She turned Garreck on his side but continued to work on him, calling out to any other Aelish healers who were not off celebrating.

"I swear to Rasha's god, Garreck, if you die I'll never forgive you. Cal will, but I won't. In fact, I'll never speak to you again." The yelling was inane, but it made Mauria's work tolerable, kept her hands steady as she moved to stitch up Garreck's back.

When she was done, her hands were bloody and her nerves were shot, but Garreck's pulse had strengthened infinitesimally.

Please be enough, she hoped.

Garreck

Garreck felt the pain of being alive before he opened his eyes. His entire body felt like it was on fire, and when he groaned the weakness in his voice was not surprising.

With enormous effort, Garreck managed to slightly open his eyelids. The dim light and slightly damp air told him that he was in a tent. Every fiber of his being hoped that it was not a Cantic tent. If it was, he hoped he had been taken prisoner; he wouldn't be able to face the mocking condescension if his father had saved him from the battle.

173

He knew he would learn nothing if he continued to stare at the ceiling above, but this meant he had to turn his head. Moving his body was out of the question. The pain coming from his extremities was the only indication that his limbs had not been blown off altogether.

With great effort, he turned his head to the left and found Mauria asleep in the chair next to him. Her eyes were red and puffy, and he could tell that she had been crying for some time.

"Man up, will you?" he rasped as loudly as he could in an attempt to wake her.

It worked. Her eyes fluttered briefly before she stretched deep in her chair. When she opened her eyes fully and saw Garreck conscious she burst into tears, throwing herself onto his bed.

"Mauria, get off, before you actually kill me…" he grunted at her. The pain of her embrace was excruciating.

She jumped away, but rather than an apology she muttered, "Hm. Perhaps I should have let you rot."

He gave her a rye smile. "So you're the one responsible for this mess?" he asked, eyeballing what was presumably a mangled body underneath a mound of blankets. Garreck was convinced he would never feel well enough to actually lift his arms and check on the rest of him.

She rolled her eyes, "I saved your life, you idiot. I deserve at least a thank you."

And for that he dropped his sarcasm. "Thank you Mauria, truly." This seemed to placate her so he added, "Now, tell me what happened."'

She seemed unsure of how to answer. After a few seconds deliberation, she said, "I'm not sure who injured you. It was a Cantic soldier, but it's impossible to know who."

"You didn't find a body? Or someone willing to admit to the attack?" Garreck knew how battle went, and surely if the man were alive he would have bragged about striking the final blow against Marten's son.

Mauria continued to look uncomfortable with the questions. "Garreck," she said quietly, "There are no bodies. There's no one left at all, in fact."

Garreck did not understand. "What do you mean—no one?"

"I mean the Cantics. We're all still here of course. We lost eleven

Aelish soldiers and six Cratians during the struggle, but the rest of us are accounted for." She looked at him with haunted eyes. "The others though, they just vanished."

If she had thought this would serve to address Garreck's misunderstanding, she was wrong. "I still don't understand Mauria, what…"

"Rasha destroyed them!" Her voice was wild, but dropped instantly to a whisper, as if anything louder would evoke whatever power she spoke of. "He said he broke their *connections*. I don't entirely understand it, but one second we were losing and I was fighting for my life, and the next second there was nothing but a shimmer, and then there was *nothing*."

Of all the many outcomes Garreck had imagined during their months and months of planning and struggle, this had never been an option. He had never had to grapple with the idea of not having a body to bring home to his mother. There was no love between the spouses, surely, but Jana deserved the opportunity to grieve in whatever way she needed.

"What about the moridium?" he managed to ask. "Is it gone, too?

"Not gone, no. It's currently being guarded by a rotation of Cardit's troops. When it's time to go, I will lead a small group and return it to Devoran. It belongs there, where it can't be misused."

"There's something else," Mauria started to tell him, but Garreck cut her off.

"But that means we won, doesn't it? Rien is safe and Rasha's people have nothing to fear. We did it!" Whatever loss the bizarre events had cost him was outshone by the truth of their success.

"Rasha …," Garreck continued, with as much animation as his state would allow. "He never let on that he was able to do something of this magnitude. It must have been a sacrifice for him to do … whatever the hell he did." Garreck closed his eyes and let the reality of their win sink in, "He saved us."

Mauria nodded, looking at him with searching eyes.

"What? Why aren't you happy?" Garreck could not understand why she wasn't dancing for joy. "I'm not dead and Rien isn't obliterated and we can actually go back to our lives. And Cal, he can finally get back to his lessons. It's going to take him ages to catch up on the work he's missed."

As he thought about it, Garreck realized that while he was grateful for Mauria's care and attention, she was not the person he had expected to see when he woke up.

"Where is he?" he asked Mauria, sharply.

Her expression told him everything he needed to know.

"I told you there were six Cratian deaths," she said, holding back tears. "One of them... one of them was Cal." She lost control and wept as Garreck lay there, unable to process what she was saying. "We didn't realize it until we had brought you back to the healer's tent. I was so focused on you, and Rasha was hardly speaking. It was when I saw Jane that I knew something was wrong. We went back out and searched through the wreckage of the battle, and that's ... that's where we found him."

"How?" The word sounded foggy and foreign on his lips.

"A dagger. Because of what Rasha did, it's hard to tell what happened for sure, but," she paused to take a breath. "I think it was probably thrown."

Cal had been the one person who Garreck knew was safe. He was the only one from their group who had agreed to run back with the others, to hide and stay out of harm's way and wait until the storm had passed. But he hadn't retreated. For whatever reason Cal had remained, unarmed, in a wild scene of violence and hate. And now he was dead ... and Garreck did not know whether his grief or fury was stronger in that moment of realization.

Tears poured from him, and his body ached as his back arched and curled in devastated convulsions. Mauria stayed with him, but did not attempt to comfort that which could not be consoled. Eventually, the worst of his lamentation subsided, and he was shocked to feel a manic laugh burbling up during this, the darkest moment of his life.

With vile humor, he realized that Cal would have been so happy to see him cry.

Rasha

They stayed in Marcan South for a few nights after their victory. While they were there, Rasha kept as close to the others as he possibly could. He rarely spoke, but Rasha found solace in the dull roar of the Cratians and the Aelish as they packed and chatted, coming down from the glory of their victory. At night Rasha willed himself awake, trying desperately to fight against sleep. Silence was his enemy and unconsciousness his hell. He had tried to explain his suffering to Mauria, but it was difficult for her to understand. She treated him differently than she had before, no longer patting his hair or gracing him with a quick hug as she used to. Rasha didn't blame her. He was not the boy she had met all those months ago.

Over the summer Rasha had evolved from a scared child running from a crisis of faith, to a young man who traded monotheism for a spirituality that provided him with strength and purpose. The growth had been enriching, and he'd been proud of that new man. Unfortunately, his most recent transformation had not been as progressive, and Rasha feared that he had become something monstrous, rather than the hero the others believed him to be.

Each time he closed his eyes or experienced a quiet moment, he felt every last one of the lives he had destroyed in his fury. At the time of his decision, Rasha had been fueled by both a selfish need to save his friends, as well as a righteousness that demanded justice against the wicked. Now, however, he saw the truth in Damean's teachings and knew that the consequences of his actions would stay with him— shadow accompanying him forever more.

He dared not speak it out loud for Garreck would have surely punched him, but Rasha almost envied Cal his peace. Rasha knew enough of magic to know that death was not an end. It was simply a restructuring. Whatever Cal's soul had gone on to become was surely brighter and more vibrant.

Rasha, however, felt eons older. He'd made a connection with each Cantic soldier, and those connections would forever be a part of him— their hauntings a constant reminder of the price of such power.

He resolved to take this new-normal day by day, and for the duration of their time in Marcan South he would test his ability to survive.

Rasha was happy to find that he had some resiliency in him. When the time finally came for all of them to depart, Mauria found Rasha and Garreck and brought them all together.

"I needed to make sure we all saw each other," Mauria said in explanation, but it was not necessary. Rasha would have been just as devastated if they had left without a proper farewell.

She hugged them both. Her embrace of Rasha was a long, constricting thing that lingered even after she had pulled away. Garreck's was more cautious. His wound was still tender, even though it was almost fully healed thanks to the Aelish gifts.

"Where will you both go?" she asked, taking a steadying breath and looking at each in turn.

"I'm going to visit my mother, and then I'll begin the journey back to Devoran." The others looked surprised, but for Rasha it was the only future that fit.

Even though it pained him to admit it, his mother had been right in her letter; Rasha knew that he could not move back to Rien permanently. The peaceful bustle of his homeland would be welcome and soothing, but it would not help him to heal, only to avoid. And although it would pain him to leave his mother yet again, he knew that Devoran was the only place he could ever truly begin to confront his failings. There would be space to breathe there, and he would have no choice but to become acquainted with the Cantic connections that were now a part of him.

"I have to go to Cratos," Garreck said quietly. His voice held none of his old sarcasm. However, Rasha was at least happy to hear emotion in the somber words, rather than the dearth of feeling that often accompanies grief. "I have to tell Cal's family what happened," Garreck continued. "I only wish I could bring his body."

"You can't, Garreck, you know that," Mauria said in a soft tone meant to comfort rather than reprimand. Rasha tried to forget the uncomfortable moment when Jane and Mauria had been forced to remind Garreck that Cal's body would not remain in an appropriate condition if they attempted to return it to Cratos. It was terrible watching Garreck's realization, as if the truth of what happens to a human body after death was some shocking revelation. Eventually, Garreck had begrudgingly agreed to a burial in Marcan South. He'd chosen a plot that, to Rasha, seemed entirely random. After some discussion, Cal was placed out in the spot where the Cratians had kept their horses before the battle, beside the remains of a long forgotten fire.

"I know I can't bring him, Mauria" Garreck said in a clipped tone. "That doesn't mean I don't want to. His poor family." Garreck shook his head as if to sling away all the unwelcome thoughts from his mind. "After I leave Cratos, though, I suppose I'll go ho..., well, back to Cantor." There was a reluctant tone in Garreck's voice when he spoke of his homeland that Rasha understood all too well. Neither of them thought of their countries as "home" anymore.

"You will find a place where you belong, Garreck." Rasha did not tell him this to pity or to coddle, but because it was the truth. As certain as he was that he had a place with the sorcerers of Devoran and that Mauria had found her calling in Marcan South, Rasha knew that Garreck would find his way. His was just a longer road.

"I *had* a home," Garreck retorted, and the depth of his sadness was almost overwhelming.

With gentle eyes, Rasha simply nodded. For that, he had no response.

Garreck

Jane and the other Cratians had been gone for over an hour, but Garreck was not ready to leave with them. After promising to catch up, he stayed, lying next to Cal's grave and watching wisps of clouds blow smooth and crisp with the autumn air.

The large stone that marked Cal's grave was rough and plain. They had been unable to come to a decision on the inscription, and Garreck refused to abandon the plot without marking it appropriately.

The problem was that nothing about the stupid boulder or the ugliness of death had anything to do with the type of person Cal had been. Garreck had loved a man who was vibrant and caring and eternally excited about life. Rasha believed that Cal's connections had gone into everything, and that they should feel grateful for his continued presence. But Garreck felt nothing of Cal but his absence.

Exhaling forcefully, he rolled into a sitting position and stared straight at the stone. What would Cal have wanted? What could Garreck write that might even partially encapsulate who Cal had been in life?

The answer came to Garreck in a sudden thought, and when it did he dared not hesitate. Grabbing the sharpest dagger that he owned, he etched the epitaph that would have to be enough.

When he was done, Garreck looked once upon his work and stood up. Without turning back, he walked away. There would be time to visit again someday, but in that moment he could not afford anything but a clean, finite break from the most amazing person he had ever known.

EPILOGUE

9 years after

Mauria was the first to arrive. She wasn't entirely surprised, as she had the shortest distance to travel. Rasha's trip from Devoran was double her journey, and Garreck was coming from Cratos.

To pass the time, Mauria meandered about the wide expanse of road and field that she had not seen in so long. It was her first time back after the battle over the moridium, and if the site hadn't held so much significance she might not have recognized it for what it was. It was late spring, and tall grass and weeds grew dense over much of the land. Emerald hues sprouted up in every direction, and white petals bloomed over long stretches of earth. The renewed relations between Cantor and Rien had resulted in a recobbling of the wide street, and while the occasional dandelion peeked through the round edges of polished stone, it appeared to be well kept.

She walked along, feeling the curve of each rock under her steps, and bracing for old memories as they came flooding back. Mauria paused when she came to what appeared to be a well-worn path etched into grass that led off to toward a vast, green space.

The way was about the width of a man, and Mauria wondered who would have revisited a spot so far from the main road. Her confusion evaporated as she turned and came upon an all-to-familiar, mossy mass. It was smaller than she remembered, and was surrounded by a crop of wildflowers that had been planted in deliberate sprigs on either side of the rock.

Mauria leaned in close, noticing after a second glance that a few words had been etched deep into the face of Cal's headstone.

Cal Hanson: away on his next grand adventure.

"I carve down a little deeper each year." A quiet voice from just behind Mauria sent her reeling, and she spun to address its owner.

Her heart settled when she saw that it was Garreck. He looked so much older than the last time she had seen him. His hair had receded ever so slightly, so that his forehead was larger than she remembered, and the dark skin of his face was creased at the edges of his eyes. Mauria wondered, momentarily, if she had changed that much, but shrugged it aside without a second thought. She had never once paid attention to her looks, and this was not the time to begin.

"You could have said hello, instead of sneaking up like that. What did you do, float over to me?" She barked the words at Garreck, who was smirking at her reaction.

"Nah, that's more of a Rasha thing, I expect. You just have especially poor reflexes."

That earned him a soft smack across the face as Mauria grumbled, "Now who has poor reflexes?"

They glared at each other before breaking into wide grins and colliding in a hug that spanned nine years of separation.

When they broke apart, Garreck scanned the area behind Mauria. "Is Rasha not here?" He asked her.

"Not yet," she relied. "I was the first one."

"I guess it's just as well," Garreck said. "It's going to take all of my attention to follow whatever incredible stories he's got for us. This gives us a chance to talk about things a little less magical." He smiled at her, and she returned it, taking his hand and guiding him back toward the road.

Together, they pitched their tents and started a fire. The warm spring air was fragile as night slowly crept towards them, and every hour brought them a few inches closer to the warmth of the flames. By midnight they were huddled close, Mauria's head leaning on Garreck's shoulder in a companionable way.

"Tell me more about your family, Garreck. You say it is large; how many children do you have?"

182

"Melli and I have six children," he told her with a smile. Mauria's heart thrilled at the look of total satisfaction that Garreck had when he spoke of all his many kids. "Landon, Remi, and Madie came first. We were actually relieved to know there had been three babies waiting to burst out. Melli had been so big, the medics in Cratos thought something was wrong. They're five years old this year."

Mauria shuddered at the thought of having one child inside her, never mind three, but she let Garreck continue without voicing her horror.

"Miles and Ellie are three years old, and when they were born we suddenly had five babies when we had only originally planned for two." He laughed and shook his head. "Still, Melli thought that there was someone missing, so we tried for another. Fortunately it was just one baby this last time. He's only six months old. I dropped the rest with my mother on my way through Cantor to come here, but the youngest is still home with his mother." Garreck paused and shifted so that he could look at Mauria, "We named him Cal."

Mauria looked at Garreck with a sad smile, which Garreck returned.

"You should have seen him when he was just born, Mauria, he was so happy. He didn't cry like others. It was like he had been waiting so long to see what all the fuss was about, and when he got out he was thoroughly taken over by this world." Garreck shook his head fondly and added, "I think he's got Cal's intrepid nature."

Mauria laughed along with him, but there was another question nagging at her. Trying hard not to be offensive, she asked, "Garreck, how did you and Melli get together?"

Garreck chuckled at this. Far from offended, he simply shrugged to himself, as if he wasn't quite sure either.

"Honestly, Mauria, I have no idea. When Cal died I was relatively sure I wouldn't find another person I could be happy with, but I was also fairly certain that if I did, he'd be a man." His eyes travelled off in the direction of Cal's headstone, and Mauria followed his gaze. "I guess you love who you love. I knew from being with Cal what it felt like to really, truly, love someone. So, when I started to feel like that about Melli, I didn't hesitate. I snatched it up because I know how rare such a connection is."

"We met through Cal's moms. Did I tell you that?" Garreck asked, and Mauria shook her head. She knew that Garreck had spent some time with his family in Cantor before deciding to move to Cratos permanently, but she hadn't known of the connection with Melli.

Garreck nodded, "She was a clerk in Caroline's office. I'd been staying with the Hansons while I worked at the capital. Melli came over now and again for dinner, and along the way something just clicked for us."

He shifted so that he was sitting cross legged in front of her, and she was forced to support her own neck again. "What about you, Maur? Do you think you will ever find someone?"

With anyone else, Mauria would have defaulted to the same empty words she used with her family and friends when they asked about her love life. With Garreck, though, she felt no need for pretense. "Truthfully? No, I don't think I'll ever find someone like that. When I hear you talk about your feelings for Cal and Melli, it sounds so wonderful, but it is not who I am. I have people like you and Rasha and Cardit who feel like soulmates, who *are* my soulmates, but I have never wanted to be anything more than the deepest of friends with anyone." Saying it out loud for the first time made Mauria realize how absolute this statement was.

Garreck seemed to accept this, even if he did not understand it. "Is it lonely?" he asked.

"Not for me," Mauria replied. "I'm complete in myself," she said simply. "I always have been."

Garreck nodded, and both he and Mauria let the conversation drift to silence. The last thing Mauria remembered was the warmth of a blanket being placed over her, and the sound of Garreck's footsteps walking slowly away.

When Mauria woke, Rasha was sitting next to her, tending to the long-chilled coals with a wooden poker. She didn't say anything at first, attempting to read as much as she could from a few silent, stolen glances.

Unlike Garreck, he looked nearly the same as last she saw him, except that he was taller. Because he was seated, she couldn't be sure how *much* taller he had gotten. Then again, Rasha had been only fourteen when they had all met, and she knew from Trent that men's growth spurts tend to come later.

His eyes, she was pleased to see, did not have their old heaviness. She hoped he was at peace. As Mauria gazed upon him, she realized that she had never known a version of Rasha that was content.

Unable to gauge anything else, Mauria decided it was time to wake. She gave a deep groan and a stretch that even she didn't believe and slowly sat up, facing Rasha and feigning surprise.

"Rasha! You made it!"

Rasha rolled his eyes and laughed, "How long have you *actually* been awake?" he asked.

"Only a bit," Mauria told him in as innocent a voice as possible.

Rasha scooted towards her and gave her a hug. It was a new hug. It wasn't the innocent embrace of a scared Rie boy, or the rigid grasp of a burdened young man. It was warm, and felt like home. Mauria leaned in and returned the gesture.

"How was your trip?" Mauria asked him.

"Long, but relatively uneventful," Rasha told her. "I stopped by my mother's to say hello to her, Adal, and little Chelem. She seems so happy; it's wonderful to visit and know that she's taken care of."

"Would you ever think about staying with them? It must have felt good to be around people who love you again." Mauria couldn't imagine living a life as isolating as Damean's was. She wanted more for Rasha than quiet solitude.

But Rasha was already shaking his head. "It's not my world anymore. I've seen what I am capable of, and I don't belong somewhere as peaceful as Rien. Plus, I don't believe in their god anymore. I would feel tainted surrounded by their faith."

Mauria began to object, but Rasha cut her off. "I murdered so many people over the moridium that day. And I did it out of rage and anger and fear. I found a monster lurking inside me, and in Devoran I can work to tame that creature without the temptations I would find in the rest of Colliptia. Can you honestly tell me, Mauria, that I would never be tempted to act in such a way again? Can you claim that there is no more evil in this world?"

Of course, she couldn't. There would be evil as long as there were men. "I guess I understand," she finally conceded. "But there are bad people in Devoran and Rien just as surely as there are in the rest of the world." As an afterthought she added, "Basta's not a saint."

Rasha laughed. "No, indeed he is not. But he is passionate and devout, and though you think him a coward, I actually admire his conviction to adhere to Rie faith when it comes time to make state decisions."

Mauria made a noise that was somewhere between a cough and an expletive, but Rasha pretended not to hear her. Instead he tactfully changed the subject.

"Where is Garreck?" he asked.

"He went off while I was sleeping. His tent is pitched just over there, but I have a feeling he's not in it."

She reached out and used Rasha to pull herself up. When he stood to join her, she realized just how tall he'd actually grown.

"Rasha, you're a giant!" He struck a regal pose, and in that movement Mauria saw a glimpse of the boy he used to be. They laughed together, and then Mauria lead him to Cal's grave, in front of which Garreck was sitting, as expected.

Garreck turned as they approached. There were tears in his eyes. "Cal always wanted me to show my emotions," he said in explanation. "I swear I cry more on these trips than I do any other time of the year."

Rasha knelt down and put his hand on Garreck's shoulder. "He'd be proud of the person you are, Garreck. I know we don't write often, but from what I've read you are doing work that Cal would have loved."

"Thanks, Rasha," Garreck said, standing up as he did so.

"That's actually why I wanted us all to meet today," he told them. "I know this is the first time in nine years that we've all been together, and I want to give us time to enjoy that." He hesitated before adding, "But, there is also something I need to talk to you both about."

Mauria had suspected a separate reason for their reunion when she'd received Garreck's note, but hadn't wanted to push him until Rasha arrived. Now that he was there, she itched to know more.

"Go on then," she said. "We'll have the rest of the day to reminisce. Tell us what's going on.

Rasha nodded in agreement.

"All right," Garreck began. "For the last few years there has been talk floating throughout Cratos about a reconciliation with Devoran."

Mauria saw Rasha's eyebrows raise, but he said nothing.

"While no one knows exactly what Rasha did nine years ago, they understand enough to know that there is power in Devoran that should not be accessible to the rest of the countries in Colliptia. Cratos is logical; they don't want the responsibility that comes with unlimited magic." Garreck paused a moment to give Rasha a gentle squeeze on the arm, but then continued. "They do, however, hope that Devoran will be willing to join in global talks. They believe there is value in unity."

Mauria could feel Rasha's rejection of this, even before the words came out of him.

"It would never work, Garreck. History has shown us that Cantor is more susceptible than any to the lure of Devoran's power. And as logical as the Cratians are, they don't know how they would react when given the opportunity to wield our form of magic."

Garreck nodded, "I told them you would say that, and I don't disagree. Even so, in the coming years I think everyone needs to be ready for the world to start showing their interest in Devoran. Mauria," Garreck shifted his glance as he addressed her. "Aelemia is the only way to reach Devoran from the other parts of Colliptia. While I expect these first visits to be uneventful, it will be important for the Aelish to stay diligent as things progress."

She nodded at him and thought of the shock it would be for her family in Marcan West, and communities like it, to be all at once subjected to frequent trips and travelers. She had never seen their hospitality fail, but this would surely push the bounds of their kindness.

"The world's beginning to change, isn't it?" Mauria asked them.

Rasha nodded. "It's astounding that it has taken this long," he agreed. "Now that it's happening, this seems the natural progression after what happened nine years ago."

"And we will be there to guide each country during the transition," Garreck told them. "That's why I wanted to make sure we were all ready and aware. Together, we can help keep things civil as our nations learn to exist together."

"Cheers!" Mauria said, and she meant it. Perhaps it was being back

187

in a place where she'd felt brave and valiant, or perhaps it was the company of two people she trusted more than almost any other, but she welcomed the prospect of tackling this task together.

Garreck grinned at her. "I'm sorry that this is the first time we're all getting together like this. It should have happened before."

"Well, we are here now," Rasha told him, and together the three of them sat, making a circle that included Cal's tombstone, and they talked. Mauria knew there would be plenty of time in the future to worry about greater things. In that moment, they needed to be the children they once were.

And they got to be. They laughed about the many ridiculous things that Garreck's offspring had done while he raised them. They wondered at Rasha's tales of learning advanced magic, and cried as he told them how hard it had been to come to terms with his own wickedness. The boys gawked as Mauria demonstrated new techniques she had learned in Marcan South and teased her when she tripped and had to heal her own scraped knee.

And then, all too soon, and even though there was still so much to say, it was time to go.

They hugged each other, and promised to write more frequently. Garreck swore to send updates as Cratos progressed in their plans, Rasha agreed to come if a representative from Devoran was needed.

And just as the world shifted from yellow to purple, they left, and the evening was quiet. Somewhere in Aelemia, men and women huddled close for communal songs, and in Devoran a woman turned the pages of her evening read. In Cantor, someone took a long sip of a drink, thinking of a hard day's work and of family waiting back home. To their north, a window in Cratos was closing, the occupants within long-settled for a good night's sleep and productive tomorrow.

And all about, in every land, human hearts yearned for their next grand adventure.

ABOUT THE AUTHOR

Kathleen Evans is a writer and high school English teacher from Whitman, Massachusetts. She graduated from Northeastern University with a degree in English, and has published several short stories including "A Right Good Workman" and "Filtered." In her spare time, Kathleen enjoys playing soccer, beating her husband at board games, and taking portrait mode pictures of her dog.